HOW I SURVIVED MIDDLE SCHOOL

COLLECTION

Volume One

Check out all of the books in the
HOW I SURVIVED MIDDLE SCHOOL
series by Nancy Krulik:

Can You Get an F in Lunch?

Madame President

I Heard a Rumor

The New Girl

Cheat Sheet

P.S. I Really Like You

Who's Got Spirit?

HOW I SURVIVED MIDDLE SCHOOL COLLECTION

By Nancy Krulik

SCHOLASTIC INC.

New York   Toronto   London   Auckland   Sydney
Mexico City   New Delhi   Hong Kong   Buenos Aires

No part of this publication may be reproduced, stored in a retrieval system, or transmitted in any form or by any means, electronic, mechanical, photocopying, recording, or otherwise, without written permission of the publisher. For information regarding permission, write to Scholastic Inc., Attention: Permissions Department, 557 Broadway, New York, NY 10012.

Can You Get an F in Lunch?, ISBN 0-439-02555-9, copyright © 2006 by Nancy Krulik.
Madame President, ISBN 0-439-02556-7, copyright © 2006 by Nancy Krulik.
I Heard a Rumor, ISBN 0-439-02557-5, copyright © 2007 by Nancy Krulik.

These books were originally published by Apple Paperbacks.

ISBN-13: 978-0-545-08840-4
ISBN-10: 0-545-08840-2

All rights reserved. Published by Scholastic Inc. SCHOLASTIC, APPLE PAPERBACKS, and associated logos are trademarks and/or registered trademarks of Scholastic Inc.

12 11 10 9 8 7 6 5 4 3 2 1   8 9 10 11 12 13/0

Printed in the U.S.A.   40
This collection first printing, May 2008

Book design by Jennifer Rinaldi and Alison Klapthor

This special edition includes the following three books!

Contents

Can You Get an F in Lunch? 1

Madame President 105

I Heard a Rumor 215

HOW I SURVIVED MIDDLE SCHOOL

Can You Get an F in Lunch?

BY NANCY KRULIK

**For Mandy and Ian,
always my inspiration**

Are You Ready for Middle School?

It's the night before your first day in sixth grade. Do you:

A. Call all your pals and arrange to walk to school together — there's safety in numbers?

B. Spend the whole night opening and closing your combination lock so you won't have trouble at your locker first thing in the morning?

C. Scarf down a pint of rocky road ice cream — nothing soothes stress like marshmallows, chocolate, nuts, and nougat?

You wake up in the morning and discover a massive zit in the middle of your forehead. Do you:

A. Get your best friend to swipe her big sister's makeup and then help you cover up the big bad blemish?

B. Put a Band-Aid over it and tell everyone you had a head-on collision with a door?

C. Hide under your bed?

Your math teacher has asked everyone to find a study partner to work with for the first marking period. Math is not your best subject. Do you:

A. Choose your best friend as your partner? You might not get the best grades, but at least you'll have fun working together.

B. Team up with the class math whiz? Then, once he's got your grades up, you can show him the ins and outs of coolness.

C. Find the most popular girl in your class and suggest the two of you become partners? Being seen together will definitely raise your social status.

So, How Ready Are You?

If most of your answers were A's, you're a lucky girl. You're headed for middle school with a BFF. So no matter how weird things get, you two will always be able to help each other pick up the pieces.

If most of your answers were B's, you're a creative gal who's got a solution for every problem. You'll be off to a great new year.

If most of your answers were C's, take a chill pill. You're going to middle school, not war. It's gonna be just fine, as long as you learn to relax, feel good about who you are, and trust your own judgment.

Chapter
ONE

THE FIRST THING I NOTICED when I walked into Joyce Kilmer Middle School was Addie Wilson's red-and-white T-shirt.

Well, not the T-shirt actually. It was more the way Addie looked in the T-shirt. It was kind of short and moved up just past Addie's belly button when she raised her arm to wave to somebody down the hall. She looked like a pop star on MTV.

I looked down at my oversize green-and-white Camp Kendale T-shirt, the one with the lizard and the mountain on the front, and freaked out. I looked bad. Really bad. Like a big green tent with a head popping out of the top.

It's not like I'd planned on looking so bad when I'd picked out my clothes for the first day of school. When I left for school in the morning, I thought that wearing a T-shirt from a sleepaway camp was kinda cool. Not too many other sixth graders had been brave enough to go away to camp for a whole summer.

But me, I hadn't been afraid. Not at all. (Okay, at least not after the first few nights, when the homesickness had worn off.)

So you see, that was why I'd put on the T-shirt. I thought it made me seem very cool. Wrong!

MIDDLE SCHOOL RULE #1:

A BIG GREEN T-SHIRT WITH A LIZARD ON THE FRONT IS NOT MATURE.

Not at all. Especially not compared to Addie's teenage — or at least *almost* teenage — shirt.

Well, maybe everyone would be too excited about the first day of school to notice how lame my shirt was.

At that moment, I really wished I'd called Addie last night to see what she'd planned on wearing. Then maybe we could have coordinated, and Addie could have saved me from looking like such a dork.

It wouldn't have been the first time Addie had come to my rescue. There was the time I'd fallen off my bike and cracked my front tooth. (Good thing it had only been a baby tooth!) She'd been the one to come to the dentist with me and hold my hand when the dentist pulled out what was left of my baby tooth.

And then there was the time she'd seen that skunk hiding in the bushes and pulled me away before I could be sprayed with stinky skunk juice.

Of course, I'd done a lot of nice things for Addie, too. After all, she only lived two blocks away and we'd been best friends practically all our lives. We were almost the same age — I was three months older — and we'd always been in the same class at George Washington Elementary School.

In fact, the first time Addie and I had ever been apart for more than a week was this summer. I went to sleep-away camp, while she stayed home and went to day camp at the community center. I hadn't seen her since the morning I left for camp. When I got home in August, she and her family were already away on their annual beach vacation. Addie hadn't gotten back until yesterday morning, and I was excited to finally see her.

"Hey, Addie!" I shouted out as I ran down the hall toward her.

Addie turned and gave me a funny little grin. "Oh, hi, Jenny," she replied casually. Then, glancing at my T-shirt, she added, "I guess you had a good time at camp."

So much for no one noticing my shirt. But it was okay if Addie did. She knew me better than anyone.

"It was awesome," I told her excitedly. "Lots of hiking and outdoor camping. I even went on a canoe trip on the Delaware River. We went over real rapids! And when we went hiking, we got to go down a mud slide. It was the most incredible experience I ever had."

Addie made a face. "Mud slide? Like actually sliding down a hill of mud?"

"Yeah." I giggled, remembering what my bunk mates and I had all looked like after sloshing down the muddy slope. "It was awesome. We looked like mud monsters! I have some amazing pictures! I can't wait to show you."

When I finished talking, an uncomfortable silence fell over us like an itchy wool blanket. It was so strange. Usually Addie and I talked and talked and talked. We barely took time to breathe. Ordinarily, Addie would have had a million questions for me about what it had been like to be away from home for so long, and what kinds of activities I'd signed up for while I was at Camp Kendale.

At the very least, Addie would have told me all about her summer — especially since she'd been so busy she hadn't even had time to answer any of my letters. I frowned slightly, remembering how bummed out I'd been at mail call. On most days there would be a letter from my parents (usually with a dollar for the soda machine tucked inside the note) and a letter from a cousin, my grandmother, or maybe my friends Rachel and Felicia from school. But Addie never got a chance to write me. She must have had a really busy summer.

Still, that was okay. I figured Addie and I would talk when I got home. But things had been so crazy getting ready for school that we hadn't gotten the chance to talk at all — until now. And even now, Addie didn't have much to say to me. She was just biting her lip and playing with her hair.

Then, suddenly, it became totally clear. Addie was just as nervous about starting middle school as I was. Whoa. Addie Wilson, scared. *Incredible.*

It was almost impossible for me to picture Addie being nervous about anything. Usually Addie's the bravest person

I know. She always has been. In third grade, Addie became the first kid to ride a two-wheeler with no hands. Sure, she'd fallen off the bike and sprained her wrist, but still, she'd been the first. And then last year she'd been the only kid brave enough to go trick-or-treating at old Mrs. Morrison's creepy house. Addie was fearless.

But now, Addie was actually scared. I was absolutely, positively sure of it. The first day in sixth grade had her all freaked out. Why else would she be playing with her hair and looking nervously around the hallway.

"This is really exciting, isn't it?" I said finally, breaking the silence. I was trying to help Addie relax. "I mean, we're actually in middle school. *Sixth* grade. Wow. Just look at this place. There are lockers and everything. It's just like one of those schools on TV, you know?"

"Yeah," Addie agreed flatly. "The lockers are pretty cool."

"Where's yours?" I asked. "Hopefully we're right near each other. I've got locker 307."

"I'm 260," Addie said. "And I really should get there and put my things away. So . . ." she turned and started down the hallway.

"Oh, yeah, totally," I agreed. I looked at Addie. She still seemed kind of nervous. Sort of the way my pet mice look when they get spooked by a loud noise. "If you need any help opening your lock, just ask me. My dad and I were practicing all night. You just spin the dial a few times to the right, then stop on the first number. Then you turn the dial to the left and —"

"Jenny, I know how to open a lock," Addie said, as if she was annoyed with me. "Everybody knows how to open a lock." She sighed heavily. "Look, I have to —"

"Hey, Addie."

Just then, a tall boy with light brown hair and green eyes walked up beside us. He was wearing a community center swim team T-shirt. I guess Addie must have met him over the summer.

I waited for her to introduce us, but she didn't.

"What period do you have lunch?" the boy asked Addie.

"Fifth," Addie replied, her face suddenly lighting up. "How about you?"

"Me, too. Fifth period," he said. "Save me a seat?"

"Sure, Jeffrey," Addie promised.

"I have fifth period lunch, too," I said, trying to get into the conversation. "It must be a really popular lunch period."

Jeffrey stared at me for a minute. "Do I know you?" he asked.

"I don't think so," I answered. "I went to Washington Elementary School. You?"

Jeffrey turned his head. "I went to Lincoln. I'm in seventh grade."

"We probably never met then," I told him. "'Cause I went to Washington. But I'm in sixth grade now. Here, at Kilmer Middle School."

Jeffrey laughed. "Yeah, I kind of guessed you went here. After all, you're standing in the hallway."

Oh, man! I could feel the blood rushing into my cheeks. *Here, at Kilmer Middle School.* How could I have said something that stupid?

"This is Jenny McAfee," Addie told Jeffrey, finally introducing us. "She and I were in the same class last year."

"And the year before that, and the year before that," I added cheerfully. "Addie and I have always been in the same class."

"Oh, " Jeffrey said, immediately looking back at Addie. "I think Claire has fifth period lunch, too."

Addie nodded. "And Dana and Aaron. It's like the whole swim team got the same lunch period."

"Cool," Jeffrey said.

I'd only been away at Camp Kendale eight short weeks, but it looked like Addie had made a whole bunch of new friends. I obviously had a lot of catching up to do. But no problem. I'd just start meeting her new friends at lunch that afternoon. Before long, things would be back to normal.

"You know, I have English first period with Ms. Jaffe," Addie said, smiling at Jeffrey. "But I can't find the classroom anywhere."

"That's because Ms. Jaffe is in B wing, and this is C wing," Jeffrey told her. "I have to pass by her room on the way to my Spanish class. I'll take you there."

"I have Ms. Jaffe first period, too," I told Addie. "I know where her room is. My mom and dad took me on a tour of the building two days ago. I can show you —"

"That's okay," Addie said, turning down my offer with a strange little smile. "See you in class, Jenny," she added, as she turned and walked down the hallway with Jeffrey.

"Wait, I'll go with you," I called after her. But Addie must not have heard me, because she and Jeffrey never even turned around.

Chapter
TWO

MIDDLE SCHOOL MORNINGS ARE LONG. Really long. In elementary school I ate lunch at 11:00 A.M. every day. And if the class got hungry before then, the teacher usually gave the class a snack at around 10:00 A.M. But not in middle school. No snacks here. And I had to wait until fifth period — 12:30 P.M. — to eat lunch.

It's not that 12:30 P.M. is that late or anything. But after spending the morning going up and down the stairs and from C wing to B wing and over to A wing, I'd worked up a big appetite. I was starved. So when the bell rang for fifth period I ran to my locker, got out my lunch, and . . .

Uh-oh. Slight problem.

I had no idea how to get to the cafeteria. The map in the school handbook was really confusing, and I had already taken so many wrong turns that most everyone had cleared out of the hallway. The only way I was gonna get to the cafeteria was ask someone for directions.

I'm not usually good at asking strangers for help. I'm kind of shy that way. But right then I was way hungrier than I was shy. When I spotted a group of older kids hanging out in the hall, I knew exactly what I had to do.

I took a deep breath and tried to think brave thoughts.

That was what my counselor at camp had told me to do whenever I had to try something new. At the time I had been scared to climb the high ropes or swim out to the far dock. But now I was going to have to think supercolossal brave thoughts if I was going to have to ask those kids where the cafeteria was. As I walked toward them I saw that both girls were wearing makeup, and the tall boy had dark fuzz peeking out from beneath his nose. I figured they were eighth graders. And everyone knew that eighth graders had no use for sixth graders.

Still, the way I looked at it, these eighth graders were my only hope of finding the cafeteria. It was either talk to them or starve!

"Um, excuse me," I said quietly as I walked up to them. My voice cracked just slightly, and I could feel my cheeks getting red-hot at the sound of it.

"Oh, Sonia, look, it's a sixth grader," laughed the red-haired girl.

"Nice shirt," her friend said sarcastically. She was thin, with brown hair and black eyeliner circling her eyes. "I like the chameleon."

"Actually, it's a lizard," I corrected her. "That's my camp's mascot. Camp Kendale. It's a *sleepaway* camp," I added, hoping to sound more cool.

It didn't work.

"Oh, a lizard," the brunette remarked. "Pardon me. I didn't mean to be insulting."

"Do you think lizards are insulted by being called chameleons, Kristin?" the redhead asked.

"I don't know, Sonia. I think maybe it's the other way around," Kristin replied with a giggle.

My cheeks were burning and I think a few beads of nervous sweat were forming on my forehead. I really hate it when people make fun of me. Not that anybody likes it, but I have a real problem with being made fun of. My mom says I have a "red button" when it comes to that. I don't know about a button, but I do know that my cheeks blush red faster than anyone in the universe! "It doesn't really matter . . ." I started to say, but my voice was suddenly drowned out by a large gurgling noise coming from my empty stomach.

"Ooh, I think the lizard's angry," Sonia joked. "It growled."

"Reptiles can be so sensitive." Kristin laughed.

I bit my lip really hard and blinked my eyes so I wouldn't cry.

"Did you want something, Lizard Girl?" the boy asked me.

"I'm . . . uh . . . I'm trying to find the cafeteria," I said in a voice so quiet it was almost a whisper. "I've been following this map they gave us in homeroom, but it just takes me around in circles and —"

"Oh, that's an old map," Kristin told me. "I think my mother had that one."

"Yeah, you'll never find the cafeteria from that thing," Sonia agreed. "That thing's so old, they don't even have the pool on that map."

"We have a pool?" I asked, amazed. No one said anything at orientation about a pool. I would have definitely remembered that.

"Sure," Kristin said. "You just take the elevator to the second floor, and it lets you off right near the pool. The cafeteria's right around the corner from there."

"Wow!" I exclaimed. "I didn't know we had an elevator, either."

"Lucky you bumped into us, huh?" the boy said. "Here's how you get to the elevator. Go all the way down this hall. Make a right. Then follow that hallway to the windows. Make a left and then a quick right. The elevator's right there. It'll take you to the pool and the cafeteria."

"Yeah, you can't miss it," Kristin added. "The elevator's the big gray metal door."

"Thanks!" I told them gratefully.

"No prob," Sonia answered.

As I walked down the hall toward the elevator, I held my head high. I had done it! I'd talked to eighth graders and lived to tell about it. Not only that, but because I'd been so brave I'd been rewarded with some facts that no other sixth grader seemed to know. We had a pool and an elevator in our school! I couldn't wait to tell Addie.

As I reached the end of the hallway I made a right turn. Then I headed for the windows, turned left, and then right.

Sure enough, there was the big gray door. Quickly, I looked around for the call button.

But there weren't any buttons or arrows or anything else on the door. Just the knob. *Maybe you have to open the door first*, I thought to myself as I reached to turn the doorknob. But the door wouldn't open. I jiggled the knob harder.

No luck. It was locked.

"Can I help you?"

I jumped as a tall man in a green uniform snuck up behind me.

"You okay?" The man asked me.

I gulped. "Yeah. Fine, I guess. I mean . . . um . . . you just scared me."

"Sorry. I was wondering what you were doing at my supply closet."

"Your what?"

"My supply closet. I'm the school janitor and that's my closet," he told me. "I don't know what you could possibly want in there."

"Nothing," I answered him quickly. "I mean, nothing but the elevator. I must have made a wrong turn or something. But these kids told me the elevator was at the end of this hall and it had a big gray door, so I figured . . ."

The janitor began to laugh. "The elevator," he repeated. "Those eighth graders do it every year."

Oh, man. I'd been punked. "So I guess there's no pool, either, huh?"

The janitor shook his head. "Nope. We do get some pretty deep puddles out on the soccer field, though."

I couldn't believe I'd fallen for that. Those eighth graders were probably laughing their heads off at me right now. They'd probably told half the school about the stupid sixth grader who'd fallen for the old elevator and pool trick.

"Don't feel too bad," he told me. "They only played that joke on you because someone did it to them when they were in sixth grade. And when you're in eighth grade, you'll probably do the same thing to some unsuspecting sixth grader."

But I wouldn't. Never.

"So what were you looking for?" the janitor asked, smiling.

"The cafeteria."

"You're about as far from that as you can get," he said.

Once again I could feel tears welling up in my eyes. I was such an idiot for believing them. And I was starving. Now it would take me forever to get to the other end of the school . . . if I could even find my way there. After all, I'd thrown out my map after those eighth graders told me it was outdated.

"Of course, you could cut through the teacher's parking lot and get there real fast," the janitor continued.

"But I can't leave the school building unless it's to go to the yard for recess," I insisted. "I saw it in the school handbook."

"You actually read that thing?" the janitor asked, surprised.

Of course I had read it. The whole thing. From cover to cover. I'd wanted to know everything about the school before I got there.

Unfortunately, the most important things you needed to know weren't in the handbook. Like what to wear on the first day or how to avoid being punked by eighth graders.

The janitor smiled kindly at me. "You can go anywhere in the school if you're accompanied by a staff member. So if you go through the parking lot with me, you'll be okay."

"You'd take me to the cafeteria?"

"Sure. Why not? I could go for a tuna hoagie right around now, anyhow," he replied. Then he held out his hand. "I'm Mr. Collins."

"Jenny McAfee." I shook his hand.

"Well, nice to meet you, Jenny," Mr. Collins said. "I think we're going to get along just fine. Most people say I'm a good person to know around here."

I smiled for the first time since I'd arrived at school. That was one thing I'd already figured out for myself.

Here's something else I figured out really quickly: A middle school cafeteria is nothing like an elementary school one. In elementary school, the kids sit with their class at long tables. And the teachers eat with their classes, too. Everyone is calm and quiet, using their "indoor voices."

But this cafeteria wasn't quiet or organized at all.

People were sitting all over the place — at tables, on the radiators, wherever they wanted. And they were loud. No indoor voices here.

Oh, yeah, I thought excitedly to myself. This was what middle school was all about!

"You gonna be all right?" Mr. Collins asked me.

I nodded. "I'm just looking for my friend's table. Thanks for getting me here."

"No problem," Mr. Collins replied. "I'm just gonna go get some lunch. Come find me if you need anything, okay?"

I nodded and smiled up at him. I was glad to finally know someone.

When Mr. Collins went to get his sandwich I was all alone again. I recognized a few of the kids at the tables, but I didn't see any of the kids Addie and I used to hang out with in our old school, like Rachel Schumacher or Felicia Liguori. They must have had lunch at a different period.

Most of the kids looked older than me. That was kind of scary. Back in elementary school, the fifth graders were the big kids. But now we were back to a place we hadn't been since kindergarten — we were the babies of the school.

When I spotted Addie in the crowd I felt relieved. She was sitting at a round table near the windows with Dana Harrison, a girl from our old school, Jeffrey the kid I'd met this morning, and a boy and a girl I didn't know, but they looked like seventh graders. I figured they had to be Claire and Aaron, the kids Addie had mentioned earlier.

I hurried over to the table, but as I got closer I noticed something kind of strange. There were no empty chairs. Had Addie forgotten to save me a seat? Nah. That couldn't be it. Back in elementary school Addie and I always sat together at lunch, usually with Felicia and Rachel. One of the older kids must've grabbed the last chair, and Addie was too nervous to explain that the seat was saved. I totally understood that.

"Hi, Addie," I said as I walked up to the table. "Sorry it took me so long to get here. I kind of got lost."

Suddenly everyone at the table stopped talking. They just stared at me.

"Oh, hi, Jenny," Addie said quietly.

"I'll just get a chair, and sit with you guys," I continued cheerfully. "I don't have to wait in line or anything. I brought my lunch."

"A brown bag lunch," Dana muttered. "Give me a break."

"What's wrong with a brown bag lunch?" I asked.

Dana shrugged. "Nothing, I guess. It's just that most people *buy* their lunch in middle school, you know?"

MIDDLE SCHOOL RULE #2:

No Brown Bag Lunches.

In fact, as I looked around the cafeteria, I did notice that most of the kids had cafeteria lunch trays in front of them. It was like a secret memo had been sent out to all the new sixth graders except me.

Okay. Starting tomorrow I'd bring money instead of lunch. But today I just wanted to eat. I was starving. I turned to the table next to Addie's and reached for an empty chair. "Are you using this?" I asked one of the boys who was sitting there.

"Nah. It's all yours," he replied.

"Cool," I said, taking the chair and swinging it over to where Addie was sitting. I stood there for a moment, waiting for Addie to move her chair and make room for me. But Addie didn't move over. No one at the table did.

"Um, we're kind of squished already," Addie told me quietly. "You got here kind of late."

Huh? I stood there for a moment. Had I heard Addie correctly? There was no room for me — *me* — at the table?

But judging by the way the other kids at the table ignored me, I'd heard her loud and clear.

Oh, man, the tears were coming again. How many times had I almost cried today? "Oh," I said quietly, blinking quickly to make sure none of the tears that were forming in my eyes would leak out onto my cheeks. "Sure. No problem. I'll . . . um . . . see you guys later."

I walked away from that table as fast as I could, with my brown bag lunch clutched in my hand. I looked around the cafeteria again, hoping to see someone I knew. Okay, so there was Mark Morgan and Justin Abramowitz, but I'd never really been friends with them. I spotted Olivia Becks sitting with some of her friends near the cafeteria door. Olivia had always been nice to me, even though she was a year older. But I hadn't seen her in a while and I didn't want to take a chance at getting rejected again.

Not that Addie had completely rejected me. I mean, it was sort of my own fault. I was the one who had come late, and the truth was, if I'd added another seat to that table, everyone would have been really squished.

But no matter what the reason, I was still without a lunch table. That meant I was going to have to eat lunch alone. But I couldn't. I just couldn't. What could possibly be more embarrassing than sitting all alone in the middle of this cafeteria while everyone else was eating with their friends? Everyone would be staring at me, wondering who the weird girl in the lizard shirt with no friends was.

I might as well stick a sign on my back that said LOSER. No way I was going to let that happen!

Then my stomach rumbled again — as if I needed a reminder that I was hungry. I had to eat lunch. I wasn't going to make it through the rest of the day without it.

And then I spotted it. A safe place. A place where no one would know what I was doing or saying. The phone booth! It was located in the corner of the cafeteria, right near the back exit of the school. I remembered from my school handbook that kids weren't allowed to use their cell phones in the school building, but we could make calls during lunch using the pay phone.

That was the answer! I zoomed over to the booth,

stepped inside, and shut the door. Then I took the phone off the hook and pretended to dial a phone number. As I gripped the phone between my shoulder and my ear, I sat down on the seat, opened up my brown bag, and took out my sandwich.

This was definitely not how I'd pictured my first lunch in middle school. I thought I would be sitting with friends, swapping stories, and laughing. But instead of hearing about summer vacations and school shopping sprees, the only conversation I heard was the sound of a recorded voice giving me the same message over and over: "If you'd like to make a call, please hang up and try again."

Chapter
THREE

BY THE END OF THE SCHOOL DAY, my fingers were killing me from taking notes in class, my back hurt from carrying my book bag up and down the stairs, and my head ached from trying to remember the names of all my new teachers and classmates. As I shut my locker door for the last time, all I could think about was how much I just wanted to go home and forget this whole day had ever happened.

Then I spotted Addie at her locker. She was all alone, and she seemed to be having trouble opening the lock. I took a deep breath. Addie was my friend and I wasn't going to abandon her. "Hey, can I help you with that?" I asked, coming to her rescue. "I'm pretty good with them, like I told you this morning. Just tell me your combination and —"

"My combination is supposed to be secret, Jenny," Addie reminded me.

"Yeah, but it's just me," I said. "And I would never tell."

"It's okay. I'll get it," Addie assured me. "I should practice, anyway."

I nodded. "So, um, you want to come over after school today?" I asked her. "I want to hear all about your summer. And I know Cody and Sam are anxious to see you. I think they really missed you."

Addie rolled her eyes. "Mice don't miss people, Jenny."

"Sure they do," I said. "You should have seen how excited they were when I got home from camp. They came running over to the side of the cage."

"Oh, that's nice," Addie replied absentmindedly.

"So, can you?" I asked her.

"Can I what?"

"Come over after school."

Addie shook her head. "I have plans with Dana. We're going school supply shopping at the mall."

First lunch and now shopping? Since when were Addie and Dana Harrison such good friends? They hadn't even had one playdate the whole time we were in elementary school. We both thought she was kind of stuck-up, actually.

Then I remembered that they'd both spent the summer at the community center day camp, and swimming on the swim club team.

Well, if Addie liked Dana, maybe I would, too. People changed, didn't they?

"So maybe I could come shopping with you guys," I suggested to Addie. "My mom could drive and take all three of us to the mall to get notebooks and stuff." *There.* Now Addie would invite me to come along, and we could all three be friends.

But Addie *didn't* invite me. She just looked around anxiously and pulled on her long, curly blond hair.

There it was. That awful silence. I wanted to ask Addie

why she was being so mean, but instead I just kept talking. Maybe I was just reading her wrong.

"So, um, what did you think of Ms. Jaffe?" I asked her finally, just to break the silence.

"She was okay," Addie replied. "Just not as funny as Ms. Strapp. She was a riot. Remember when she came in and did that rap song about adjectives last year?"

I giggled. Ms. Strapp had been our fifth grade teacher. She'd always been able to make even the most boring things — like grammar — seem hilarious. "What about the time she taught us all how to do those dances from when she was a kid, because 'dance' was a verb?"

Before long, Addie and I were laughing together, talking about old times. It was like nothing had changed.

Except for how she had treated me earlier.

"Addie, how come you didn't save me a seat at lunch?" I asked her finally.

Addie got quiet and looked at the ground. "I was sitting with some of my other friends," she said plainly.

"But we always sit together at lunch."

"I know we used to," Addie admitted. "But I wanted to sit with my friends from the swim team."

"But aren't we friends?" I asked her.

"Sure," Addie said. And she didn't sound like she was lying or anything. "But we don't have to do everything together, you know. This is middle school. Things are different."

Just then, Dana appeared at the end of the hall. She

waved at Addie. Addie smiled back. "Look, I gotta go. I'll see ya later, okay?" Addie told me.

I watched as Addie ran off to go shopping with Dana, and not me.

Addie wasn't kidding. Things were different.

Suddenly, a tall thin girl in long cargo shorts and a tank top came up beside me. "Hey, aren't you in my English class?" she asked in a voice so loud it echoed through the nearly empty hallway.

I looked at her for a minute, surprised. Then I nodded. "I think so," I said quietly. "Ms. Jaffe. First period, right?"

"Ms. Jaffe's kind of boring, huh?" the girl said. "I almost fell asleep today when she was explaining how she wanted us to set up our notebooks."

"That was kind of boring," I agreed.

"My name's Chloe," the girl said. "What's yours?"

"Jenny."

"Cool. So, I guess I'll see you tomorrow."

I smiled at Chloe. The first real smile I could remember giving anybody all day. I was really glad that someone was finally being nice to me. "You bet," I told Chloe. "First period. I'll be there."

"Hi, honey. How was your first day in middle school?" my mom eagerly greeted me as soon as I walked through the door.

"Fine," I grumbled.

"Tough teachers?" Mom wondered.

I shook my head. "Nah. They're okay."

"Did you make any new friends?"

I thought about Chloe, but a twenty-second conversation did not count as friendship.

"Not yet."

"Do you have classes with Addie or any of your old friends?"

"I have English and gym with Addie, but I didn't see Felicia or Rachel at all today."

"Oh." She studied my face for a moment. "Are you okay? Did something happen?"

"It's just . . . forget it. You wouldn't understand." I really didn't want to talk about this anymore. I just wanted to go up to my room to be alone.

"Okay, well, whenever you want to go school supply shopping, let me know," she said, changing the subject. My mom's pretty good about letting things drop. "Do you have a list of the things you need?"

"I just need to check a few things before we go," I said.

"No problem, but I only have time for a quick trip. Any big stuff will have to wait until the weekend, okay?"

I scowled as I made my way up the blue-carpeted stairs to my room. Then I shut my bedroom and flopped down on the red-and-white gingham comforter on my bed. There was something kind of soothing about being in my room. It had looked this way for as long as I could remember. Yellow furniture, red carpet, red-and-white gingham comforter and curtains. Nothing ever changed in my room.

It would be nice if everything in the world was like that, too.

At the sound of the door opening and closing, my two white mice, Cody and Sam, began squeaking wildly. "At least you guys are glad to see me," I said as I pulled two mouse treats from the container near the cage. "No one else was today. I just don't get it." I took Cody from the cage and held him close as I stroked his soft white fur. "Addie was so mean to me. She's never acted like that before."

Cody snuggled in against my Camp Kendale T-shirt and gnawed happily on his treat. I looked down at him for a moment, and then it hit me. The T-shirt! That had to be it. Addie and Dana had been all dressed up today in cute tops and low-slung jeans. They had fit right in with seventh graders.

But not me. I hadn't been dressed like a seventh grader at all. Actually, I didn't look any different than I had in fifth grade. No wonder Addie didn't want me sitting with her at lunch. She didn't want the older kids to think her best friend was a little kid.

Suddenly, I felt a lot better. Once I understood what was probably going on in Addie's mind I could forgive her. In fact, I could do better than that. I could help her. From now on, I was going to have to act and look more grown-up, so that Addie wouldn't have to choose between me and the seventh graders anymore.

A bright smile formed on my lips as I placed Cody back in his cage and raced over to my computer. I logged on and quickly Googled the words "teen fashions." Almost instantly a huge list of websites appeared on the screen.

I scanned the names of the websites and saw www.middleschoolsurvival.com

Hmm . . . that sounded like what I was looking for.

I clicked on the site and immediately saw links for quizzes and advice columns. There were also tons of photos.

Instantly, I clicked on the section called "Fierce Fashions." Pictures of low-slung jeans, funky hats, and boots appeared. They were awesome. Just the kinds of things Addie and her new friends had been wearing today.

I hit the PRINT button on my computer, and pictures of really cool clothes began shooting out of the printer.

I smiled to myself as I stared at the photos. It looked like I'd be adding a few extra things to my school supply shopping list!

Chapter
FOUR

IT'S NOT EASY finding different places to hide and eat your lunch. But that's what I had to do the whole first week of school. Tuesday the stairwell. Wednesday the library. Thursday the hallway near Mr. Collins's supply closet. Friday I was back to the phone booth.

It didn't exactly make for the perfect school dining experience. But I'd had no choice since I couldn't go clothes shopping until the weekend.

But when Monday came, I was ready to rock! "Oh, yeah," I murmured excitedly to myself as I headed to the school entrance for my second week in sixth grade. Things were already starting to look up.

To begin with, I already knew where all my classes were located so I wouldn't have to ask directions again. And some of the kids' faces were already beginning to look familiar. As I walked up the steps toward the school, I spotted two other sixth graders who had been in my math and Spanish classes. They smiled at me and I smiled back. A connection. Cool. And I hadn't even gone inside the school building yet.

I reached down and patted the pocket of my new jeans.

The five-dollar bill was still there. Dana had been right. A bag lunch was sooooo elementary school.

As I walked down the hallway of C Wing I felt *transformed*, mostly because of what I was wearing. My new outfit totally rocked. Somehow I'd been able to convince my mom that things like a newsboy cap, low-slung ripped jeans, and cowboy boots were every bit as important for school as a binder and pencils. And believe me, that hadn't been easy.

As I walked down the hallway toward my locker, I could feel the eyes of some of the other kids on me. My make-over was definitely working. I looked every bit as cool as the other kids now. Maybe even cooler. Now Addie wouldn't have to choose between her new friends and me.

As I headed down the hall, I saw Addie with Claire and Dana. They seemed to be having a very intense conversation. I reached out my arm just high enough so that when I waved to Addie, my new lemon yellow tank top scooted up just above my belly button.

But Addie, Dana, and Claire didn't wave back. Instead, they remained clustered together, giggling wildly about something.

"Check out the granny panties," Claire said, giggling. "Why would anyone wear them with low-slung jeans? You can totally see her Fruit of the Loomies."

"She's walking all bowlegged, like she's been riding a horse too long," Dana added with a laugh.

Addie giggled.

I looked around to see who they were talking about, but it was hard to tell who it could be. I didn't see anyone who was walking bowlegged or wearing Fruit of the Loom underwear.

For a minute I wondered if maybe they were talking about me. But I knew that couldn't be it. For one thing, I looked too cool. And for another, Addie would never let anyone make fun of me.

At least I didn't think she would.

"Hi, Addie," I said, as I came closer. "What's up, Dana? Claire?"

Dana and Claire looked at each other.

"Uh, hi," Dana said.

"Yeah. Um, hi," Claire added.

They looked at each other again. "We'll . . . uh . . . we'll see you later, Ad," Claire said. "Gotta go."

"Bye," I said, as they walked away. I was glad to see them go. Now it was just me and Addie.

"So, I went shopping this weekend, and got a bunch of new clothes," I said, pointing to the gray cap on my head.

"I noticed," Addie said.

"So, now we both have cool tees and new jeans," I pointed out to her. "Awesome, huh?"

Addie looked at my new clothes. "Well, it's not like we're wearing the same outfit or anything, Jenny," she pointed out. "And everyone gets new school clothes in September."

"Yeah, that's the best part of the new school year," I said. "Getting new clothes. I think half of the school was in Green Oz on Saturday." I purposely let Addie know that I had been shopping in Green Oz. Addie and I had always wanted to shop there, but our moms had always said the clothes were too grown-up for us.

Not anymore!

"Oh, Green Oz," Addie said. "That's a nice store, I guess. Dana and I like Rosie's better, though. It's got much cooler stuff. You should check it out sometime."

I sighed. Once again I had been just one step behind Addie and Dana on the coolness meter. At least Addie had told me about Rosie's having better stuff. Next time I would shop there. I smiled at her gratefully. "Thanks for the tip," I said.

Addie shrugged. "Sure. I gotta run. See ya later, okay?"

"Yeah," I said. "Maybe at . . ."

I was going to say maybe at lunch, but I never got to finish my sentence. Addie was gone before I could. I took that as a hint that she wouldn't be saving a seat for me at her table today.

I'd been dreading the fifth period bell all morning. In fact, for the first time in my life I was actually praying that science class would go on forever. I figured it was better to face the basics of how electricity works than to start another week facing the crowds of unfriendly faces in the cafeteria.

But all the wishes and prayers in the world can't stop the clock from turning, and before I knew what was happening that bell rang.

As I walked into the cafeteria, I made a point of not looking toward Addie's table in the back of the room. Instead, I hurried over to the lunch line and looked at my choices: bagels with butter, turkey sandwiches, pasta with tomato sauce, and some sort of brownish mystery-meat. It all looked really nasty and it smelled even worse. A brown bag lunch would be better than this. Finally I decided on the bagel — I figured that would be pretty hard for the cafeteria staff to mess up — a container of milk, and some red Jell-O. I paid my three dollars and took my tray.

Now came the hard part. Where was I supposed to sit? The stairwell? The library? Or maybe for something completely different, how about a stall in the girls' room?

"Hey, Jenny!"

Suddenly I heard someone screaming my name — *really screaming* — across the cafeteria. I blushed when I noticed how many people had stopped talking and turned to see what was going on.

But Chloe, the girl who had actually done all the yelling, didn't seem to be embarrassed at all.

"How ya doin'?" she asked as she caught up with me.

"Hi, Chloe," I answered quietly.

"So, are you sitting with anyone?" Chloe asked me, her voice still at top volume.

"I . . . um . . . well, not really. I don't know too many people in this school yet," I whispered.

Okay, that wasn't a hundred percent true. But the people in the school I did know either had lunch during another period or had ditched me. So it wasn't a complete lie, right?

"I know tons of people. My next-door neighbor, Marc, is in seventh grade and he kind of introduced me around," Chloe said. " I'm sitting with him, his friend Liza, and some kids from my old school. I went to Stevenson Elementary."

"I went to Washington Elementary School," I said.

"Oh, so you must live on the east side of town," Chloe said.

I nodded yes.

"No wonder I've never met you," Chloe continued. "Although I think maybe I saw you at the community center a couple of times."

"It's possible. I took pottery classes there last spring."

"Pottery. Cool," Chloe said. "So you wanna sit with us?"

I didn't have to think that over for too long. It wasn't like I had anyone else begging me to come sit with them. And besides, sitting with seventh graders would be kind of impressive. Addie wouldn't be the only one eating lunch with older kids.

"Sure," I said finally. "That'd be great."

I followed Chloe over to a table near the fruit-vending machines. Her friends looked up as we walked over.

"Hey, everybody, this is Jenny. She's stuck in Ms. Jaffe's English class with me. Jenny, this is everybody," Chloe introduced me.

A guy in a black vintage Led Zeppelin T-shirt laughed. "Very classy intros, Chloe," he said. "What's she supposed to call me? 'Every' or 'body'?"

I giggled. That one was actually kind of funny.

"So introduce *yourself*, big shot," Chloe told him, taking a huge bite of her turkey sandwich before she even sat down. "I'm hungry."

"Close your mouth, Chloe," one of two twins groaned.

"Ooh, gross," her sister added.

Chloe opened her mouth wide, and displayed her half-chewed food, her brown eyes laughing with delight.

"Okay, we're not all that nasty," the guy in the Zeppelin shirt told her. "I'm Marc."

"Hi," I said. "You're the one in the seventh grade, right?" I blushed the minute the words were out of my mouth. How stupid did *that* sound?

But Marc didn't seem to think it was stupid. "Yeah. I got here early and kind of scoped the place out before Chloe arrived."

"Hey, we were here last year, too, you know," one of the twins reminded him. She smiled at me. "I'm Marilyn."

"And I'm Carolyn," her sister added.

"You can tell us apart because I'm the cute one." Marilyn laughed.

"No, I am." Carolyn giggled.

I smiled. Considering both girls had the same long blond hair, small blue eyes, and rosy pudgy cheeks, any argument over who was the cutest seemed kind of ridiculous to me. If they weren't wearing different-color T-shirts, I doubt anyone would be able to tell them apart.

"And the genius over there, the one looking over his algebra textbook, is Josh. He's a total whiz," Chloe told me, pointing to her left at a dark-haired guy in wire-frame glasses and a black-and-white rugby shirt. "He's taking seventh grade math, even though he's just a puny sixth grader like us."

"Who are you calling puny?" Josh demanded. "I'm a black belt now, remember?"

"Sorry, Karate Kid," Chloe apologized sarcastically.

"Wow, do you really have a black belt in karate?" I asked Josh. Now that was impressive.

"It's actually in tae kwon do," Josh corrected her. "But I can never get Chloe to get it right."

"Whatever," Chloe replied with a shrug. "It's still a bunch of kicking, screaming, and breaking wood."

"I'd like to see you break a piece of wood," Josh shot back.

Chloe laughed. "No thanks. That's not my idea of a good time."

I turned to the only person who had not introduced herself. She was petite and had short brown hair that fell just below her ears. She'd been sitting there completely silent, watching us all with her intense brown eyes.

"And you are . . . ?" I asked her, amazed at how relaxed I had suddenly become in this new group of strangers.

"Liza," the girl replied so quietly that I could barely hear her. "I'm in seventh grade, too."

"Liza's the shy, mysterious type," Chloe said, obviously unaware that she was embarrassing Liza. Liza's face turned as pink as the stripes on her shirt. I knew just how she felt.

"So how come we didn't see you at lunch last week?" Marc asked me.

"Oh, I was here, but I had a lot of stuff to do. Like one day I had to make an important phone call, and another I had to go to the . . ."

"Yeah, I made the same phone call the first day I was in this place," Marc interrupted me with a knowing wink.

Now it was my turn to blush. Marc had obviously figured out my lunchtime secret. So much for seeming cool around seventh graders.

"Hey, it's okay," Marc told her. "The first week is always the worst."

I took a deep breath and let it out. He had no idea just how bad things had been.

"I like your hat," Liza interrupted shyly.

"Me, too," Chloe said. "It's the first thing I noticed when I got into English class this morning. Maybe I should get one."

Josh shook his head. "You don't need any help getting

noticed, Chloe," he assured her. "With that mouth of yours, you're hard to miss."

"Yeah, well, with that —" Chloe began.

"So, are you guys going to stay in your own classrooms this year?" Marc interrupted, turning the conversation to Marilyn and Carolyn in an obvious effort to stop an argument between Josh and Chloe before it started.

"What fun would that be?" Marilyn said. (At least I *thought* it was Marilyn. I couldn't remember which twin was in the green shirt and which was in the blue one.)

"Seriously. Why should I have to take a math test when she's so much better at math than I am?" Carolyn wondered.

"Yeah. But if I take your math tests, you've got to take my Spanish tests," Marilyn reminded her sister.

"No problemo," Carolyn replied.

"You two will get in big trouble if you get caught," Liza pointed out quietly.

"No one's caught us yet," Marilyn assured Liza. "Hey, even our mom gets us confused sometimes."

As everyone continued talking, my eyes sort of drifted off toward the windows. Addie and Dana were sitting there, whispering to each other, while Claire and Aaron blew the wrappers from their straws at each other, and Jeffrey seemed to be hurrying to finish some last-minute homework. It was pretty much the same kind of thing that was happening at our table, and yet somehow they seemed so much cooler.

"Forget about it, Jenny," Marc remarked from across the table.

"What?"

"I said forget about it," he repeated. "They never let anybody in. That group's set."

"Who?" I asked, embarrassed at having been caught staring. More blushing. *Great.*

Marc nodded over in the direction of Addie's table. "Those guys. The Pops."

"The *Pops*?"

"Yeah. 'Pop' as in popular. They're just a bunch of snobs who spend their whole lives trying to impress everybody. They're not really that great."

I shrugged. Deep down, I knew Marc was probably right. So how come I still really wanted to be one of them?

Chapter FIVE

IT'S JUST THE THING TO DO. Or at least it's the thing the *Pops* do.

I found that out when I went there after lunch. There were like a hundred girls in the bathroom. Okay, maybe not a hundred, but you know what I mean.

Not that I had to wait for a stall or anything. I was the only girl in there who was actually using the bathroom. For everyone else it was just a place to talk about other people and put on makeup. Addie, Dana, and Claire were there giggling, and putting on layers of eye shadow, mascara, and lip gloss before their next classes.

As soon as I stepped out of the stall and walked over to the sink, Dana and Claire stopped talking. Ha! As if I'd really want to hear about some cute boy they spotted in the gym or who they were making fun of now.

Okay, I admit it. I probably would have really liked to have heard it. But there was no way I was going to let them know it! I just focused on the water flowing from the faucet and stared at the soap dispenser.

"Uh, nice boots," Dana said, barely trying to choke back a giggle.

"Thanks," I murmured.

"Value Shoe, right?" Dana asked.

"Huh?"

"I mean you got them at Value Shoe, didn't you?" Dana explained. "You must have. They're cheap copies of the designer boots my mother wears."

Ouch. Okay, that one hurt. There's nothing worse than being told you were dressed like somebody's mother!

Dana had definitely changed over the summer. Now she wasn't just boring — she was mean and boring!

"Of course, my mom's boots are made of a much better leather," Dana told Addie and Claire. "Those cheap imitations are so hard to walk in." She bent her legs slightly outward and pretended to walk like a cowboy with sore thighs.

I walked over to the paper-towel dispenser and wiped my hands, refusing to say anything more. I glanced over at Addie to see if maybe she would tell Dana to cut it out, but Addie seemed to be ignoring me all together. It was like she hadn't even heard the conversation.

And maybe she hadn't. She was incredibly focused on brushing some pale blue eye shadow on her eyelid.

I watched with amazement as an eighth grader walked over to talk to her.

"You're Addie Wilson, right?" she asked.

Addie nodded.

"I'm Sabrina Rosen," the eighth grader introduced herself. "I went to Washington Elementary."

"I remember," Addie replied. "You had Mr. Plotkin in fifth grade, right?"

Sabrina nodded. "Yeah. The one who spit when he talked. It was awful talking about space in science." She spit slightly when she said the word *space.*

Addie giggled, and Sabrina laughed along with her.

Now that was definitely impressive. Sabrina was an eighth grader, and yet, she had been the one to come over and talk to Addie. Not the other way around. That was huge!

Soon, Addie, Dana, and Claire were exchanging pots of eye shadow and blush with the older girls, bonding over their collections of Cover Girl, Hard Candy, and Jessica Simpson Dessert makeup. No one even seemed to notice I was there anymore. Not that I could have joined in on the conversation even if they had. The only thing I had that even remotely resembled makeup was a beeswax lip balm I'd bought at the drugstore.

I bumped into Chloe, Marc, and Liza again later in the day, while I was on my way to Spanish class. They were standing by the D wing lockers talking. Unlike Addie and her friends, these guys actually waved for me to come over and join the conversation.

"Hi, Jenny," Marc said, holding up a small video camera. "What's up?"

"What're you doing?" I asked him, turning away from the camera. I don't usually like having my picture taken, especially when I'm not ready for it. I always seem to wind up with a doofy grin on my face or something.

"I'm making a movie," Marc explained. "It's kind of like reality TV," Marc told me. "You know: 'What is it really like to go to Joyce Kilmer Middle School?'"

"Who'd watch that?" Chloe asked him. "School's boring."

"Not necessarily," Marc said. "You just have to know what to look for."

"Marc, turn off the camera, okay?" Liza asked him in her soft voice.

I smiled gratefully at Liza. It seemed like we had a lot in common — besides the blushing.

"Yeah, Jenny doesn't look like she's in the mood to be interviewed by *you*, Mr. Spielberg," Chloe teased him.

"Hey, don't make fun of Steven Spielberg," Marc warned.

"I wasn't," Chloe assured him. "I was making fun of you. And I was protecting Jenny." She turned to me and studied my face. "You don't look so good. Are you okay?"

No. I wasn't okay. Not by a long shot. My feet hurt from

walking up and down stairs all day in my new boots, and my head was hot from being under a hat. But I didn't say that. I didn't say anything at all.

"Oh, that was real nice of you, Chloe," Marc said, shaking his head.

Chloe frowned. "I didn't mean you don't look nice or anything, Jenny," she apologized. "I just meant your face was a little gray."

"Not much better, Chloe," Marc said, coming to my defense.

"Well, I'm just worried," Chloe continued. "She looked a lot better at lunch than she does now and —"

"Chloe," Marc interrupted her. "Quit while you're behind, will you?"

I had to laugh at that one. "I think I'm just tired," I told Chloe, letting her off the hook.

"Well, you'd better wake up," Chloe said. "We've got Spanish next. And I think we're getting our first vocabulary sheet."

"So soon?" I asked.

"Marc says señorita Gonzalez gets started right away," Chloe replied.

"*Sí*," Marc agreed. "*Trabajamos mucho en la clase de español.*"

"Huh?" Liza, Chloe, and I all said at once.

"I said, there's a lot of work in Spanish class," Marc replied.

"Are you taking Spanish, too?" I asked Liza.

She shook her head. "French. I started last year, and I'm sticking with it."

Just then the bell rang.

"Okay, that's *adiós* for me," Marc said, moving away from the lockers. "I'm gonna be late for science." He turned to me before he left. "Let me know if you need any help with Spanish, okay?"

"Thanks," I said.

"De nada," he replied.

"Huh?"

"It means 'you're welcome.'" He held up his video camera. "Say bye to the camera."

I put my hand over the lens of his camera.

"Too late," he teased. "You're already part of the movie."

Great. So here I was, with a gray face, tired feet, and sweaty hair recorded for all time on camera. Just what I wanted.

As Marc walked away, I thought of something else they don't tell you in the school handbook. Beware of seventh graders who carry cameras.

Chapter
SIX

"JENNY, I SAVED YOU A SEAT!" Felicia Liguori shouted as I climbed into the school bus at the end of the school day.

Seeing her at the end of the school day had really kept me going — especially since Addie and I hadn't been talking or sitting together on the bus, either. Talking to Felicia made it seem like everything was back to normal. No confusing halls, makeup parties in the bathroom, or girls making fun of my Fruit of the Loomies. Just Felicia and me riding the school bus together. Like the good old days.

"Check this out," Felicia said as I sat down.

Felicia opened her mouth wide, so I could see the thin metal band stretching over her front teeth. "I went to the orthodontist this weekend and got a retainer."

"Oh. Does it hurt?"

Felicia shook her head. "It's just kind of annoying. It makes it hard to talk."

She wasn't kidding. Suddenly all of Felicia's s's sounded like sh's.

"Are you gonna need braces?" Felicia asked me.

"Dr. Benton says he's not sure yet," I told her. "I still need to lose some more baby teeth." I frowned slightly. As if I hadn't felt like a baby enough these past two days, right?

But Felicia didn't make fun of my still having baby teeth. Instead, she started to laugh. "Oh, man, check that out," she whispered to me as Addie got on the bus.

"What?"

"Doesn't Addie look ridiculous?" Felicia said. "Rachel and I were talking about it at lunch. All that makeup and stuff. She's trying to look older, but I think she looks like a clown."

I stared at Felicia with surprise. Usually she was really kind to everyone. But that wasn't a nice thing to say at all. Especially since she and Addie had been friends for a long time, too.

"You were away all summer," Felicia continued in a low whisper. "You don't know what happened to Addie, do you?"

I leaned over closer so I could hear her better. I didn't want to miss a word.

"She and Dana are good swimmers," Felicia said. "And when they took the swim team test, they were really, really fast. So the coaches put them on the older team. The next thing you know Addie and Dana started getting really tight with all these seventh graders on the team. Addie stopped talking to Rachel and me, and started dressing like . . . like . . . that!" Felicia laughed. "She looks like how we looked when we got into my mom's makeup kit. Remember?"

I laughed at the thought of that. We'd looked pretty ridiculous with red lipstick all over our faces, and bright green eye shadow going from our eyelids all the way up to our foreheads.

"She puts all that makeup on at school so her mom won't find out," Felicia continued. "But she must have forgotten to take it off. Her mom's gonna kill her when she sees!"

I looked at Felicia strangely. She sounded like she was happy that Addie was going to get in trouble.

"Well, this is my stop," Felicia announced as the bus turned the corner. "Call me tonight?" she asked.

"Sure," I agreed. "Maybe we can do something this weekend, you, me, and Rachel."

"But not Addie," Felicia whispered.

I shook my head. No. *Not Addie.*

A few minutes later, the school bus stopped at the corner near my house. I walked down the stairs, and Addie followed close behind. I didn't even try to talk to her. I could take a hint.

But Addie hurried to catch up to me as we got off the bus.

"Hi, Jenny," she said.

"Hi," I answered, but not too nicely.

"What are you doing?"

"Walking home," I answered her.

"No, I mean this afternoon," Addie continued. "Do you have a pottery class or something?"

I shook my head. "It doesn't start for another week or so. I'm just going to do homework, I guess."

Addie nodded. "I have a lot of homework, too. Maybe we could do it together."

Huh? Now I was totally confused. We hadn't talked in days.

"I figure I haven't seen Cody and Sam in a while, and you and I haven't gotten a lot of time to talk since you got back . . ." Addie let her voice trail off.

And whose fault is that? I wanted to say. But I didn't. Addie sounded so much like her old self all of a sudden. I didn't want that to change, so I just answered, "Sure. You can come over."

"Great. We'll do homework together, and play with Sam and Cody," Addie said as she happily walked up the stairs toward my front porch. "But first, I've gotta use your bathroom."

When Addie walked out of the bathroom, the eye shadow, blush, mascara, and lip gloss were gone. She'd washed it all off. Now her mom would never know.

"So I guess you like middle school a lot," I said, walking over to Cody and Sam's cage and giving them their mouse treats.

"It's okay. I mean, it's still school."

"Yeah, but you have so many new friends and all. " I picked up Sam and stroked his soft white fur.

Addie pulled Cody from the cage and began to pet his

back. "You've got a lotta friends, too," she said. "I saw you at lunch."

So Addie had been noticing me at lunch, too. Wow. I'd never even thought about that possibility.

"Anyway, it was pretty cool that Sabrina Rosen came over to talk to you in the bathroom today," I said.

"I guess," Addie said. "No big deal."

Those were the words that came out of her mouth. But the smile on her face let me know that Addie thought it was a *huge* deal.

For the first time since school began, I was starting to relax around Addie. Things seemed almost the way they'd used to. And yet, there was something really nagging at me. And the more I stared at Addie's clean face, the more I just had to ask her.

"Hey, Ad?"

"Yeah?"

"Can I ask you something?"

Addie shrugged. "Sure."

"Did you really come over here to hang out and do homework?"

"Why else would I come over?" Addie asked.

"I don't know. To wash your makeup off before your mom saw you with it?" I asked.

I regretted the words the minute they came out of my mouth. Addie turned white. She looked like I had just punched her in the stomach.

"I mean . . . I didn't mean, well, you know, I was just

wondering because . . . oh, never mind," I stammered nervously. "I know you wanted to see Cody and Sam."

Of course she did. She was cuddling Cody, wasn't she?

Addie nodded and petted Cody once more before gently placing him back in the cage. "I love your mice."

I smiled. Of course she did.

Addie asked, "Did you hear about the school dance next week?"

"I know — next Friday," I said, relieved that Addie had moved on to another topic. I was also happy to have known something before Addie did. "It was on the calendar in the back of the school handbook."

Addie giggled. "I can't believe you read that thing."

I blushed a little. "So, I guess you're going to the dance," I said.

She nodded. "Claire, Dana, and I are going shopping for new outfits on Saturday."

"Oh, that sounds fun," I said.

"Um . . . yeah. I guess," Addie murmured.

"I could probably use some new clothes, too," I suggested. "Does your mom have any more room in the car?"

Usually, I didn't like to invite myself somewhere. But Addie had brought it up. And she wouldn't have done that if she hadn't wanted me to come.

Addie shrugged. "Yeah, I guess. We're probably taking the minivan."

"Cool," I said excitedly. Then I stopped. I remembered I had said I would do something with Felicia and Rachel this weekend. But that was okay. I could shop with Addie on Saturday and hang out with them on Sunday or something.

"Oh, hi, girls."

Addie and I stopped talking when my mother appeared at my bedroom door. Not that we were saying anything too private. It just seemed weird to be talking about school stuff when my mom was around.

"It's great to see you, Addie," my mother continued. "It's been so long since you two have had a playdate."

I groaned slightly. I couldn't believe my mother had said that. *Playdate.* Even I knew that once you were in middle school you didn't call them that. I wasn't sure what you called what Addie and I were doing – hanging out, I guess – but it was *not* a playdate.

Luckily, Addie didn't seem upset at what my mother had said. "I know," she told my mother. "I've been crazy busy, with vacation and the start of school and all that."

"Well, I hope when things calm down, you'll come over more often. Maybe I'll take you two to the teddy bear factory store in the mall. I know you two love making those bears," my mother told her.

Oh, man. This was just getting worse and worse. Teddy bears? If Addie didn't think I was a baby before, she would now.

"Um, Mom," I said. "Addie and I are going to do some homework now. We have a lot of work. *Middle school* work."

"Oh, okay," my mother said sweetly. "Let me know if you two want a snack or something."

"Sorry about that," I said, as soon as the coast was clear.

"My mom's like that, too," Addie said. "She still thinks I want to go to the movies with her. Now why would I want to be seen at a movie theater with my mother?"

I looked at Addie with surprise. "Have you gone to the movies just with friends?" I asked her excitedly.

"Not yet," Addie admitted. "But soon . . . I hope."

I felt a little better. Maybe I wasn't as far behind Addie as I felt.

Addie didn't stay at my house long enough for us to get our homework done. We talked for a little longer, and then Addie went home. She said she had to make a few phone calls. *Probably to Claire and Dana,* I thought to myself as she left.

Still, maybe it was better to do homework alone. One thing I'd learned pretty quickly about middle school, the work is a whole lot harder. It wasn't the kind of stuff you could do with a friend — or even a semi-friend — in your room with you.

Semi-friend. I guess that's what Addie was to me now.

I sat down at the computer and tried to do my English homework, but I couldn't focus. I kept thinking about

Addie and if she came over just to wash off her makeup. How could you tell if someone was really your friend?

I thought about what my English teacher, Ms. Jaffe, had told us today about tests. She said they were a way to prove how much you knew.

That was it. A quiz. There were tons of them on that website I'd found the other day. Quickly I typed in www.middleschoolsurvival.com.

As soon as the website popped up, I searched the screen for the list of online quizzes. Finally, I found the one I wanted.

Is Your Friend Poison?

To find out, click the answer that best describes your friend. The results will follow.

If you told your friend a secret, what would she do?

    A. Keep it to herself even if she was tortured by the enemy.

    B. Try to keep the secret, but let it slip out by mistake.

    C. Blab your deepest, darkest secret to the whole world just to make herself seem cool.

That was a tough one. Before the summer, I would have said A. But I wondered if Addie would tell Claire and Dana about all the stupid things my mom had said about playdates and the teddy bear factory. Maybe they were laughing at me right now.

    I decided to click B. It was sort of a compromise.

You and your pal are in the mall, trying on clothes. You put on an outfit that doesn't really look that great on you. Which is your friend most likely to do?

    A. Say that you look nice, but you could look better, then offer to help you pick out something more suited to you.

B. Lie and say you look awesome so she doesn't hurt your feelings.

C. Let you buy the outfit, look awful, and then laugh at you behind your back.

Okay, that one was easy. Even though I didn't know for sure, I did suspect that maybe Addie's friends had been laughing at me in the hall. And although Addie hadn't exactly been laughing, she hadn't defended me, either. C was the answer.

When you're totally bummed out, does your best friend:

A. Come to your rescue and take you out for a good cry and a big banana split?

B. Steer clear and wait for you to come to her when you want to talk?

C. Ditch you for friends who won't be a drag on her mood?

I supposed the best answer to that question was probably B. Addie did talk to me today about school — and she even said she noticed that I had new friends, too. So she wasn't totally ignoring me. I guessed I could still come to her when I was upset — as long as I did it when Dana, Claire, and Jeffrey weren't around.

When you're out of school with a cold, what does your best friend do?

    A. Bring your homework to your house, and give you all the buzz about what was going on at school.

    B. Call you from her house to talk, so she doesn't get sick.

    C. Hang out with someone else until you get better.

I read that one over and over again. I couldn't choose between B and C. I hoped Addie would at least call me if I were sick with the flu or the plague or something. But I couldn't be sure. Lately I wasn't sure of anything.

Your friend has made some new friends that you don't know. How does this affect your relationship?

    A. It's so cool because now you've got a bunch of new pals, too.

    B. You guys still hang out, just not as much because she spends some of the time hanging with the new crowd.

    C. She drop-kicks your friendship right out the window.

Definitely B. Addie would never be seen with me in school. But at home, she was still sort of like the same old Addie.
    I scrolled down for the results.

If you answered mostly A's, you can rest easy. Yours is a true-blue BFF. She'll be there for you through thick and thin.

If you answered mostly B's, it seems your friend is not the sweet, kind person she appears to be. There are a few dangerous aspects to her personality. No one's saying to steer clear of her completely, but it would be wise to keep your guard up.

If you answered mostly C's, dial 911 immediately and ask for poison control. This girl is toxic. Stay as far from her as possible.

Okay, that settled it. Addie wasn't exactly poison, but she wasn't my BFF, either. I was right. She was my semi-friend. Which I guess was better than her not being my friend at all.

Chapter
SEVEN

WHEN I WOKE UP the next morning, I had made a decision. The next step toward getting Addie back would be putting on makeup in the girl's bathroom, just like Addie and the other Pops did. That would be a good thing.

The only trouble was, I didn't really know that much about putting on makeup. Addie seemed to know exactly what colors to use, and just how to put it on. Somehow she'd learned all that over the summer.

But I didn't have any friends who could teach me about putting on makeup.

On the other hand, I did have something else. A computer. Maybe middleschoolsurvival.com had some ideas about makeup.

My mom and dad wouldn't be awake for another half hour. That gave me just enough time to check the site. Quickly, I flicked on the computer and clicked on www.middleschoolsurvival.com. It was on my bookmark list now.

Sure enough, there's a link to "Makeover Madness." I double-clicked the mouse. Almost immediately, a whole group of topics appeared on the screen. I went right to

Eye-Deal
Eye Shadow Tips

Looking for the perfect shade of shadow for your eyes? Just follow these simple rules and you can't go wrong.

BLUE-EYED BABES: Brown and rose eye shadows were made for you. Apply the eye shadow from lash lines to the creases in your eyelids. Then top it with some dark brown or black mascara.

BROWN-EYED BEAUTIES: Green and gold are the colors for you. These shades will pick up the tiny colored flecks that are often found in brown eyes. Choose a shadow with just a little bit of shimmer, and apply the green shadow from the lash lines to the crease in your eyelids. Then add a pale cream color from the crease to your eyebrow. Finish it up with brown mascara.

GREEN-EYED GALS: Go for lavender and mocha shadows. Warm mocha is the perfect color for day wear, lavender will give you a purply glow for nighttime. Either way, remember to finish off your eyes with brown mascara.

HAZEL-EYED HONEYS: Deep green and pale yellow are the shadows for you. Choose a shadow shade that matches different flecks in your eyes. For added fun, apply your eye shadow, then line eyes with the same color, using a liner brush dipped in water.

I hurried into the bathroom and found my mom's makeup bag. Well, actually I opened one of my mother's many makeup bags. My mom has tons of makeup. Most of it is little samples she gets at the mall. So she's got tons of colors.

I dug through the bag until I found a pretty shade of lavender eye shadow and some brown mascara — everything the website recommended for my green eyes. Then I grabbed one of her old blushes, and a really pretty pink lipstick. Then I closed up the bag and went back to my room.

I smiled to myself as I placed the makeup in my backpack. My journey to the top of the Pops had definitely begun.

But I wasn't feeling that confident when I walked into first period English class that morning. In fact, I was a nervous wreck. My stomach was bouncing all around. It was like waves crashing up and down in there. *Tidal* waves. *Tsunamis.*

I guess I was nervous because both Addie and Chloe were in my English class. At school, I was getting friendly with Chloe — at least I'd felt that way at lunch yesterday. But Addie and I were friends, too — at home, anyhow. So it was sort of like my two worlds were colliding.

"Yo, Jenny, I saved you a seat," Chloe shouted the minute I entered the room. "Over here."

I looked over to the back of the room where Addie and Dana were sitting. They were looking at some pictures on Dana's camera phone. They didn't even glance up when Chloe called my name.

A camera phone. Wow. Dana was really lucky. I'd practically had to beg my parents to let me have a regular cell phone. And now that I had one they wouldn't let me even bring it to school. It was just to use at night or on weekends.

"And this is a picture of my sister and me at the mall," I heard Dana tell Addie. "Her friend took it."

"Where was your mom?" Addie asked.

"She just dropped us off. My sister and I go to the mall by ourselves all the time."

I nodded to myself. Now I knew why Addie so desperately wanted to go to the movies without a grown-up. It was a Pop thing.

I wondered if Addie's mother would be hanging out with us when we all went to the mall together this Saturday to shop for the dance.

"Jenny, didn't you hear me?" Chloe shouted again from her seat in the middle of the room.

Of course I heard her. Everyone in the room had heard her. People in Timbuktu had probably heard her.

"Uh, yeah. Sorry," I said as I slipped into the seat beside her. "I guess I was daydreaming."

"Cool sneakers," Chloe said, looking down at my red-and-white canvas Converses.

"Thanks," I murmured. I actually wasn't wearing the sneakers because they were cool. I was wearing them because my feet still hurt from those boots yesterday.

I looked down at Chloe's feet. She was wearing a really old pair of pink-and-white sneakers. Chloe didn't seem at all hung up on things like expensive shoes or clothes, either. At the moment she was wearing a pair of regular jeans that weren't low-slung or anything. Her T-shirt had a picture of a frog on it. It said HOP TO IT.

"So, did you get to see *Hot New Star* last night?" I overheard Addie saying to Dana. "That girl with the short blond hair can really sing."

"Amanda," Dana replied, giving her name. "She rocks. But I just watch for that judge from England. I think he's so cute."

"I know," Addie agreed. "English accents are so awesome. No matter who you are, if you talk with a British accent you're automatically cool."

"And smart," Dana added. "English people always sound so smart."

I had to agree with that. I wished I had watched *Hot New Star* last night. Then I could join in the conversation. But I'm not allowed to watch TV on school nights. My parents record *Hot New Star*, and I watch it on the weekends. But by then, it would be too late for me to talk about that with Addie and Dana.

When the teacher came in, the class grew quiet. Addie and Dana stopped talking. But they managed to keep up their conversation throughout the rest of class by passing notes. I watched as Dana scribbled something on a piece of paper, folded it up small, and then quietly dropped it on the corner of Addie's desk.

MIDDLE SCHOOL RULE #4:
PASSING NOTES IS COOL.

"Jenny. Jenny. Hello. Earth to Jenny McAfee!"

I jumped as I heard Ms. Jaffe call out my name.

"Um . . . here," I said quickly.

"I know you're here," Ms. Jaffe said with a deep sigh. "I'm not taking attendance. I just asked you if you could explain what an epic poem was."

I could feel my face turning red. The kids in the class were all laughing at me. Addie and Dana were giggling harder than anyone else. This day was starting out terribly.

So what else was new?

I had done my homework. I knew what an epic poem

was. I really did. But I couldn't seem to get the words out. Instead, I shrunk down in my chair. And I didn't say another word the entire morning.

I sat with Chloe and her friends at lunchtime, but I barely ate anything. I was too excited. I had a plan to put into action.

I kept one eye on Addie's table as I talked to my new friends. The minute I saw Addie, Dana, and Claire head into the bathroom, I grabbed my book bag, too.

"I . . . uh . . . I gotta go," I excused myself to my new friends.

"Where are you rushing to?" Chloe asked me curiously.

"Uh, the bathroom," I told her.

"Wait a minute," Chloe said. "I'll go with you."

No. That was definitely not going to work.

"Uh, sorry. Can't wait," I told her as I grabbed my book bag and rushed off.

The bathroom was totally buzzing by the time I got there. I practically had to fight my way to one of the mirrors. But I got one. Right next to Claire. Addie was by a mirror closer to the windows.

"Hi," I said to her.

"Hi," Claire replied, without even looking in my direction as she applied shiny lip gloss to her lips.

"I guess you're here to put on makeup, too," I continued.

Claire rolled her eyes. *"Duh."*

"I have a really pretty lavender eye shadow, if you want it," I said. "Of course you have brown eyes, so a green shadow would probably work better, but . . ."

Just then, Dana peeked over my shoulder to look at my makeup selection. I moved to the side for a moment so she could get a better look. "You can borrow anything you want," I said, as I applied the lavender shadow and topped it off with black mascara, just like it said on middleschool-survival.com.

"Why would I want to borrow this stuff?" Dana asked me. She picked up the pink lipstick. "Look, she's wearing Landfield. My *grandmother* wears Landfield."

"Mine, too." Sabrina laughed.

I bit my lip and tried not to cry. Tears would smear the black mascara I had just put on. "Well, maybe you can help me get some better stuff when we all go to the mall on Saturday," I suggested to Dana, as I put some blush on my cheeks.

Dana stared at me. "*You're* going with us? Yeah, right."

"I am," I told her.

"Says who?" Dana asked.

I looked over at Addie, hoping she would back me up. After all, she was the one who'd invited me.

"Oh, Addie, you didn't . . ." Claire began.

"All I said was my mom had room in the van for one more person," Addie insisted. "I never said she was invited. . . ."

I gasped. Suddenly I felt as though I couldn't breathe. The room was spinning all around. Sure, that *was* all Addie had said. But she'd meant I could come. I knew she had. And she knew it, too. But now, in front of her friends . . .

"Oh, man, nice cheeks." Claire giggled, looking over at me. "What are you going for, that circus look?"

I looked into the mirror. She was right. The blush I had taken from my mom's bag was way too red for my face.

"Come on, you guys, let's just go," Addie said.

I stared at the floor as Dana and Claire followed Addie out of the bathroom. One by one, the other Pops made their way out of the room, too.

"I can't believe she thought she was going to the mall with us." I heard Dana laugh as she walked away.

"Like that was going to ever happen," Claire added. "Boy, Addie, you've really got to watch what you say around her."

As the door slammed shut, I could feel the tears falling down my face. I could just imagine the black stripes dripping down.

So much for my brilliant plan. I looked ridiculous. I'd definitely made a fool of myself in front of all those popular girls.

But worse than that, *Addie* had made me look like an idiot. Or at the very least, she hadn't helped me *not* look like an idiot.

This day could not get any worse.

As I bent down toward the sink to wash the makeup from my face, I heard the sixth period bell ring. It was about to get worse. I was going to be late for Spanish, which meant I would have to do an extra homework assignment tonight.

"Middle school stinks!" I shouted out into the empty bathroom.

Chapter
EIGHT

THE NOTE LANDED ON MY DESK at the exact moment señorita Gonzalez turned her back to write on the board. I grabbed it quickly, before anyone could see it, and opened it beneath my desk.

> You want to play basketball with Marc and me on Saturday? He has a hoop in his driveway.
> — C

That sounded great, but I had one problem with Chloe's invitation. I'd already made plans with Felicia and Rachel. But we hadn't decided what to do yet. That gave me an idea.

> I sort of have plans with two friends from my old school. Can they come, too?
> — J

I reached over my shoulder and passed the note back to Chloe. Not two seconds later, the paper was back on my desk.

> Sure. The more the merrier. And wait until you taste Marc's mom's lemonade. It's da bomb!

I giggled slightly as I read the note. But I stopped laughing as soon as señorita Gonzalez turned back around. There was no way I would be able to explain why I was laughing without getting in trouble. Somehow I didn't think she'd believe that I found the numbers one through twenty in Spanish all that funny.

I looked down at the note again. The more the merrier. That was so cool. Definitely not the way Addie and her friends thought. They didn't want to let anyone else in on their plans. It was just those few special people. The Pops.

Which really didn't make all that much sense when you thought about it. If Addie and Dana and the rest of their clique were supposed to be so popular, how come there were so few of them? Didn't being "popular" mean that you were liked by everyone? But that wasn't how it was at all.

Now that I thought about it, I had a lot more friends than Addie did. There was the whole crowd Chloe had introduced me to. And I was still friends with Felicia and Rachel. And we weren't snobs. We would hang out with anyone who was fun. But we stayed away from the kids who had fun making fun — of other people, that is.

But I still wondered, if any of us got a chance to be a Pop, would we take it?

"Hi, Felicia," I said as she got on the bus that afternoon. "I saved you a seat."

Felicia hopped into the seat next to me and sighed heavily. "You wouldn't believe how much homework I have! It's scary."

"I know," I agreed. "I have a Spanish test coming up on Monday, and it's only the second week of school."

"I wish I was back in elementary," Felicia groaned.

If Felicia had said that earlier in the day, I would have totally agreed with her. But right now I was in such a good mood I couldn't. "I don't know about that," I said. "Who wants to eat lunch with their teacher?"

"Good call," Felicia admitted.

"And weren't you getting sick of the same thirty kids?" I continued. "It's so much better when you can meet new people."

I stopped for a minute, realizing what I had just said. What a difference a few days made.

"Have you met a lot of people?" Felicia asked. "Rachel and I really haven't."

Maybe that was because Rachel and Felicia didn't really have to go out and make a bunch of new friends. They had each other to eat lunch and hang around with.

But not me. I *had* to meet other people. Addie had shut me out completely.

"Some of my new friends are playing basketball on Saturday," I told Felicia. "You and Rachel want to come? That way you can meet everyone and shoot hoops."

"Your friends won't mind?" Felicia asked.

I shook my head. "They're – I mean *we're* – not like that."

All Thursday and Friday I tried hard to stay away from Addie and her friends. But it wasn't easy. Addie and Dana had the same English and gym periods as I did, so I had to see them, then. And of course, Addie was on my bus. But even though I knew I was angry with Addie for being such a jerk about the trip to the mall, I couldn't help missing her. We'd been friends for a really long time. You don't just turn that off like a light switch, you know?

The only thing that kept me going was the fact that I knew that I had plans this weekend. Addie might have thought she'd ruined my life by ditching me when she went to the mall with Claire and Dana, but she hadn't. There's more to life than shopping at the mall. Like basketball, for instance.

Chapter
NINE

"SHE JUMPS. SHE SHOOTS. She . . . misses!" Marc shouted as he filmed Chloe shooting the ball at the hoop that hung over his garage door.

"Hey, big shot, if you think it's so easy, why don't you put down the camera and shoot a few?" Chloe playfully snapped back, sticking her tongue out at Marc.

"Here, Jenny, take this and tape me," Marc said, handing me his camera. "I want this recorded for all time. All you have to do is push the button until the red light goes on in the corner."

"You got it," I said, pointing the lens in his direction and catching every second of his dribbling, shooting, and — *swish* — sinking the ball right into the basket.

"Yeah, well, you're the one with the basketball hoop at your house," Chloe reminded him. "That sort of gives you an advantage."

As Marc and Chloe argued about whether or not that really was an advantage or if Marc was just a better athlete, I turned the camera toward Felicia. She'd gotten her hands on the ball and was dribbling toward the basket. Josh had his hands up and was trying to block her.

But it was no use. A whole summer of basketball camp

at the community center had trained Felicia well. She shot right over Josh, and sunk the ball into the basket.

"Josh, don't give up the karate," Chloe joked.

"It's tae kwon do," Josh replied. But he didn't really sound all that annoyed. Instead, he flopped down on the grass and wiped his forehead with the bottom of his shirt. "Man, it's hot out here," he groaned.

"Yeah, it's so hot the birds have to use potholders to pull worms out of the ground," Rachel joked.

"Ouch. That one was awful," I told her. But I laughed anyway. I was used to Rachel's bad jokes.

"Then how about, it's so hot you have to eat chili peppers to cool your mouth off," Rachel tried.

Chloe scowled at that one. "It doesn't seem fair that there should be school when it still feels like summer," she said, obviously trying to turn the attention away from Rachel and her jokes.

"It *is* still summer," Josh corrected her. "Until September twenty-first."

Felicia was still standing by the basketball court. "Hey, Rache," she called out. "Wanna shoot a few more?"

Rachel shook her head. "This game's been canceled on account of sweat," she told her.

Marc wiped a few beads of sweat from his forehead and then started to walk toward the side of his house.

"Where are you going?" Josh asked him.

"Be right back," Marc assured us with a chuckle.

"I don't like the sound of that," Chloe said.

I looked at her strangely. What was the big deal about Marc going around to the side of his house?

Chloe definitely knew her next-door neighbor a whole lot better than the rest of us. Sure enough, Marc was up to no good. A moment later he returned. And instead of holding his camera in his hand, he was holding the garden hose.

"GOTCHA!" he shouted out, spraying us all with icy-cold water.

The first shock of the water was awful. It was freezing. But after a few seconds, we were all happy to be jumping around in the spray.

Still, it didn't seem fair that Marc could get us, when we couldn't get him back. And since he had the hose, there could be no element of surprise. Unless . . .

Suddenly a plan hatched in my brain. "I'm gonna get Chloe," I whispered to Marc as I grabbed the empty bucket from near the side of the house.

He smiled mischievously. "Go for it," he whispered back, filling the bucket to the brim with icy water.

I pretended to race over toward Chloe. But at the last minute, I turned back and dumped the whole bucket of icy-cold water right on Marc's head.

"Oh, that's it, J," Marc shouted. He pointed the hose at me. I tried to run, but it was impossible to escape the stream of water that was flying in my direction.

By the time my mother arrived to take Felicia, Rachel, and me home, I was soaking wet. And so was everyone else. We were all sitting on the grass, sipping cold lemonade.

"Boy, I'm glad I didn't bring the car," my mother said, laughing as she walked up onto the lawn. "You two would have destroyed the seats."

At that moment, all the joy washed out of my face. "What do you mean you didn't bring the car?"

"It's a nice day. I figured we could walk. We'll cut through the park," my mom explained.

"Cool. Can we get an ice cream on the way?" Felicia didn't seem to have any problem with that, but I sure did.

"Sure," my mom agreed.

"Awesome. Thanks, Mrs. McAfee," Rachel added.

I looked at Felicia and Rachel with amazement. Didn't they get it? My mother was walking us home – like we were babies or something. What if we ran into Addie or Dana along the way?

I watched as my mom and Marc's mother introduced themselves and spoke for a few minutes. Then, as my mom turned to leave, I thanked Mrs. Newman for having me over.

"I see Marc hasn't beaten those manners out of you yet," Mrs. Newman told me with a grin.

"Give me time," Marc called over to her.

"Leave Jenny alone. I love nice manners," Mrs. Newman said.

My mother smiled proudly at that. You know how it is with parents. Whenever you get a compliment they act like it's for them or something.

"Well, we're off," my mother remarked finally.

"Bye, you guys," Chloe said.

"See you at school," Marc added.

"Yeah," Josh said. He smiled at all three of us, but the way he grinned at Felicia tipped us off that he liked her.

"Bye," she answered him in a kind of shy voice.

"Yeah. Bye," I added. Then I turned to Felicia and Rachel. "Race ya!" I shouted.

"Okay!" Felicia agreed excitedly.

"You're on," Rachel added.

As we took off down the street I smiled slightly. I figured if we ran far enough ahead of my mom, people would think we were really running home by ourselves.

Of course, that only lasted as far as the park. The minute my mother spotted the ice-cream stand, she called out to us. "Jenny, Rachel, Felicia, don't you want an ice cream?" she asked.

Rachel and Felicia stopped right away. Neither of them would ever give up a chance for an ice-cream cone. So I had to stop, too. I figured I might as well get a cherry Popsicle. I mean, it's not like I could race myself, right?

By some miracle, we managed to drop Felicia and Rachel at their houses without bumping into one person we knew from school. But as soon as my mom and I reached my neighborhood, we passed right by Addie, who was sitting on her front steps. She was wearing a cute little denim miniskirt and a white tank top. Her hair was pin straight, which was weird, because her hair is usually so curly.

I looked down at my old pink T-shirt, which was still sopping wet and now had a big red Popsicle stain on it. I knew my hair was a disaster, too — that's what happens when you have icy water sprayed right on your head.

"Hi, Addie," my mother called over to her. "How are you doing?"

Addie shrugged. "I wanted to go to the mall, but my mom is busy gardening."

I smiled to myself. So Addie and the Pops hadn't made it to the mall after all.

"Your mother's right. It's too nice out for you to be inside at the mall all day," my mother told Addie. "It's too bad Jenny didn't know you had no plans. You could have gone with her to play basketball and have a water fight at her friend Marc's house."

I gasped. I couldn't believe my mother. How could she have said something like that? But I guess that wasn't her fault. She thought Addie and I were still friends.

"Well, I just straightened my hair," Addie said slowly. "It took a long time. I don't know if I would have wanted to get it all wet."

"Your hair does look lovely," my mother assured her.

"But I guess it doesn't really matter," Addie continued. "It's just going to curl up in all this heat, anyway."

"True," my mom continued. "But there's nothing like a good water fight on a hot day." She started to walk down the block toward our street.

"Yeah," Addie said quietly.

For a second I got the feeling that she would have rather spent the morning shooting hoops and having a water fight than straightening her hair.

Not that Addie would ever admit being jealous of anything I'd done. Why should she? It's not like I would ever admit to anyone that I was jealous of Addie and the Pops, right?

"See you later," I mumbled to Addie as I followed my mom.

"Sure, later," Addie said.

Chapter
TEN

WHEN THE PHONE RANG early on Sunday morning I knew it had to be for me. My parents' friends never call early on the weekends. They all know that my parents love to sleep in.

I hurried to get the phone on the first ring, so it wouldn't wake up my parents. "Hello?" I said.

"Hi, Jenny. It's me, Felicia."

"Hey. What's up?"

"I just wanted to say thanks for inviting Rachel and me yesterday," she said. "I really liked your friends."

"And they liked you," I said, thinking about Josh especially.

So was Felicia.

"Josh was nice," she said. "And he's so funny."

"Yeah, he is," I agreed. "And smart, too. He's taking seventh grade math."

"Wow." Felicia was really impressed.

"And I think he likes you," I added. I stopped for a minute and took a deep breath. I'd never had a conversation like this with anyone, ever.

"I wish there was some way I could find out if Josh *really* likes me," Felicia said hopefully.

"You want me to ask him?" I suggested.

"No. It would be too embarrassing," Felicia continued.

I glanced over at the computer against the wall, and thought about the friendship test I had tried the other day. "Maybe there's an online quiz you could take? I know this really great website. . . ."

"Oh," Felicia said with a little bit of disappointment. "I'll never get near the computer today. My sister has to write a paper for her history class."

"Oh, well, I could go online and read you the questions," I suggested. I never have to wait to use the computer at my house. It's one of the advantages of being an only child.

"Could you?" Felicia asked.

"Sure. Just give me a minute," I said as I turned the computer on, and went straight to middleschoolsurvival. com. "Here's one that looks right," I said. "It's called 'Does He Like You?'"

"Perfect!" Felicia exclaimed.

"Okay, first question," I said as I began to read the quiz.

Does he tend to think about your needs before his own?
- Yes
- No

Felicia thought about that for a moment. "Well, he did give me a glass of lemonade before he took one, and he was really thirsty."

"It's yes then," I said excitedly, as I clicked the button. A new question popped up on the screen.

> Do you often catch him looking at you even when there are other things going on around him?
> ◉ Yes
> ◉ No

"I can answer that one," I said. "Definitely."

"Really?" Felicia asked. She sounded so happy.

"Oh, yeah," I said, clicking the YES button. The next question popped up.

> Does he do things to catch your attention, even if it makes him look like a fool?
> ◉ Yes
> ◉ No

"I don't think Josh looked like a fool at all yesterday," Felicia said sadly. "So I guess that one is no."

"Oh, yeah? What about trying to guard against you in basketball? He's terrible at basketball. He just did that so he could hang out with you," I insisted, hitting the YES button without even asking Felicia if she agreed.

> Does he always seem to be fixing his hair or clothes when he sees you?
> ◉ Yes
> ◉ No

"Okay, that one's a no," I admitted. "But it doesn't really count, because we were having a water fight and no one fixes their hair in a water fight."

"That's true," Felicia admitted, but she did sound kind of disappointed at having to give a no answer on the quiz.

When he's with his friends, does he spend more time talking to you than them?
⬤ Yes
⬤ No

"He played some one-on-one basketball with me," Felicia remembered. "But is that really talking? I mean, we didn't have a conversation or anything."

I didn't know how to answer that. "I won't click either button," I said, hitting the mouse so I could advance to the next part of the test. "Okay, now we're going to find out your results. You said yes to three out of five questions." I scanned the list to see what that meant.

5 out of 5 yes answers: Keep this boy away from banana peels. He's already fallen hard . . . for you!
4 out of 5 yes answers: This guy has definitely got you on the brain!
3 out of 5 yes answers: We sense the beginning of a beautiful friendship . . . or more. Only time will tell.

2 out of 5 yes answers: It's time to move on. There are plenty of fish in the sea — go buy a fishing rod.
1 or 0 yes answers: Fuggedaboutit! This guy's just not interested.

"A beautiful friendship, huh?" Felicia said, sounding disappointed.

"Or more," I corrected her. "It says only time will tell. And don't forget, we didn't really answer the last question. So you really got three out of four yeses."

"I guess." She paused for a minute. "Do you think Josh is going to the dance?"

"I could find out," I said. "Why? Are you?"

"Aren't you?" Felicia asked me.

I was quiet for a minute. I hadn't really thought about it. In fact, the only time the dance had ever come up in conversation was that day Addie came over. I guess I had assumed that it was just the Pops who went to stuff like that. Still, if Felicia was going, then maybe I would, too.

"I'm not sure yet," I said. Then I laughed. "Only time will tell."

"So, um, are you guys going to the dance?" I asked the next day as I sat down for lunch at my regular table. How cool was that? I had a regular table. With my own crowd of friends.

"I doubt it," Chloe said between bites of a baloney sandwich she'd brought from home. Apparently Chloe didn't think it was lame to bring your own lunch to school. As usual, she did whatever she wanted.

"Oh, come on," Marilyn said. "You have to come."

"Yeah," Carolyn agreed. "The dances are hilarious. You gotta see how those Pops get all dressed up . . . just to stand there and watch everyone else have a good time."

"I don't even pay attention to them," Marc said. "At most dances I end up playing Ping-Pong in the gym. They show a movie in the auditorium, too." He turned to Liza. "What movie did they show at the spring fling dance?"

"I think a bunch of stupid cartoons," Liza replied with a giggle.

"Totally G-rated," Marilyn added. "With no violence at all."

"The school's afraid of freaking out our parents," Carolyn suggested.

I smiled. I was glad I didn't have parents that freaked out too easily. My mom and dad might not let me go to the movies with my friends if there was no grown-up around, but at least they took me to good movies. Some of them were even PG-13, which was pretty cool since I was only eleven and a half.

"Yeah, but the Ping-Pong's fun, and the snacks aren't half bad. They had foot-long heroes at the last one," Marc told me.

"They were delicious," Carolyn recalled.

"So are you going to come, Jenny?" Liza asked me.

"Maybe we could go together. My big sister could drive us. She just got her license."

Wow! Liza had a sister who was old enough to drive. How cool was that? Still, I doubted my parents would let me get in a car with someone who had just learned how to drive.

"Maybe you could eat over at my house, and then my dad could drive us," I suggested, trying not to hurt her feelings. I figured it had taken a lot for her to ask me to go with her. She was so shy.

"Okay," Liza replied. "I'll ask my mom."

"So . . . um . . . are any of your other friends going to the dance?" Josh piped up nervously.

"You mean like *Felicia*," Chloe teased him.

Josh bit his lip. His cheeks turned redder than the tomato on his sandwich.

"I didn't mean anyone special," Josh murmured. "I just thought that Jenny might have friends from her old school, and you can never have enough friends."

"Yeah, right," Chloe said, laughing. "Whatever you say, Josh."

"I think Felicia and my friend Rachel are going to the dance." I glanced over at the Pops' table. I was pretty sure Addie and Dana would be at the dance, too. But I didn't say anything about that. After all, Josh had only asked about my *friends.*

"Oh, okay," Josh said, trying to sound like he didn't

notice I had said Felicia was going to the dance. He wasn't very successful. The smile on his face gave him away.

I couldn't wait to tell Felicia!

Bad news! I had gym sixth period, right after lunch, and the grilled cheese sandwich I'd eaten was stuck somewhere between my chest and my stomach, and it didn't seem to be moving. Chloe was smart to bring her own lunch. The school food was the worst!

But my undigested sandwich wasn't the worst part about gym. The worst part was that both Addie and Dana were in the class with me. That would be okay, if some of my friends were in there, too. But they weren't.

To make things worse, this was gym. It was one thing for Addie and Dana to sit near each other in English class, because they hardly got a chance to talk in there. But in gym class, kids can talk the whole time. And Dana and Addie sure did a lot of talking!

"Did you see what she was wearing today?" Dana chuckled as she and Addie walked out to the field together.

I gulped. Would they really talk about me when I was just two steps behind them? I guess it wasn't that big of a shock. They'd done it before.

"I know. Who puts on purple tie-dyed sweatpants to go to school?" Addie agreed. "Especially homemade ones."

Phew. Okay. So it wasn't me they were talking about. I was wearing jeans.

"She probably made them at the community center

this summer," Dana said. "Didn't she and Rachel have arts and crafts in the afternoons?"

She and Rachel. I frowned. I didn't get to see Felicia this morning because her mom drives her to school. But I'd bet anything she was the one in the tie-dyed sweatpants.

"And have you heard her talk lately?" Dana said. "You can't even understand her with that weird retainer in her mouth."

"I know," Addie said and giggled. "My name isch Felischia," she added, imitating her.

Now I was really mad. It had been one thing when Dana had been saying all the bad things and Addie had just been agreeing. But now Addie was being every bit as mean!

Addie had gone over to the dark side. She was lost forever!

"Well, at least she'll have straight teeth," I shouted at Addie. "Not fangs like you have coming out of the sides of your mouth!"

It was true. Addie had two teeth that were slightly longer than the others on either side of her mouth.

Addie and Dana stopped in their tracks, turned around, and stared at me.

"What did you say?" Addie demanded.

"You heard me."

Addie looked as though I had just punched her in the stomach. She was in shock. I think she found it impossible to believe that anyone would say anything like that to a Pop.

I couldn't believe I'd said it, either.

"Yeah, well, at least Addie doesn't eat lunch with the Geek Squad, the way you do," Dana spat back. "I mean, that girl, Chloe? What a loudmouth. And those twins? What are their names? Tweedledum and Tweedledummer?"

"It's Marilyn and Carolyn," I informed her. "And they're really funny and interesting. So is Chloe, for that matter. She's a riot. At least she's got a personality. She talks about more than makeup and clothes. She's unique. Not like you clones!"

My heart was pumping really hard now. My stomach was all in knots. I knew that I had just ended any chance at being part of the Pops or being best friends with Addie again.

As I stared into Addie's glaring blue eyes, I knew one thing for sure.

This was war!

Chapter
ELEVEN

"YOU KNOW WHAT, I think it's time we showed the Pops who the coolest kids in the school really are," I told Chloe and Felicia when I met up with them in the hall at the end of the school day. We were standing by Chloe's locker, which gave us a good view of the other end of the hall where Addie, Dana, and Claire were busy checking themselves out in the mirror that was attached to Addie's locker door.

"They *are* the coolest kids in the school," Felicia said.

"Oh, give me a break," I said angrily. "They just act that way. I think they're boring and stupid!"

Chloe and Felicia looked at me strangely.

"What brought all this on?" Chloe asked me.

"Um . . . nothing. I don't know. They just bug me," I said. I didn't want to tell them about the mean things Addie and Dana had said.

"I don't know why you even think about them," Chloe told me. "I never do. I just pretend they're not there."

"But doesn't it bother you that they walk around like they own this place?" I asked her. "That they have this tight little crowd and they don't let anyone else in?"

"Why would I want to be part of their crowd?" Felicia asked.

I didn't really have an answer to that. I had wanted to be a Pop, ever since the first day of school. But now, after hearing how mean Addie had become, I knew I could never be a Pop. Yeah, I had said some mean things to Addie, too, but that was in defense of my friends. I wasn't the kind of girl who liked making other people feel bad.

Which was why I couldn't tell Felicia and Chloe what Dana and Addie had said about them. It would just make them feel awful. And that wasn't who I was.

The next morning I made sure to sit as far from Addie and Dana as I could in English class. I figured they'd still be talking about me, especially since I was probably the only person in the history of the school to ever stand up to a Pop.

After English I didn't see Addie or Dana again until fifth period. So the morning sailed by pretty smoothly — I even managed to get a four out of five on my math quiz. So as I entered the cafeteria I was feeling really good about myself.

MIDDLE SCHOOL RULE #5:

NEVER FEEL TOO GOOD ABOUT YOURSELF.
SOMEONE WILL MAKE IT THEIR BUSINESS
TO KNOCK YOU DOWN AGAIN.

In this case, that person was none other than Addie herself. She was standing two people behind me in the lunch line.

"She's had those jeans for two years already," she was saying to Dana. "Look how short they are."

"I think she's expecting a flood," Dana giggled.

I knew they were talking about me. But they were wrong. My pants weren't too short. Not at all. They were just fine. And they weren't two years old, either. I'd only bought them last spring.

Anyway, I wasn't going to give Addie and Dana the satisfaction of getting all upset. I just stared straight ahead and put a container of milk on my tray.

"It's so funny that she actually thought we would take her to the mall with us," Dana continued.

"Like that was ever going to happen," Addie agreed.

I smiled to myself. I knew for a fact that they hadn't even gone to the mall.

"I think she really thinks you guys are still friends," Dana told Addie.

"Oh, please," Addie replied with a sigh. " We were only friends because our moms are friends. That's what happens in elementary school. But now I'm old enough to choose my own friends. And can you imagine me hanging out with a geek like her? Please!"

That was it. I couldn't take it anymore.

Everything that happened next is kind of a blur. All I

know is that I picked up a big cup of this purple yogurt stuff — they call it "fruit float" on the cafeteria menu — and hurled it at Addie. Purply goo oozed all over her super-straightened hair, and her brand-new blue-and-white peasant blouse.

"Are you nuts, Jenny?" Addie screamed in surprise. "This stuff stains. And I'm wearing a brand-new shirt. You are *so* dead!" She grabbed a container of fruit float and dumped it on my head.

Suddenly the fruit float was flying everywhere. Addie and I just kept throwing it, smearing it, and pushing each other into it. Dana moved out of the way — Addie may have been her new BFF, but she wasn't about to get fruit float in her hair.

My friends, however, had come racing over. They were cheering me on from the sidelines.

"Yeah! Go, Jenny!" I could hear Chloe shouting out over the rest of the noise. And then, Mr. Collins, the janitor, jumped between Addie and me. "Whoa. What's going on here?"

Addie and I just stood there for a minute, staring — no make that *glaring* — at each other.

"She started it," I said finally.

"No, you did," Addie shouted back. "You threw that whole big thing of fruit float at me."

"Only because you and Dana were saying horrible things about me."

"Well, it's all true," Addie responded.

"Okay," Mr. Collins said. "That's enough. I don't care who started it. It's finished right now. Do you girls have any idea what a mess you've made? It's hard enough cleaning this cafeteria after lunch. Now I've got all this extra purple goop to clean up, as well."

I frowned as I looked around. The place was kind of a mess now. It would take a while to clean up. Mr. Collins shouldn't have had to clean all that up on his own.

Come to think of it, I was kind of a mess, too. I had fruit float in my hair, my pants, and even in my shoes. And it was starting to stink like spoiled milk.

"I'll help you clean up," I told Mr. Collins. And I meant it.

"You bet you will," he replied, looking angrily at Addie and me. "You both will. And then we'll see what other punishment the principal can come up with."

"So how much trouble did you get in?" Chloe asked me that night on the phone.

"My parents were pretty mad," I admitted. "I'm grounded for the whole week and I can only talk on the phone for a few minutes each night."

"Oh, man, that stinks," Chloe commiserated with me. "That means you can't go to the dance."

"Well, not exactly," I said slowly. "I can go to the dance. I just can't have any fun there."

"Huh?" Chloe sounded confused.

"It's part of the principal's punishment. Addie and I have to spend all night serving snacks at the refreshment table."

"Well, at least you'll be there," she said, trying to make me feel better. "And you'll get first dibs on the best food."

"I guess," I admitted.

"And you can save the best snacks for us," Chloe continued. "Just stick 'em under the table or something."

I giggled. "You got it," I assured her.

"That was pretty cool, what you did today," Chloe complimented me. "I couldn't believe you did that to that Pop girl."

"I told you yesterday I was getting sick of those Pops being jerks to everyone," I reminded her.

"Yeah. But everybody feels that way. You were the only one who did anything about it."

That was true. And despite the fact that I was in big trouble with my parents, I wasn't sorry about it at all.

"You're like a celebrity," Chloe gushed. "A legend. The first girl ever to cover a Pop with fruit float."

"Come on, Chloe," I said, pretending I wanted her to stop. But I really didn't.

"I'm telling you, this is going down in Joyce Kilmer Middle School history," Chloe assured me. "Marc says he got some great shots of you dumping that purple gunk all over Addie's head. You're the new hero in his film."

"A hero?" I repeated.

"Totally," Chloe agreed.

"Wow," I murmured. What more could I say?

*　　*　　*

When I walked into school on Wednesday morning, I knew everything had changed. Kids were smiling at me in the halls. Even eighth graders!

"Yo, Jenny! How are you?" an eighth grade girl with long red hair greeted me as I walked into C wing.

I stopped for a minute and looked at her with surprise. It was Sonia, one of the eighth graders who had sent me on a wild-goose chase for the elevators on the first day of school.

"Hello?" I said, more as a question than a greeting.

"Nice food fight," she complimented me. "You got that Pop big-time."

"Uh . . . thanks," I said. I turned to walk away.

"Hey, you're still not mad about that whole pool and elevator thing are you?" Sonia asked.

I shook my head no. I wasn't mad anymore. It seemed like it happened forever ago.

"'Cause it was just a joke," Sonia assured me. "We play it on all the sixth graders. But if we had known back then how cool you are . . ."

Whoa. Me? Cool?

"Well, anyway, see you at the dance," Sonia said. "You'll be there, won't you?"

I nodded. "I have to be. It's part of my punishment."

Sonia laughed. "Well, I'll see you there, 'kay?"

"Okay," I said. And as I walked away, all I could think was: Lizard Girl was gone for good. Long live Jenny . . . hero of the non-Pops!

Chapter

TWELVE

SERVING PIZZA AND JUICE was definitely better than doing extra chores around the house. It was good to be out with other kids and listening to music, even if the dance wasn't exactly all I'd dreamed it would be.

"I can't believe the principal made you wear that." Rachel giggled as she walked up to the refreshment table with Marc. She was pointing at the hairnets Addie and I had been required to wear.

"I think it's cool," Marc teased. "We should all wear one. We could start a new fashion trend."

"Oh, yeah. That'll happen," I answered him.

"I think pizza is a great snack," Rachel said, taking a slice and changing the subject.

"Yeah, it's definitely better than anything they serve in the cafeteria during the day," Felicia added.

"But do you know where the best place to have pizza is?" Rachel asked.

"Where?" I wondered.

"In your mouth!" she declared with a grin as she took a huge bite of her slice.

"Oh man, Rachel, your jokes are getting worse," Felicia said. But she was laughing just like the rest of us.

All of my friends took turns visiting me at the table, which was more than I could say for Addie's crowd. They hadn't come over to the refreshment table once. The Pops were all too busy standing against the wall of the cafeteria in their new clothes. They weren't dancing or anything. They were just standing there, listening to the music, and acting bored.

Besides, I was pretty sure they didn't want to be seen around Addie while she was wearing a hairnet. You should have seen Addie's face when the principal handed her that net — she almost died. She'd spent at least an hour straightening her hair. And now she had to cover it up.

I glanced over at Addie and tried to smile. I actually felt kind of sorry for her. *But only for a minute.* You wouldn't believe the nasty look she gave me. Like I didn't have the right to look at her or anything.

"Hardly anyone's dancing," I noted, turning my attention back to my friends.

"No one ever does at these things. Maybe a few eighth grade girls, but that's about it," Marc said. "I told you. Everyone's either watching a movie or playing Ping-Pong and basketball."

"Or eating," Josh said, coming over to stand next to Felicia. "Can I have another slice, Jenny?"

"Sure." I put a fresh slice of pizza on a paper plate.

"I'm so hungry," Josh continued. "We've been playing basketball all night."

"He's really getting good," Felicia told me.

"Nah. You and Rachel slaughtered me," Josh admitted.

"But you're getting better," Felicia assured him.

"Definitely," Rachel agreed.

"You should see me in tae kwon do. That's when I really rock," Josh boasted.

"I'd love to see you do tae kwon do," Felicia said sincerely.

Josh grinned at her.

Wow. I could tell Josh and Felicia were getting along really, really well.

So could Addie. She was pretending like she didn't care enough to listen to our conversation, but she was. Addie was totally surprised that Felicia had someone who liked her, and *she* didn't!

"So you guys want to play basketball tomorrow at my house?" Marc asked everyone.

"Sorry, I can't," I said. "I'm grounded, remember?"

"Oh, yeah," Marc recalled.

"It's going to rain, anyway," Josh pointed out.

"Maybe we can all hang out at your house," Felicia suggested to me. "Watch a movie or something."

"I guess that would be okay," I said. "My folks said I had to stay home. But they didn't say I couldn't have anybody over to keep me company."

"Cool," Marc said. "I'll tell Chloe, Liza, and the twins."

As he walked off, I smiled to myself. There was going to be a whole crowd of kids hanging out in my house tomorrow. My friends. My *middle school* friends.

I looked over at Addie. She was standing all by herself pouring apple juice into little paper cups. She seemed miserable and lonely. *Just the way I'd looked on the first day of school.*

I guess being a Pop isn't always all it's cracked up to be.

Are Your Friends True Blue . . . or Just Using You?

It's a Friday night, and your pals all want to go to the movies. But you're totally grounded. What does your clique do?

A. Choose one representative to hang with you while the others hit the cineplex.

B. Go over to your house and rent a flick instead.

C. Go to the movies and leave you at home, but promise to hang with you when your grounding is up.

The most popular girl in school hates you. She vows to socially destroy anyone who is friendly with you. What do your friends do?

A. Take a stand and stick with you, willing to risk total social disaster.
B. Leave you all alone to fend for yourself.
C. Hang with you, but only when no one is watching.

You drop your tray in the lunchroom and spill spaghetti sauce all over your new shirt. What do your friends do?

A. Applaud and laugh with the rest of the kids in the caf.
B. Go to the bathroom with you and help you wash the red stuff off your shirt.
C. Hurry to their lockers to loan you anything they can find.

You spent Saturday night at a sleepover with a bunch of your friends. But now it's Sunday and you're totally not prepped for that big history test tomorrow. What do your pals do?

A. Even though they're all totally fried from lack of sleep, they haul over to your house for a Sunday cram session.
B. Tell you you're on your own, they're too tired to be of any help to you.
C. Loan you their notes and then head home to crash.

How Great Are Your Friends?

Add up your score by checking your answers to this point system.

1. A = 2 points   B = 3 points   C = 1 point
2. A = 3 points   B = 1 point   C = 2 points
3. A = 1 point   B = 2 points   C = 3 points
4. A = 3 points   B = 1 point   C = 2 points

Now see how your group measures up:

0–5 points: Call it quits on the clique. They're not real friends at all.

6–9 points: You're hangin' with some cool kids, but you may not always be able to rely on them. You can still remain friends, but be ready for some tough times along the way.

10–12 points: Lucky you! These friends are true blue. Hope you are, too!

HOW I SURVIVED MIDDLE SCHOOL

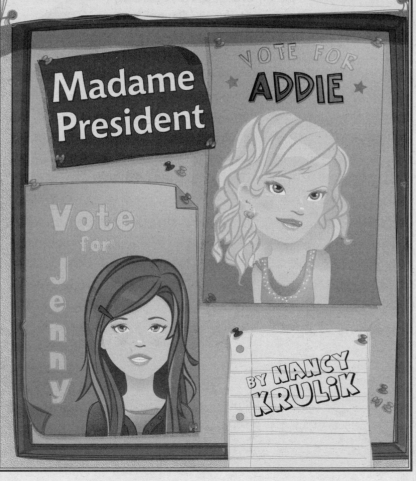

Madame President

VOTE FOR ADDIE

Vote for Jenny

BY NANCY KRULIK

For my ever-supportive parents,
Gladys and Steve

What Kind of Girl Are You?

1. **There's a new boy in school and you think he's really hot. Do you**

    A. Offer to show him around, since you know how hard it is to be the new kid?

    B. Ask your best buds if they think he's cute, too? If they agree, you introduce yourself. Otherwise, forget about it.

    C. Flash him a big smile and hope he introduces himself to you?

2. **You see one of the snobbiest girls in school walk out of the bathroom with the back of her skirt stuck in her underwear. What do you do?**

    A. Start laughing so loudly that everyone looks in her direction.

    B. Let her know quietly, so she can run into the bathroom and fix things.

C. Say nothing — someone in her crowd is bound to tell her sooner or later.

3. When it's test time, what's your usual reaction?

A. You copy off the smart kid next to you — 20/20 vision's got to be good for something!
B. You're really nervous. You don't usually do well on tests.
C. You are totally confident. You studied really hard.

4. At a sleepover party, you can usually be found:

A. Sleeping. You're always the first one zzz-ing at these things.
B. Gossiping about all the kids that you didn't invite to the party.
C. Taking charge and coordinating the evening's triple-M entertainment: makeovers, manicures, and munchies.

Check your answers
and add up your points.

1. A) 3 B) 1 C) 2
2. A) 1 B) 3 C) 2
3. A) 1 B) 2 C) 3
4. A) 2 B) 1 C) 3

10–12 points: Flap those wings, you social butterfly! You're the kind of girl everyone loves — confident and cool. Rock on, girl!

7–9 points: You may be shy, but it's those quiet girls who have all the surprises. Come on, gain some confidence! Let the kids at school see that amazing person you've been hiding inside.

4–6 points: You can be nice when you want to, but for some reason, you often choose to show your nastier side to others. Try making an effort to say something nice to someone today. You may just discover it makes you feel good, too.

Chapter
ONE

THE FIRST PERSON I SAW when I walked into school on Monday morning was Addie Wilson. What a terrible way to start the week!

Addie was standing in front of her locker in C wing of Joyce Kilmer Middle School, with her friends, Dana and Claire. As I walked by, they started to giggle.

"Loser," Dana coughed into her hand.

"Geek," Claire added, coughing over her word as well.

"Did you see those sneakers?" Dana asked. "Nobody ever wears high-tops. How uncool."

"Jenny *is* uncool," Addie told her. "So the sneakers are perfect for her."

It's not hard to see why Addie and I aren't friends anymore.

Luckily, not everyone in my school is so obnoxious. I've got lots of friends. And none of them spend their time making fun of people.

"I see the Pops are at it again," my friend Felicia Liguori said, as she walked over to my locker with Chloe Samson, another one of my pals.

That's what we call Addie and her friends. The Pops. As

in popular. Why they're popular, I'm not quite sure. Most people think they're jerks. Of course, most people wish they could be one of them, too. I can't explain it. It's just the way it is.

"Yeah, it's makeup madness at locker 260 . . . again," I replied.

The Pops put on their makeup at Addie's locker mirror every morning. Then they wash it all off again at the end of the school day. That's because none of them are really allowed to wear makeup. If their moms saw them with all that blush, eye shadow, and lip gloss on they'd be in so much trouble.

"I don't know why Dana's laughing," Felicia said. "We got our first math test back last Friday, and she failed hers. I saw it. If I were her I'd be flipping out."

"Yeah, well, as long as her best friend Addie's by her side, Dana's happy," Chloe said. "Who needs math when you've got popularity?"

Felicia laughed at that. But I didn't. All I could think about was that Chloe had called Dana Addie's "best friend." That used to be me.

All through elementary school, Addie and I were best friends. I mean total BFF. You'd never see Addie Wilson without me — Jenny McAfee — by her side.

Then last summer I went away to summer camp, and Addie started hanging out with Dana. By the time I came back home, Addie was more interested in makeup and shopping than riding bikes around the neighborhood or building shoe-box playgrounds for my pet mice, Cody and Sam. *Those* were the kinds of things Addie and I used to do when we were together.

But we aren't friends anymore. That's because the more Addie hung out with Dana, the more Addie started to be like her. And there's just one word that can be used to describe Dana — *mean*. Now that's pretty much how I'd describe Addie, too.

"I wonder how happy Dana would be to know that Addie went to the movies with Claire and not her this weekend," Chloe said.

"Were they there by themselves?" I asked her. I knew that Addie had been bugging her mother to let her go to the movies without a grown-up. I wondered if she'd had any success. Addie's mom and my mom were friends. I figured that if Addie was allowed to go to the movies without her parents, maybe my mom would say it was okay for me to do that, too.

"Nah," Chloe said. "They wanted everyone to think they were, but I saw Claire's mom sitting two rows behind them."

Okay, so much for that.

"I've got to get to math class," Felicia said. "I'll see you on the bus after school, Jen."

"Save me a seat," I replied. Not that I had to say that. Felicia and I always sat together on the bus ride home.

"We've gotta get to English," Chloe said, as she adjusted the strap on her overalls.

I nodded, and followed Chloe down the hallway. Suddenly I spotted a huge yellow sign on the wall.

AFTER-SCHOOL CLUBS
sign-up this afternoon

Cafeteria
3:00–4:30

"Marc told me all about them," Chloe interrupted. Marc Newman was Chloe's next-door neighbor, and a seventh grader. Because he was a year older, he knew the deal about middle school. Chloe got all her information from him.

Of course, I knew about the after-school clubs, too. I'd read all about them in the handbook the school had given out at sixth grade orientation. I think I was the only kid in the school who had actually read that thing – cover to cover.

"There are all kinds of clubs," Chloe continued, as we walked down the hallway. "Like the theater club, the chess club, the art club, the Spanish club, the French club, student government . . ."

"I know. It sounds so cool," I said.

"It is," Chloe agreed. "I'm signing up for the theater club. I heard they're going to do *You're a Good Man, Charlie Brown* this year. Don't you think I'd make the perfect Lucy?"

I didn't know if Chloe could sing, dance, or act, but I did know that she had a pretty big mouth — just like the Lucy character in the *Peanuts* comics. "You're a natural," I teased.

Chloe laughed. She knew exactly what I meant. But she wasn't insulted. She knew she was loud — she was actually kind of proud of it. "So what are *you* going to sign up for?" she asked me.

"I don't know," I said. "I haven't even thought about it."

"Well, you'd better *get* thinking," Chloe warned. "The best clubs always fill up fast. Marc said that last year he wanted to be in the movie club, but he couldn't because the older kids had gotten to the cafeteria right after school and taken all the spots. He wound up having to choose between the yearbook committee and the chess club."

"Which did he choose?" I wondered.

"Yearbook," Chloe said. "He figured that way he'd at least be able to make sure there weren't any dorky pictures of him in there."

I nodded. I knew how he felt. I hated having my picture taken for just that reason.

"And besides, he doesn't play chess," Chloe continued.

Neither did I. And acting wasn't my thing, either. "I guess we'd better get to the cafeteria right after school," I said.

"Uh-huh," Chloe agreed. "I'm going to call my mom at lunch and tell her I'll be taking the late bus home today."

"Me, too," I agreed. Then I looked up at the clock. "And speaking of late . . ." I began.

Chloe got my drift. "We gotta roll!" she exclaimed, as we both took off down the hall at top speed.

By lunchtime, everyone was buzzing about the after-school clubs. It was all anyone could talk about.

"This year, I'm getting into the movie club," Marc said. "No matter what."

Marc wanted to be a movie director when he grew up. Actually, he wasn't even waiting until he grew up. He was already making a movie. It was a documentary about being in middle school.

It was so cool that Marc already knew what he wanted to be when he grew up. The last time *I* had any idea about that, I was three years old and wanted to be a fairy princess.

"I'm going to join the Spanish club," my friend Carolyn said. She flipped her long blond hair behind her shoulder and took a bite of her hot dog. "They go out for Spanish and Mexican food a lot," she added.

"That sounds like a good idea," Carolyn's identical twin sister, Marilyn, agreed. "Anything not to have to eat this slop."

"I know," I agreed, holding up my hot dog. "This tastes

like it's made of rubber. If I dropped it, I'll bet it would bounce."

Marilyn giggled. "Anyway, I'm signing up for field hockey."

"I didn't know you liked sports," I said.

"She doesn't," Carolyn interrupted. "She just likes the uniforms the girls on the team get to wear. Marilyn's much more into fashion than I am."

That made me laugh, because at that moment, the twins were wearing the exact same thing — gauzy peasant blouses. Marilyn's was yellow and Carolyn's was blue.

"What are you going to sign up for?" my friend Josh asked me.

I shrugged. "I have no idea."

"Have you talked about it with anyone else?" he wondered.

I smiled. By "anyone else" I knew he meant Felicia. He had a huge crush on her. "Well, I'm pretty sure Felicia's going to join the basketball team," I told him. "She and Rachel spent all summer playing at the community center."

"They're really good," Josh agreed. "Especially Felicia. She's promised to teach me how to make a jump shot."

"So what are you joining, Mr. Wizard?" Chloe asked. She loved to tease Josh about being smart.

"My algebra teacher asked me to sign up for the Mathletes," he replied shyly.

"I thought that was only for seventh and eighth graders," our friend Liza said.

"It is . . . usually," Josh agreed. "But since I'm already taking seventh grade algebra, I guess it's okay for me to be in it."

As Liza started talking about how she wanted to join the art club, Addie, Dana, and Claire passed by our table on their way to the bathroom. That's where all the Pops go after lunch. They hang out in there, putting on makeup, and gossiping about people. I know because I'd tried to join them at the very beginning of the school year.

What a mess that had been. They had said all kinds of mean things about me. And not when I left the room, either. Right to my face. They did stuff like that all the time.

"Check out the overalls," Dana said as she passed behind Chloe. She was pretending to whisper, but she was being loud enough for everyone to hear.

"Maybe she's going to milk the cows after school," Claire joked. "Mooo."

Addie giggled. "Too bad there's no farm club. She could be the president."

"Or the mascot," Claire added. "Moooo."

"Mooo, mooo," Dana chimed in, so loudly that a bunch of kids started staring.

Chloe just ignored them. She didn't say a word. She didn't even frown. I thought that was pretty impressive.

"Gee, I wonder what club those three are going to join?" Marilyn asked. "Maybe the moron club?"

Hmm . . . I thought about that for a minute. Addie may

have turned into a class-A jerk, but she wasn't a moron. She was actually pretty smart. I didn't know Claire very well, so I couldn't say. But Dana on the other hand . . . Well, after what Felicia had told me this morning, maybe Marilyn wasn't too far off.

Everyone at our lunch table was staring at Chloe now. Sure, she'd stayed really cool while the Pops were talking about her, but we all knew she had to be upset.

It was Liza who knew exactly what to do to cheer her up. "Check this out," she said in her soft, quiet voice. She took her hot dog out of its bun and dropped it on the floor.

The hot dog bounced! It really did. We were all hysterical. And no one laughed harder than Chloe.

I smiled happily to myself. Let the Pops spend their lunch hour staring at themselves in the bathroom mirror.

There was no way they were having more fun than we were right now!

Chapter
TWO

"AND HERE THEY COME, three more wild animals, fighting for survival in the jungle that is club sign-ups!" Marc said in a deep newscaster-type voice, as Chloe, Liza, and I walked into the cafeteria at the end of the school day.

I giggled as Marc shoved his video camera in our faces. Chloe let out a giant wild-animal-type roar. Liza put her hand in front of her face. She really hated being on camera. "Whoa, I thought we'd be one of the first ones," I said, looking around the room.

Obviously, I'd been wrong. It seemed like half the school was there already. Most of the kids had come right after the bell rang.

I sighed and added another rule to my growing list of things they never tell you at sixth grade orientation.

MIDDLE SCHOOL RULE # 6:
Don't Stop at Your Locker
Before Club Sign-ups.

"You guys are going to have to fight your way to the front of the line if you're going to get anything good now," Marc noted.

He wasn't kidding. Already there were at least a half dozen tables with big CLUB FILLED signs on them.

"I'd better get moving before the theater club is full," Chloe said as she zoomed off.

"Yeah, I'd better hurry over to where the art club table is," Liza said, glancing across the room. The line was already snaking around the corner.

As Liza left, Marc shook his head. "She's a seventh grader. She should have known better than to get here so late. After last year, I wasn't taking any chances."

"Did you get into the movie club?" I asked him.

Marc nodded. "I was one of the first ones here. I asked to go to the nurse in the middle of my last period class. I stopped there, got my cough drop, and ran to the cafeteria."

I giggled. That was a big joke at our school. No matter what you had wrong with you, the nurse would give you a cough drop. Sore throat — cough drop. Headache — cough drop. Broken leg — cough drop. That was pretty much all she had in there.

"So what did you decide on?" Marc asked me.

"I haven't," I admitted. "There are so many choices. I don't know. . . ."

Before I could finish my sentence, Liza reappeared at my side. Her eyes had welled up with tears. "I was too late. I got closed out of the art club . . . again," she told us quietly.

Marc pulled out his camera and started filming. "Disappointment runs rampant during club sign-ups," he said into the microphone.

"Turn that off," I told him. Sometimes boys can be so insensitive.

"Sorry," he replied sheepishly as he lowered the camera.

"There are other clubs," I told Liza gently.

Liza shook her head. "Drawing and painting are the only things I'm good at."

"Maybe you're good at something else and you just don't know it yet," I suggested. "You could find out you're great at chess or field hockey or cooking. . . ."

Liza shook her head. "Forget it," she said. "I'll just ask my mom if I can take an art class at the community center."

But Liza wanted to be in an after-school club. I could tell. There had to be something left for her.

I looked around the room. Suddenly I spotted Chloe, happily signing her name to a club list. "That's it!" I shouted out. "Liza, you're going to join the theater club."

"What?" Liza looked at me as though I had three heads. So did Marc.

I smiled, knowing what they were thinking. Shy Liza in a play? No way! But that wasn't what I had in mind at all. "You can draw and paint scenery for the show," I told her. "I'm sure they need a lot of people to do that. It would still be art. Just a different kind."

Liza thought about that for a minute. "I don't know . . ." she began.

"Come on, Liza," Marc urged. "It'll be fun. Jenny's right. They need someone who can really draw. And you can draw."

"I guess," she said slowly.

"I'll walk you over," I told her.

"But don't *you* want to get in a line for something?" Liza asked me.

I shrugged. "I still don't know what club I want to be in."

"It's okay. You just pick something and sign up," Liza said. "I can go over by myself."

I smiled as I watched her go. Liza would be really happy working on the sets for the play. Now the question was, what would *I* be happy doing?

I didn't even have time to think about that before Felicia and Rachel Schumacher came running over to me. They looked really upset.

"Jenny, please tell me you haven't signed up for anything yet," Rachel exclaimed.

I shook my head. "No. I still haven't de —"

"Oh, thank goodness!" Felicia exclaimed. "This is great!"

"It's great that I don't know what club I want to be in?"

"You've got to go sign up for student government," Felicia said, practically begging.

"What?" I asked. Student government? That hadn't even been on my short list. (Not that I really *had* a short list.) "Me? Why?"

"Because Addie just decided to run for sixth grade

president," Rachel explained. "And so far no one's running against her."

"That means Addie could be our representative in student council," Felicia added. "And no Pop is going to represent me!"

"I'm sure someone else will sign up to run," I told them.

"Not someone who will win," Felicia argued. "You have lots of friends. You could beat her."

I smiled to myself. *You have lots of friends.* That sounded really nice. Like I was popular or something. Not in a Pops way, of course. But popular just the same.

"I don't know," I said. "Being class president is a big deal. I don't think I want to do something that huge."

"Well, somebody has to," Rachel said. "Think about it. Addie's already walking around like she's queen of the school. If she wins this . . ."

Rachel had a point. Addie would be completely unbearable if she won. But I wasn't sure I was the one to take her on. "What about one of you two?" I suggested.

"We're already signed up for basketball," Rachel said. "That means after-school practice three days a week."

"That's a lot of practicing," I said.

"It's cool. We love playing hoops," Felicia told me.

"And speaking of basketball, do you know why you can't play hoops with pigs?" Rachel asked.

I smiled. I knew just what was coming — another one of Rachel's bad jokes. "Why?" I asked her.

"Because they *hog* the ball," Rachel joked.

Ouch.

"Can we get back to the election?" Felicia urged, turning back toward me. "Jenny, you gotta run. You're our only hope."

"What about Josh?" I asked. "He's a sixth grader, and he's really smart. You should be smart if you're going to be class president."

"He's in the Mathletes club, remember?" Felicia said. "And besides, you're smart, too. Not as smart as Josh, but . . ."

I sighed. No one was as smart as Josh. At least not as far as Felicia was concerned.

"Come on," Rachel urged. "Just put your name on the list. Then you can think about it tonight. If you decide not to do it, you can always cross it off."

I shrugged. It's not like I'd put my name on any other list. Judging by all the FILLED signs that were popping up around the cafeteria, I'd run out of options, anyway.

"All right, I'll sign up," I said finally. "But I'm not saying I'll actually run."

My heart was racing as I got off the late bus and headed toward my house. Me? President of the sixth grade? Impossible. Especially if Addie was running. She was a Pop. *Maybe even the poppest sixth grade Pop of all.* I didn't have a chance against her.

Or did I? There really weren't that many Pops in the

sixth grade. And there were a whole lot of the rest of us. If I could get those people to vote for me . . .

But would they?

And if they didn't, and Addie won, would she ever let me forget that I'd tried to beat her?

Talk about a tough decision. I was going to need some help with this one. And since I already knew what all my friends wanted me to do — you should have heard Chloe squeal when Felicia told her I'd signed up — I would have to go to someone who didn't have any opinion at all. Someone who could help me decide this scientifically.

I would have to ask for help from my computer. Well, actually a website on my computer called middleschool-survival.com. That site is awesome. It's got all kinds of quizzes and advice columns just for middle-schoolers. I knew I could find a quiz on there that would tell me exactly what to do.

I raced over to the computer and quickly typed in the Web site. I clicked on the link for quizzes and almost immediately a whole list appeared on the screen. I scanned down past quizzes like *Are You Really What You Eat?*, *Is He Heinous or Harmless?*, and *Are You a Diva or a Dud?*, until I found just the one I needed.

Were You Born to Lead?

1. **It's Saturday afternoon, and you're bored out of your skull. Do you**

   A. Curl up on the couch and watch a marathon of MTV's *My Super Sweet 16*?

   B. Send a text message to your friends to see if they have something planned . . . and if you can tag along?

   C. Round up your friends for an afternoon hike? Nature is calling!

That was easy. My answer was definitely C. A few weeks ago, when school had just started, I probably would have checked A or B, because I would have been too shy to call any of my new friends and suggest a plan. But now I felt totally comfortable with them.

2. **Dinner's over. The dishes are piled in the sink. What's your game plan?**

   A. Call a friend and hope your mom will be too nice to interrupt your call to ask you to do the dishes.

   B. Hurry upstairs and start your homework, successfully avoiding your chores.

C. Hop to it and immediately start rinsing off the grease and grime.

Okay, if I were being completely honest, I'd have to click B here. I could never just lie around and watch my mom and dad do all the work, but I wouldn't volunteer for chores, either. At least doing my homework would be a good thing, right?

3. It's oral report time in English class! What's your plan of action?

A. Sink down low in your chair and hope the teacher doesn't notice you.

B. Make sure you've got your report out and ready just in case you get called on.

C. Volunteer to go first — better to get it over with than to have the whole thing hanging over your head.

I guess it was another B for me. I always have my work ready to go, but I don't usually volunteer to go first for anything.

4. There's a school dance coming. Do you

A. Start planning what you're going to wear, and let others plan the dance.

B. Wait to see if a planning committee forms, and then sign up to help.

C. Start your own planning committee, so you can be sure it'll be the hottest night of the year.

I wasn't sure what to click for this one. The only school dance we'd had was planned by the faculty, since it was held the second week of school. But it sounded like an excellent idea to start a planning committee with my friends, because then we could make sure we had a good time. But I didn't know about starting the committee. Was that the kind of thing sixth graders did? After thinking about it for a while, I clicked B. It was sort of a compromise.

5. **Your study group is ready to take a chow break. The trouble is, two of you are arguing over whether to go with pepperoni or mushrooms on the pizza. How do you handle this?**

   A. Ignore the fighting duo. You hate getting in the middle of things, and besides, you'll eat anything.
   B. Tell your friends you think arguing over pizza is totally ridiculous and suggest you get half with pepperoni and half with mushrooms.
   C. Suggest that everyone in the study group vote for his or her favorite. The topping with the most votes wins.

Definitely C. I hate being around people who are fighting. And I'll do just about anything to stop it. The voting thing worked for me.

   That was the last question. I clicked the SUBMIT button and held my breath as I waited for the computer to decide my future.

You have chosen three B's and two C's.
How Do You Measure Up?

If you answered mostly A's, you tend to shy away from the spotlight. Leading's not your thing. You're also not a big joiner.

It's okay to do things on your own, but you might want to give getting involved a shot. You'd be surprised how much fun it can be!

If you answered mostly B's, you are a team player. You may not be a natural-born leader, but you're not one to shirk responsibility, either. Don't be surprised if your friends come to you for a helping hand.

If you answered mostly C's, baby you were born to lead!

Okay, so now what was I supposed to do? I was stuck somewhere between being a team player and a natural-born leader.

Maybe that meant I shouldn't run for president. Maybe I should just sign up to be on a bunch of committees during the year. That way I could help out, but I wouldn't have to be in charge.

Still, the website did say that my friends would come looking for me to lend a helping hand. And that's exactly what they'd done. They'd asked me to stop Addie from becoming the president of our grade.

How could I let them down?

Chapter
THREE

"OKAY, SO IT'S SETTLED. Liza and I will make the posters. Felicia's going to help you with the speech, and Josh is going to . . ." Chloe stopped for a minute. "Josh, what *are* you going to do?"

Everyone at our lunch table turned toward Josh. It was the day after I'd signed up to run in the election, and already Chloe had named herself my campaign manager.

"I could set up a 'Vote for Jenny' website," Josh suggested. "I'm good with computers."

"I could videotape you talking about the issues," Marc volunteered, holding up his camera, "and then feed the video into the website."

The issues. Yikes. I hadn't thought about that. I was going to have to come up with a platform — my feelings on how to make the school a better place. I didn't have any feelings about that. I'd only been at this school a few weeks.

"I wonder what issues Addie's going to talk about in *her* campaign," I said.

"Probably bigger mirrors in the bathrooms," Chloe joked.

I giggled. Addie did spend a lot of time looking at herself these days.

"More like how to improve the cafeteria's dessert menu," Liza said. "Looks like she's already handing out her own treats." Liza pointed across the room. Addie and Dana were passing out little bags of candy.

Eventually, Dana made her way over to our side of the cafeteria. As she passed our table, she glared at Chloe and me. She didn't give us any candy, either. In fact, the only person at our table she did give candy to was Josh.

"What's that about?" Chloe demanded. "Are you some sort of double agent spying for the other side?"

Josh looked at her. "No. I don't know why she gave me this. Honest."

"She's probably trying to divide and conquer," Marilyn suggested.

"Yeah. Maybe she's hoping she can get us so mad at Josh that we won't focus on the campaign," Carolyn added.

"But we'll never be divided," Marilyn swore.

"Yeah, we'll stick together," Carolyn vowed.

I looked down at the bag of candy on Josh's tray. There were four chocolate kisses in the bag. It was sealed with a sticker that read:

> From Addie, here's a kiss.
> Vote for her. She can't miss.

"I can't believe she's already campaigning," I groaned. "We just signed up for the election yesterday."

"It's okay," Chloe said. "We're pacing ourselves." She thought for a moment. "But we'd better come up with something for lunchtime tomorrow."

"I can't believe we only have one week. Next Monday is the campaign speech assembly and then everyone votes on Tuesday," I said nervously.

"I know," Chloe nodded. "We've got to get thinking. What kinds of snacks can we give out?"

"How about if we bake cookies?" Carolyn suggested.

"Yeah, everyone loves cookies," Marilyn agreed.

"But are you guys allowed to help me?" I asked the twins, glancing at Liza and Marc, too. "I mean, these are the sixth grade elections."

"There are no rules about that," Marc said. "You can help anyone you want. It's a free country."

Chloe looked over toward where Addie was handing out her candy treats. "Not if Addie gets elected. Then it'll be free only if you're a Pop. The rest of us will have to do what Addie says. That's what we've gotta stop." She paused for a moment. "Hey, that's a pretty good campaign slogan: Stop the Pop . . . Before She Stops You!"

Stop the Pop. Yeah. I liked that.

My house turned into election central after school that day. Liza, Felicia, Rachel, and Chloe were at my dining room table making signs. Josh and Marc were in the living room, working on the website on Josh's laptop. Marilyn, Carolyn, and I were in the kitchen, getting ready to bake cookies.

"Do you guys know a good recipe for cookies?" I asked the twins.

They both shook their heads. "At our house it's slice and bake," Carolyn said.

"Yeah. Our mom's not big on making stuff from scratch," Marilyn added.

"Well, we can't just buy cookies," I said. "These have to be homemade and delicious. It's the only way our campaign snack will be better than Addie's. I mean, what did she do? Buy a few candies and shove them into bags?"

"Maybe your mom has a good recipe," Marilyn said.

"I doubt it. We don't bake much around here, either," I admitted.

"We could check the computer," Carolyn suggested.

The computer! That was it! "I know just the site," I said.

Sure enough, middleschoolsurvival.com had a whole recipe section. "Let's see," I said, looking at the list. "Oh, yuck. Amazing Artichoke Hearts . . ."

"Ugh," Chloe shouted from the other room. "We don't want to make everyone throw up."

Agreed. "Marvelous Milk Shakes . . ." I continued, scanning all the recipes on the site.

"Too hard to bring to school," Felicia warned.

"But easy to make," Rachel told her. "All you gotta do

to make a milk shake is sneak up behind a cow and yell boo!" Rachel giggled. "Get it?"

"That was awful," Felicia groaned.

I smiled and changed the subject from bad jokes back to cookies. "Oh, here we go," I said when I came across some cookie recipes.

The twins and I scanned the list.

"Mmm . . . chocolate chip," I noted, looking at one recipe.

Marilyn shook her head. "Chocolate equals zits," she pointed out.

"You don't want kids blaming their lousy skin on you," Carolyn warned.

"How about sugar cookies?" I suggested, glancing down the list of recipes. "Everyone loves them."

"That's true," Marilyn agreed.

"Print it out," Carolyn told me.

With two clicks of the mouse, I did just that.

A few minutes after Marilyn, Carolyn, and I put the first batch of cookies in the oven, I heard Josh's cell phone ring.

He flipped it open. "Hello?" he said. He paused while the person on the other end said something, and then he asked, "Why are you calling me? How'd you get this number?"

Okay, that sounded a little mysterious. I couldn't help but eavesdrop.

"Um . . . well . . . I don't know," Josh stammered. "I

Yummy in the Tummy
Sugar Cookies

INGREDIENTS:
- $1/_2$ cup butter, softened
- $1/_2$ cup margarine, softened
- 1 egg
- 1 teaspoon orange extract
- 2 cups white sugar
- 2 $1/_2$ cups self-rising flour
- *Optional: Sprinkles or small candies*

YOU'LL ALSO NEED:
- Large mixing bowl
- An electric mixer
- Measuring cup
- Baking sheet
- Spatula

DIRECTIONS:
1. Preheat oven to 350 degrees F.
2. Beat all ingredients in the mixing bowl, except self-rising flour, with an electric mixer until fluffy.
3. Add self-rising flour and mix well.
4. Shape dough into balls, coat in sprinkles or favorite toppings, and flatten on an ungreased cookie sheet.
5. Bake for 5 to 8 minutes until cookies are light golden brown.

Makes 24 cookies.

mean. Why me?" He listened to the person on the other end and then said, "Look, I can't talk about this right now. I'm . . . uh . . . well, I'm busy. We can talk about this tonight."

There was complete silence as he hung up the phone. It was kind of obvious that we'd all been listening in on his conversation.

"That, uh, that was my cousin," he said quickly.

I looked across the kitchen and into the dining room. Chloe and I made eye contact. She shook her head. I knew exactly what she meant. That wasn't a cousin kind of conversation. It was too suspicious.

I glanced over at Felicia to see if she had noticed how weird Josh had sounded on the phone. But she was happily putting glitter on a poster. She didn't seem to think there was anything strange about the call.

"Oh, no! Pull out those cookies, fast!" Carolyn shouted to me.

"They're gonna burn," Marilyn screamed out.

The sound of their voices brought my attention back to the baking. Quickly, I grabbed two pot holders, and pulled out the sheet of cookies.

Phew. I'd gotten to them just in time.

When I went to bed that night, there were 120 little bags of cookies in a box in my living room. Every one of them was sealed with a sticker that said, "Be a Smart

Cookie — Vote for Jenny!" Chloe had come up with that one, too. She sure was good with slogans.

I was so tired that I practically fell asleep before my head hit the pillow. And all night long I dreamed of round sugar cookies — except these cookies all had Addie's face on them. And every Addie-faced cookie was laughing at me!

I'd only been a candidate for 24 hours, and already the campaign was stressing me out.

Felicia and I giggled as we stared at the poster that Addie and her friends had posted in C wing the next morning. There was a photo of Addie and below it it read, "Vote for Addie. She's Rad-die."

"Rad-die?" Felicia chuckled. "Give me a break."

"That is pretty bad," I agreed.

Just then Chloe came rushing over to us. She was carrying a pile of posters and some masking tape. "Come on, you guys, start putting these up," she said, plopping the posters into our arms. She was in total campaign-manager mode. "This election isn't going to win itself, you know."

As I placed my poster on the wall across from Addie's, I frowned. The photograph on Addie's poster was of Addie in a long black dress, with her blond hair pulled back in a tight bun. She looked like a model.

I was wearing a pink-and-green polo shirt and jeans in my photo. My hair was in a ponytail. I didn't look like a dork or anything. I just didn't look very cool. At least not the way Addie did.

"I look like a baby in that picture," I groaned.

"No, you don't," Felicia said. "You look eleven."

"But I don't *want* to look eleven," I insisted. "Check out Addie's poster. She looks like a teenager."

"Addie and Dana are the only ones in the whole grade who look like that," Chloe pointed out. "Everyone else is more like you. Trust me. It's perfect. People will relate to this picture. It shows you're one of them."

I shrugged. Chloe sounded so sure of herself. But I wasn't quite as certain. I still wished I could look more like Addie. And I bet other people did, too.

Would that make them vote for her?

Chapter
FOUR

"HI, I'M JENNY MCAFEE. I'm in a few of your classes. I hope you'll vote for me for sixth grade class president," I said to two girls I recognized from my Spanish and math classes, as I handed them cookies. That was how I was spending my lunch period — handing out cookies and introducing myself to people. Chloe called it a "meet-and-greet opportunity."

I don't know where she gets this stuff.

"Mmm . . . cookies," Celina, one of the girls, remarked.

"Homemade," I assured her. "They're delicious."

"Oh, yum," her friend Emily said, taking a bite. "I love sugar cookies."

"These are totally better than those candies Addie gave out yesterday," Celina said. "I'm not a big chocolate eater."

"It gives you zits," Emily added.

I smiled. Marilyn and Carolyn had been right.

"I bet Addie's really surprised someone had the guts to run against her," Emily continued.

"I have no idea," I told her. "But I do know that I have some ideas about how to make this school great. And I want everyone to hear them. That's why I'm running."

Wow. I was really starting to sound like a politician.

"Well, I think you're really brave. Addie can be pretty mean when she wants to be," Emily remarked.

I frowned slightly. No one knew that better than I did.

"Mmmm," Celina sighed, as she licked the cookie crumbs from her fingers. "That was yummy. Can I have some more?"

Before I could hand her a second bag of cookie, Chloe grabbed me by the arm. "Sorry, guys, but I have to talk to the future Madame President right away."

"Oh, okay," Emily said as Chloe dragged me off. "Thanks again, Jenny."

"What's so important?" I asked, as Chloe and I moved away from Celina and Emily.

"You can't give out seconds on the cookies," Chloe said. "You have to give everyone just one. Otherwise it'll look like you're playing favorites with people. You can't make it look like you're the kind of person who would treat some people better than others."

"But she asked for more and —" I began.

"Look, Jenny, we're trying to show that Addie will run the school only for the Pops. *You're* the candidate who will represent everyone," Chloe explained.

"I doubt the Pops want me to represent them," I corrected her.

"Yeah, but there aren't that many of them. And besides, they're all gonna vote for Addie. We're campaigning for the other —" Chloe stopped mid-sentence and stared at the doorway in the front of the cafeteria. "What's going on over there?" she asked.

I followed her glance. Whoa! Josh was standing by the door, talking to Dana. I watched in amazement as she wrote something on a slip of paper and handed it to him. He nodded and then tucked it in his jeans pocket.

"Josh and Dana?" Chloe asked. "Since when?"

I shook my head. "Nah. It can't be. Josh likes Felicia. Everyone knows that."

"It sure doesn't look that way," Chloe said. "Look at how close she's standing to him. And he's not backing away."

"Maybe she's whispering and he has to stand that close to hear what she's saying," I suggested.

"What could Dana have to say to Josh that would be so interesting he'd want to hear it?" Chloe countered. "Unless . . ."

"Unless what?" I asked.

"Unless *he's* the one who's doing the whispering," Chloe said.

"Huh?"

"Maybe he's actually on Addie's side in this election," Chloe continued. "Maybe he's a double agent."

"Oh, come on," I said. "Josh? Spying for the Pops? Give me a break."

"Dana did give him that bag of candy yesterday," Chloe pointed out. "And he got that weird phone call."

"Yeah, but if he was a spy, wouldn't she be pretending she *didn't* like him?" I asked. "This is too obvious. Spies are supposed to be sneaky."

"Maybe," Chloe said. "But I wouldn't talk about our campaign secrets in front of him . . . just in case."

"What campaign secrets?" I asked her.

"Well, if we get any, we're not going to share them with Josh," Chloe told me. Then she pushed me back into the lunchroom. "Come on, we still have a lot of cookies to give out. You're going to win this election, with or without Josh's help."

At the end of the school day, I was walking happily through C wing, minding my own business, when Addie and Dana leaped out from behind a classroom door and blocked my path.

"You're such a baby, Jenny," Addie shouted at me.

"What are you talking about?" I asked her.

"You know exactly what I'm talking about," Addie said. "My posters."

"What about them?"

Addie moved aside so I could see the wall. There was her photograph, the one with her in the black dress and the bun in her hair. But someone had drawn a mustache and beard on her face with a black marker. The words had been changed, too. Now they read: *Don't* Vote for Addie. She's *a Bad*-die!

I choked back a laugh.

"It's not funny," Dana said. "We worked hard on those posters."

"I'm sure you did," I told her. "And I didn't do anything to them."

"Oh, come on, Jenny. You're jealous of how good I look in my picture," Addie insisted. "That's why you ruined it."

"You're so conceited," I replied. "I'm not jealous of you."

Okay, so maybe I was a little jealous of Addie. But I wasn't about to tell her that.

"Yeah, well, if you didn't do it, one of your stupid friends must have," Addie insisted.

"They're not stupid. And they wouldn't do something like this, either," I defended them. "Anyone could have drawn on your poster, Addie."

Dana stepped a little closer to me — too close.

But just then, Marc, Chloe, and Felicia walked up behind me. Suddenly it was four of us against two of them. Apparently Dana didn't like those odds, because she took a step back.

MIDDLE SCHOOL RULE # 7:
THERE'S SAFETY IN NUMBERS.

"Which one of you losers ruined Addie's poster?" Dana demanded.

"You're the only loser I see around here," Marc shot back. "So it must have been you."

"I'm not a loser," Dana told him. "I'm on Addie's team. *The winning team.*"

"Don't count on it," Felicia said.

"You guys had better watch out," Addie warned us.

"No, *you'd* better watch out," Chloe replied. "We're gonna beat you on election day."

Addie and Dana started to laugh. "Yeah, like that'll ever happen."

"We've got a few tricks up our sleeves," Chloe told them.

"Oh, so do we," Dana assured her. "Trust me."

"Is that a threat?" Marc demanded.

Addie shook her head. Her eyes grew small and mean. "No. It's a promise," she said.

I didn't like the sound of that.

As Dana and Addie walked away, I turned to Chloe. "What tricks?" I asked her.

Chloe shrugged. "I don't know. I just wanted to scare them."

"Well, we'd better come up with something," Felicia said. "I don't trust Dana and Addie. They fight dirty."

Suddenly I felt a nervous twinge in my stomach. My mind switched back to that whole Josh and Dana in the cafeteria thing. What if that was the trick Addie had been talking about?

"Hey, don't worry," Marc assured me. "We'll come up with something. You're gonna win. You'll see."

I sure hoped he was right.

Chapter

FIVE

"OKAY, SO HERE ARE the points you want to make," Felicia said as she and Chloe sat down beside me underneath the tree in my front yard late that afternoon. "Even though sixth graders are the youngest in the school, our voice really counts, because the changes that are made this year are the ones we'll have to live with for the next three years."

"Right. Then go into the plans you have. Like to put a jukebox in the cafeteria as a way to raise money," Chloe added.

"And field days," Felicia continued.

"Oh, yeah. Definitely don't forget field days," Chloe agreed. "When the whole school goes to the park instead of classes and has races and plays games and things. It's a great way to get to know each other and boost school spirit."

"That's an important one," Felicia agreed. "Who *wouldn't* vote for someone who can get everyone out of classes for a day?"

"I don't think the principal will go for that," I said.

"She doesn't have to," Chloe explained. "You're just saying that's what you want. You'll bring it up at student council meetings. You're not actually promising you'll make it happen."

"But if we know it won't . . ." I began.

"We *don't* know," Chloe said. "The principal might think it's a great idea. *We* all do."

"That's true," I said slowly. I looked up at Marc. "Let's go," I said.

"All right," he said, aiming his digital video camera in my direction. "And . . . action!"

It took me about three tries to get the speech just right, but finally, everyone was happy with what I said on camera.

"Okay, let's bring the camera inside so we can download this," Felicia said cheerfully. "Josh must have the website almost up and running by now. I don't know how he does it. He's so smart."

"Let's hope he doesn't *out*smart us," Chloe murmured to me.

"What?" Felicia asked.

"Nothing," I assured her. "Come on, let's get inside and give this to him right away. I can't wait to see the website and those other posters Liza's making."

"Liza's an amazing artist," Chloe told me. "She's already working on some scenery designs for *You're a Good Man, Charlie Brown.* They're awesome."

"When are the auditions?" I asked her.

"Next Friday. Three days after the election. So I have plenty of time to get ready," she answered.

Wow. It was hard to believe the elections were next Tuesday.

"Okay, we're here," Marc called out as we headed for the living room. "You ready for the video yet, Josh?"

"Yeah, in a minute." He moved aside so we could see the screen on his laptop. "Here, check out what I've done so far."

Josh clicked the mouse, and my picture appeared on the screen. Underneath my face it said: JENNY MCAFEE, OF THE PEOPLE, FOR THE PEOPLE." Then a balloon came on the screen with a picture of Addie on it. A giant sewing needle suddenly appeared, popping the balloon. The caption read: POP THE POP. VOTE FOR JENNY.

"That's hilarious, Josh," Felicia laughed. "I love that whole balloon thing."

Marc handed Josh his camera and a connecting cable. "Here you go," he said. "The video's all ready for you to download."

Josh nodded, and connected the cable to the computer and the camera. He waited for the video icon to appear on the screen, then he double-clicked the mouse and waited.

And waited. And waited.

But nothing happened. At least not at first. Then, suddenly, the computer shut down.

"Oh, man. It crashed," Josh said. He pushed a few buttons, and turned the computer on again.

"It's all right, just pull up the file and try again," Felicia urged him.

Josh nodded and began searching. But after a few moments he frowned and said, "It's not here."

"What do you mean it's not there?" Chloe demanded.

"I mean I can't find the file. It's missing," Josh said.

"The file just can't be missing," Marc insisted.

"I know," Josh said. "It's probably just in a different folder or something. It's going to take some time, but I'll find it," he assured me, as he shut down the computer.

"What are you doing?" Chloe demanded.

"I gotta go," Josh told her.

"But the website . . ." I mumbled.

"Don't worry. I'll find it," Josh promised again.

"You have to fix it now," Chloe insisted. "There are only six days until the election. Kids have to be able to go on the site right away."

"And I've already put the address on the posters," Liza told him. She pointed to the bottom of the glittery poster she was working on.

"Come on, man, just try and find it now," Marc urged.

"I'm sorry, but I gotta do something important," Josh said.

"What's more important than this?" Chloe demanded.

Josh bit his lip and looked down at the floor. "I'll call you guys later," he said as he left.

"See, I told you," Chloe said to me the minute we heard the front door close behind him.

"Told you what?" Felicia asked suspiciously.

I sighed. "Chloe thinks Josh is a spy for Addie's side."

"That's ridiculous!" Felicia exclaimed. "How could you say that about him?"

"Look, everyone knows you like Josh, so I can't expect you to be objective about this," Chloe told her. "But first there was the candy thing, and then that whole freaky conversation he was having with Dana, and now this —"

"What candy thing? What freaky conversation with Dana?" Felicia asked nervously.

"It was nothing," I told her.

"Some nothing," Chloe argued. "First Dana gives him a bag of candy —"

"It was campaign candy," I corrected her. "She gave it to lots of people."

"Not at our table," Marc pointed out.

"Exactly," Chloe said. "And let's not forget about the mystery phone call he got yesterday. Then at lunch today, there he was, talking to Dana. And she gave him that note, and he put it in his pocket. . . ."

Felicia stared at Liza and me. "Did you guys see this, too?"

Liza shook her head. "I didn't. But Chloe told me about it."

"Jenny?" Felicia asked.

I nodded slowly. "I saw them. But, Felicia, we don't know what he was talking about with her."

"I'll bet he's with Addie and Dana right now," Chloe insisted. "He's probably telling them all about our website."

"Our *crashed* website . . ." Marc said.

"I'm just glad he didn't get a chance to download the video," Chloe said. "We don't want them to know our campaign platform."

"I don't believe you guys!" Felicia shouted. "Josh is our friend. You can't really believe he'd do this."

"Oh, yes I can," Chloe said. "And you'd better believe it, too."

I could see tears forming in Felicia's eyes. "I'm going home!" She glared at Chloe and then stormed off.

I sighed, remembering what Marilyn had said about Dana trying to divide and conquer us by giving Josh candy.

That was definitely what was happening. Except we didn't need Dana's help. We were doing it all by ourselves.

That night, Felicia called me. I could hear in her voice that she'd been crying.

"You don't really believe all that stuff Chloe was saying about Josh, do you?" she asked me.

"I don't want to think one of my best friends is a spy," I said. "But you gotta admit . . ."

"No, I don't. I don't have to admit anything!" Felicia insisted. She paused for a minute. "Do you think Josh likes Dana now?" she asked quietly.

"I don't know," I told her honestly. "I'm not really good when it comes to stuff like that."

"Well, how am I supposed to know?" Felicia asked.

I thought about that for a minute. "Remember when we did that quiz on the computer together at the beginning of school?" I asked her.

"You mean the one that told you if a boy likes you or not?" Felicia recalled.

"Uh-huh," I said. "Maybe there's another quiz to see if he *still* likes you."

"Sounds good," Felicia said hopefully.

"Hold on. I'll see if I can find one," I said, booting up my computer and going directly to www.middleschool survival.com. "Here it is. . . ."

Is He Still Into You?
True or False: Lately you've discovered that he's being very secretive.

"I don't think Josh is secretive," Felicia said.

I sighed. It was going to be hard to get Felicia to answer these questions honestly. "How about today when he wouldn't tell us where he had to go? Or yesterday, when he wouldn't tell us who called him?"

"He said it was his cousin on the phone, remember?" Felicia insisted.

"Come on, Felicia," I said. "Is that how you talk to your cousin?"

"Okay," Felicia admitted finally. "Check true."

True or false: He's stopped using your pet name.

"That's definitely false," Felicia said.

"It is?" I asked.

"He never had a pet name for me," Felicia explained. "So he couldn't stop using it."

I guess I had to give her that one. I clicked on the FALSE button.

True or false: Lately you've seen him hanging around with other girls.

"I haven't," Felicia said. "Except for you, Liza, and the twins. And that's nothing new. You guys always have lunch together."

"What about that whole thing with Dana?" I pointed out. I didn't want to be cruel. But you can't get a good answer from a computer quiz if you don't answer the questions honestly.

"I didn't see that. Chloe did. And I don't believe anything I don't see with my own eyes."

Well, the questions did say "Lately *you've* seen him . . ." So I had to click FALSE.

True or false: He's stopped paying you compliments.

"False. False. Totally false!" Felicia said excitedly. "Just this morning he told me that I was the best basketball player in the school. Girl or boy. That's a huge compliment. You have to put false this time, Jenny."

"Okay, okay," I said. "False it is." I clicked the button, and then waited. A few seconds later, the results popped up on the screen.

You answered one true and three false.

Mostly true: Sorry, but it's time to say bye-bye to your guy. He's got his sights set on someone else.

Mostly false: Don't worry, this guy's still totally into you.

"Phew," Felicia said, taking a deep breath. "That was a close one. But now that we've proved Josh still likes me, that means he could never be a spy."

"Mmm-hmm," I said, trying hard to sound as positive as Felicia did. But I wasn't sure at all. There was definitely something weird about how Josh was acting. And no computer quiz could convince me differently.

Chapter
SIX

MY CELL PHONE BEGAN TO RING even before my alarm clock went off the following morning. I rolled over and answered groggily.

"Hello?"

"I told you Josh was on our side," the voice on the other end said excitedly.

"Hi, Felicia. What are you talking about?"

"The website. It's up and running. And it's great."

I sat up in bed. This was pretty exciting. I'd never had my own website before. "I can't believe you got up so early just to check," I told Felicia.

"I didn't. Josh called me to tell me," she explained. "That's how I woke up."

I smiled. Felicia probably didn't mind being woken up by a call from Josh.

"Go take a look," Felicia said excitedly. "I'm gonna call Chloe and tell her she was wrong about Josh."

I laughed. I didn't know which Felicia was more excited about — that Chloe was wrong, or that the website was up and running. Probably both.

I hung up the phone and ran downstairs to the

computer. As soon as the website loaded, the video of me speaking popped up.

"Hi, I'm Jenny McAfee. And I'm running for sixth grade president . . ."

Did you ever notice how different you sound when you hear a recording of your voice? You spend your whole life thinking you sound one way, and then you hear yourself in a recording, and it's a lot squeakier. I guess that's why so many people think they can sing really well, when they can't even carry a tune.

But even though my voice was kind of high-pitched, I thought it still sounded pretty nice. And the video *looked* really professional. Marc had done a great job filming me as I talked. I didn't look like a dork at all. I sounded like I knew what I was talking about — thanks to all that coaching from Felicia and Chloe.

Watching myself on the screen, I was kind of amazed. I had to admit, I actually looked presidential. Maybe I could do this after all.

By the time I got to school in the morning, Liza and Rachel had already placed posters with my new campaign website address all over the halls. They were really nice posters — covered with glitter and drawn with neon markers. There was no chance of missing them as you walked around the school.

Unfortunately, there was also no missing Addie, either.

She was standing in the middle of C wing handing out key chains with her picture on them. "While they were thinking about *their* website, *I* was out making presents for all of you, my fellow sixth graders," I heard her say as she handed a key chain to one girl.

She turned to a boy passing by. "I'm always thinking about you," she said, pressing a key chain into his palm and winking.

I frowned. Addie had made it seem like my friends and I were being selfish by creating a website. But that wasn't the point of the site at all. I'd made it to let everyone know how I felt about the issues. So far, Addie hadn't talked about issues at all. She'd just smiled at people and given them free stuff.

"Wow, what a great idea," I heard Celina coo as Addie handed her a key chain. "Even better than homemade cookies."

That made me mad. Celina had made me think she was on my side when I gave her my cookies. Now she was on Addie's side — just because of a stupid key chain.

Addie was trying to buy the election. And from the looks of things, it was working.

"By the way," I heard Addie say to Celina, "I love your shirt. It's just the kind of thing I would wear."

I frowned. There was nothing special about what Celina was wearing. It was just a plain sky-blue T-shirt. Addie was just saying that to get Celina to like her.

"Can I count on your vote?" I heard Addie ask her.

Celina looked at the key chain, and then at Addie's smile. "Uh, sure," she said.

"That's so cool," Addie said, thanking her in a very Pop-like way. "I always knew you were one of *us*."

Celina practically glowed at that. She looked like she'd just won the lottery or something. Which I guess she had. The middle school lottery, anyway.

MIDDLE SCHOOL RULE # 8:
Even People Who Hate Pops, Want to *Be* Pops.

"Addie's a piece of work, isn't she?" Chloe whispered, coming up behind me. "What a big, fat liar!"

I turned and nodded. "But people believe her. They even like her."

Chloe nodded. "Don't worry. They won't for long. Everyone is about to find out what Addie Wilson is really like."

I looked at her strangely. "What are you talking about?"

Chloe looked around. "I can't tell you now," she said, tipping her head to the left, where Dana and Claire were standing, watching us. "We'll meet at your house after school today."

Okay. Now I was really curious. I was dying to know what Chloe knew that I didn't. But I understood why she couldn't tell me anything now. There were spies everywhere.

I was one of the last people to get to fifth period lunch. I'd been in the library, checking on our website. According to the counter at the bottom of our screen, 47 people had logged on so far. That wasn't bad, considering it was only 12:30, and not all the sixth graders had had their study halls yet. Study hall was about the only time you could go to the library and use the computers.

As I brought my tray over to our usual lunch table, Chloe started humming "Hail to the Chief" – the song they play whenever the real president walks into a room.

"Very funny," I said, squeezing in between her and Carolyn.

"Better get used to it," Chloe said. "You'll be president before you know it."

"If I win, it'll be because of the video on the website," I said, turning to Marc. "You're an amazing filmmaker. I look like a real candidate."

"You *are* a real candidate," Liza told me.

"You know what I mean," I said, blushing at her compliment. "Like in a real election. Not a school one."

"I didn't do anything. You're the one who made the video look so professional," Marc assured me. "The first thing we learned in movie club was the camera doesn't lie."

"Thanks," I said, blushing deeper. "It was really nice of you to take time out of making your movie to help me."

"Oh, I'm still making the movie," Marc explained. "The election's going to be a featured part of it. I'm going to film you making your acceptance speech when you win the election, too."

"Don't be so sure," I told him. "I've seen lots of kids carrying Addie's key chains today."

"I told you not to worry about that," Chloe insisted. She looked across the table at Marc and smiled mysteriously.

"Where's Josh?" Marilyn asked me.

"He did an awesome job on the site," Carolyn added. "I want to congratulate him."

"I think he had a Mathletes thing in the library," Marc said.

"Just as well. We need to talk about Jenny's campaign. And we don't want him knowing any of our secrets," Chloe remarked.

"We don't have any secrets," I reminded her. "All we have is a website and a cookie recipe."

"For now," Chloe said. "But there are a few more secrets coming," she added, grinning mysteriously in Marc's direction.

"I guess we can't tell Josh about them," Marc remarked with a frown.

Chloe shook her head. "Absolutely not," she declared. "He knows too much already."

I didn't see Josh all day. In fact, the first time I noticed him was in the parking lot after school. Like everyone else, he was heading toward the buses to go home. Nothing strange there — except for the fact that he was walking with Dana.

"I'm so glad you could change your plans to come to my house this time, Josh," I heard Dana say.

Josh going to Dana's house? How weird was that?

I'm pretty sure Josh knew I was staring at him as he boarded the bus, but he didn't wave or anything. He pretended he didn't see me.

But people saw him. Lots of people.

"I don't believe it," Liza said. She was standing a few feet behind me with the twins.

"Whoa," Carolyn murmured.

"Exactly what I was thinking," Marilyn told her.

"Poor Felicia," I added. I looked around quickly, to see if Felicia had seen Josh and Dana getting on the bus together. But Felicia wasn't around. She was probably still at her locker.

Phew. That was lucky.

I walked over to my bus, and grabbed seats for Felicia and me. I made sure to sit by the window so I could block her view of Dana's bus. A few moments later, Felicia climbed onto our bus and plopped down beside me.

"I was so glad I read that English chapter last night," she told me excitedly. "I've never had a surprise quiz before. They don't do that in elementary school. Half the kids in my class were totally freaked when Ms. Jaffe handed out the papers. They hadn't read anything."

I sat there listening to Felicia chatter on and on about how well she'd done on her English test. I tried to smile and act normal, but it was really hard. I knew that Chloe and Marc were coming over later to talk to me about this big campaign secret they were working on. And even though I would ordinarily ask Felicia to come to my house and hang out with us, I didn't today. If Josh really was a Pop in disguise, I couldn't risk Felicia spilling any secrets to him.

I turned slightly in my seat and caught a glimpse of Addie. She was sitting toward the back of the bus, talking to two other sixth graders. That was unusual, because Addie always sat by herself on the bus. After all, she was the only Pop on our bus, and no Pop would ever be caught dead sitting with a non-Pop. But there she was, sitting with David and Trey. That was bizarre because I knew Addie didn't like either of them. In third grade, Trey had this weird thing about picking his nose and flicking his boogers across the room. David, his best friend, always cheered him on.

Addie thought it was disgusting. And even though Trey stopped flinging boogers by fourth grade, she never really got over it.

Until now, apparently. Because there was Addie, sitting with Trey and David, happily talking about being in middle school, and how much she could do for kids like them . . . if they voted for her for sixth grade president.

"Well, I guess we could start a *Star Wars* club, if there

were enough kids who wanted it," I overheard Addie tell Trey.

"Yeah, we could get all the members Wookiee costumes," David said excitedly. "They could wear them to meetings, the way the kids on the basketball team wear their uniforms."

"Um . . . er . . . maybe," Addie replied. "Sure. Why not? Good idea, Dave."

I frowned. *Come on!* She knew the school wouldn't buy Wookiee costumes for a club. The uniforms for sports teams were totally different. But Addie would say anything at this point to get votes. And Trey and David were eating it up. They were so excited to be sitting with a Pop, they'd believe anything.

Okay, so now Addie was spending time with the kids she used to call the "gruesome twosome," just so she could convince them to vote for her. And I was sitting with Felicia, who I couldn't invite over to my house because the boy she liked might be a spy.

I'm telling you. You can't make this stuff up. Elections are weird, weird things.

Chapter
SEVEN

"OKAY, SO WHAT'S THE BIG SECRET?"

It was already five o'clock, and I was busting at the seams to find out what Marc and Chloe had been hinting at during lunch.

Chloe got up from the living room couch and started walking around the room. She peered in between the flowers on the table, ran her hand over our mantel, and then bent down to look underneath the easy chair.

"What are you doing?" I asked her.

"Looking for bugs," Chloe replied.

"Bugs?" I asked, sounding very insulted. "We don't have bugs in our house, Chloe. We're very clean."

"Not those kinds of bugs," Chloe told me. "I meant recording devices. You know, like those tiny tape-recorder things you see in the movies."

"Are you crazy?" I asked. "Why would we have things like that in our living room?"

"Maybe Josh planted them in here," Chloe said. She was completely serious. "He's a real whiz when it comes to technology."

"Oh, cut it out," I said. I looked at Marc. "You don't believe Josh would do something like that, do you?"

Marc shook his head. "Come on, Chloe. You're going all drama queen on us."

"We can't be too careful," Chloe said. "You guys saw what happened today at lunch." She lifted up the cushions on the couch, looked around, and then proclaimed, "Okay, it's all clear. We can talk."

Marc looked at me and rolled his eyes. Then he took out his video camera. "I want to show you something," he said.

"Oh, you are gonna love this," Chloe said. "It's priceless."

"Show me!" I said excitedly.

Marc turned on the camera. In a second, Addie came on the small screen. She was dressed in shorts and a T-shirt, and she was dancing around her backyard with a garden hose.

"Oh, oh, oh, I'm singing in the sun. Just singing in the sun. Gonna laugh and play 'cause I'm number one," she sang out, using the end of the hose as a microphone. Then, suddenly, water splashed out of the hose, drenching her.

"See, I told you it was amazing," Chloe said.

"I don't get it," I said. "What's so special about a video of Addie singing and getting splashed?"

"It's just so totally un-Pop," Chloe said. "Especially because she sings so badly."

"Where'd you get this?" I asked Marc.

"I taped it while I was walking home from your house the other day," he said. "She never even noticed me. She never notices me. I'm not a Pop, so to her, I'm pretty much invisible."

"Which definitely works to our advantage," Chloe added. "Check out what Marc taped in school yesterday."

I watched as the video switched to the B wing hallway. Addie was talking to Claire. "Dana's not nearly as cool as she thinks she is," Addie was saying. "Like those goofy posters she made. *Addie's Rad-die.* I almost wanted to die."

Ouch. That was mean. Good thing Dana didn't hear her.

"And that's not all," Marc said proudly, as the video continued. This time, Addie was talking to Dana in C wing. "I loved all those posters you made," she was saying to Dana. "I'm so glad I picked you instead of Claire to be my campaign manager. I mean, Claire's not nearly as cool as we are. Sometimes when it rains and her hair frizzes up, she looks like a clown."

"I know," Dana said. "Her makeup is pretty circus-like, too."

"Yeah, being around her could really hurt our status," Addie agreed.

"Maybe we should keep away from her until after the election," Dana suggested.

"I think so," Addie told her. "I mean, we don't want to be seen with someone so ordinary. After all, people expect more out of me. They look up to me."

"They worship you," Dana told her.

"And you, too," Addie agreed with a giggle.

As Dana and Addie began to walk down the hall, it was hard to make out what they were saying.

"They moved out of range," Marc told me apologetically. "I didn't want to risk getting caught by following them."

"It's okay," Chloe assured him. "We got what we need, anyway."

I looked at them both strangely. "What do you mean?" I asked. "All you have is a tape of Addie and some Pops saying mean stuff. That's not exactly news."

"But they're saying mean stuff about each other," Marc said.

"Exactly," Chloe agreed. "Usually it's us they're trashing. But this time they're tearing one another apart."

"If we put this stuff on your website, everyone will see what the Pops are like when no one's watching," Marc explained. "Better yet, they'll hear themselves talking about each other."

"Divide and conquer," Chloe said. "That's their strategy with Josh. We can use the same strategy with these tapes. One look at these, and Addie's campaign is history. Even the Pops won't vote for her," Chloe declared triumphantly.

"I don't think the rest of the school will enjoy hearing that Addie thinks they worship her, either," Marc added.

"As if," Chloe seconded. "Nobody worships her."

But that wasn't true. Lots of people *did* worship Addie.

Still, Marc was right. They probably wouldn't want it thrown in their faces.

"Won't we get in trouble for taping Addie's conversations?" I asked Marc.

He shook his head. "The halls are a public space. I was just taping. Can I help it if she came into camera range?"

I knew that wasn't exactly true. He'd been looking for Addie.

"So how do you think we should get the news about this to everyone?" Chloe asked. "How about we e-mail everyone in the sixth grade and send them a link to your website?"

"Yeah, and we could tell them we have exclusive video they can only see there," Marc added excitedly.

"Exclusive. I like that," Chloe told him.

"Addie's history in this campaign," Marc assured me.

"Not only that, but the Pops will be furious with her," Chloe continued. "They'll ditch her. She'll be totally friendless."

I studied Chloe's face. I don't think I'd ever seen her this happy. Which was kind of weird because the thing that was making her so happy was being mean to someone else. This had gone way beyond a campaign for class president.

I frowned slightly. "Maybe we should wait and think about this."

"There's no time to waste," Chloe told me. "The

election's next week. We want people to see this tape right away."

I didn't say anything.

"Don't we?" Chloe asked me.

"I'm not sure," I said honestly. "It will hurt a lot of people's feelings to see this. And it was kind of sneaky to tape Addie when she didn't know she was being filmed."

"I was standing right there, with my camera. I can't help it if she didn't notice me," Marc defended himself.

"I know, but . . ."

"Jenny, do you want to win this election or not?" Chloe demanded.

"Of course I do."

"Then this tape is really important. Because right now, people are liking Addie . . . *a lot.*"

"That's because she's giving them key chains and telling them whatever they want to hear," I insisted. "She's not talking about any real issues."

"Apparently people don't want to hear about school dances or field days," Chloe told me. "They're voting for Addie because she's a Pop."

"And no matter how many great ideas you have, that's one thing you'll never be," Marc added.

"Neither will you!" I muttered.

"But I'm not running for class president," Marc said.

"I don't get your attitude, Jenny," Chloe told me. "This is what we've been waiting for!"

I took a deep breath. "Just let me think about it, okay?" I asked them. "I promise I'll decide what to do by tomorrow."

Chloe and Marc didn't stay at my house much longer after that. Before I knew it, I was all alone in the living room.

I had a big decision to make. And I had no clue what the right answer was. So, I did what I'd been doing lately. I went on the computer.

What was it Chloe had said? Something about how she didn't get my attitude about all this. Well, I didn't, either. Mostly because I didn't know what my attitude about all this was.

Luckily, there was a middleschoolsurvival.com quiz that could help me figure it all out.

Dude, Do You Have a Major 'Tude?

Answer these questions to find out what kind of attitude you have.

1. **You love softball and want to join the girls' team. But no one goes to girls' games at your school. What do you do?**

   A. Forget about playing and join the gang in the stands at the boys' baseball games.
   B. Try to get your friends to support the girls' team and come out to cheer.
   C. You don't need anyone's approval. Go out, join the team, and pitch that no-hitter.

I figured my answer had to be B. I'm not a great athlete, but I do think girls' teams should get attention, too.

2. **You've just walked out of the local grocery store with a cold soda in your hand. You see an older person struggling with her packages. Do you**

   A. Let the clerk in the store know so he can send someone to help.

B. Keep on going. Much as you'd like to help, you've got plans and you can't be late.

C. Put down your can of soda and give the woman a hand. How long can it take?

I would be the kind of person who would help the old woman. At least I hoped that's what I would do. I clicked C. I was pretty sure that was how I'd handle things.

3. **Okay, so you were really tired this morning and accidentally put on a purple sweater and orange socks. The fashion police at school are sure to give you a hard time. Do you**

A. Keep a low profile for the day.

B. Not care at all. You're your own person. You can wear whatever you choose with complete confidence.

C. Make a joke out of your look and beat the critics to the punch.

A few weeks ago I would have clicked A, because Addie and her friends had a way of making me feel really lousy about myself. But lately I'd learned to pretty much ignore them. I clicked C. I might not feel good about my fashion faux pas, but I could definitely laugh about it.

4. **You hear on the evening news about a horrible tornado that has destroyed a town somewhere on the other side of the country. What's your reaction?**

A. Write down the address of where your parents can send a donation.
B. Organize a relief effort at school.
C. Immediately find the remote. This is too depressing to watch.

Last year a big earthquake had destroyed a town in Asia. My whole class got together and had a bake sale and a car wash to raise money to help the people there. I was very involved in that. So my answer was a definite B.

5. There's a new girl in school who is incredibly shy. What's your game plan?

A. Ignore her completely. You've got plenty of friends already.
B. Smile at her in gym class, just to let her know you're an approachable person.
C. Invite her to sit at a table with you and your friends for lunch.

I remembered how great it felt when Chloe came up and asked me to sit with her friends at the beginning of school. Before then I'd eaten alone — in the stairwell, at the library, and even sitting in a phone booth. Eating alone at school really stinks. C, I would invite the new girl to sit with us for sure.

I clicked on the SUBMIT button and waited for the computer to tally up my points.

Check out how many points each of your answers is worth. Then add up your score, and check where you land on the 'tude meter.

Here are the point values for each answer.

1. A) 1 B) 2 C) 3
2. A) 2 B) 1 C) 3
3. A) 1 B) 3 C) 2
4. A) 2 B) 3 C) 1
5. A) 1 B) 2 C) 3

12–15 points: Congratulations! You are the queen of self-esteem. And better yet, your positive 'tude allows you the confidence to help others, even when it may not be the popular thing to do. You'd never go out of your way to hurt someone else. You don't need to do that just to build yourself up. You're already confident.

8–11 points: You're a fascinating mix. At times, you can be incredibly kind and giving, with a generous attitude that people adore. At other times, a lack of motivation keeps you thinking of yourself. Basically, you're human — not perfect, but well on your way to being the kind of gal who's not so stuck on herself that she can't take the time to help others.

5-7 points: Time for an attitude adustment. You're far too wrapped up in yourself. Open your eyes and notice the world around you. You just might like what you see.

I had scored 13 points. Wow! I had no idea I was that confident. But the part that really stuck with me was that thing about not going out of my way to hurt somebody else. That's definitely what I would be doing if I let Marc and Chloe put that video on my website. And as much as I wanted to win, I just couldn't do it that way. Fighting dirty like that was the kind of thing Addie and her friends might do. I wasn't going to sink that low. No way.

I had made my decision. I just hoped I wasn't going to be sorry about it later.

Chloe could barely even look at me as she, Felicia, Rachel, and I walked into school together on Friday morning. Instead, Chloe was laughing at Rachel's jokes, which was definitely weird, because Chloe usually thought Rachel's jokes were pretty bad.

"So what did the sock say to the foot?" Rachel asked us.

"What?" Felicia wondered.

"You're putting me on."

Felicia and I looked at each other and sighed. Another bad joke from Rachel . . . but you had to love her.

But Chloe laughed as if it were the funniest thing she'd ever heard.

If Felicia and Rachel sensed any tension between Chloe and me, they didn't show it. To break the ice, I turned to Chloe and said, "We gotta get to English. We're going to be late."

"Whatever," Chloe replied, rolling her eyes. She turned

to Felicia and Rachel. "See you later," she added. Then she stomped down the hall, leaving me three steps behind her.

Boy, Chloe really was furious about my decision not to use the tape of Addie. Which was kinda funny, because Marc wasn't angry at all. And he was the one who'd taken the video in the first place. He'd just shrugged and said he'd still help me in any way he could.

But as far as Chloe was concerned, this had turned into more than just a campaign. This was a mission. She wanted to be the one to take down the Pops. And she was mad that I'd taken away the "secret weapon."

I had always thought Chloe didn't care what the Pops said or thought about her. Obviously, I was wrong. Nobody got this mad without caring.

"So, anyway, I was thinking we could have a big party to celebrate after you win," Dana said loudly, as Chloe and I entered English class. I could tell she wanted to make sure everyone heard her conversation. "Maybe a pool party at Claire's house. It'll still be warm by next week, don't you think?"

"Mmm-hmm. We would just invite the people who voted for us, right?" Addie added in an equally loud voice.

I could see the eyes of the kids in our sixth grade English class light up. The idea of being invited to a Pops party was something that they'd barely even dared to dream about.

"I guess that doesn't include those two," Dana said, pointing to Chloe and me.

"No losers at the luau," Addie added.

"You see what we're up against?" Chloe hissed angrily in my ear. "Everyone's going to want to go to that party."

I nodded. I understood. But I also didn't want to sink that low. I wanted to be elected president because I was the right person for the job — not because I'd destroyed Addie Wilson.

Not that it hadn't been tempting.

Chapter
EIGHT

"HEY MARILYN, MOVE OVER, WOULD YOU?" Josh asked, as he walked over to our lunch table that afternoon.

Marilyn glanced at Chloe. Chloe shrugged and stared at her sandwich with intense fascination. It was like there was nothing more amazing than tuna on whole wheat. Marilyn didn't know what to do.

Josh just stood there for a minute watching everyone. Finally, Liza scooted over to make room for him. "Here you go," she said in her quiet, peaceful voice.

Usually, we're a pretty rowdy group at lunch. But today no one was talking. Chloe was too mad at me and too paranoid about Josh to say anything. Marilyn and Carolyn were pretty much convinced Josh was a spy, too, and so they kept their distance. Marc was busy reading his English book, getting ready for his test next period.

Only Liza seemed completely normal around Josh. She was too nice to believe that one of her friends could have gone over to the dark side. "How's the Mathlete club going?" she asked.

"Pretty good. I'm the youngest one in the club, but I'm holding my own," he told her.

"I'm sure you're going to be fine," Liza assured Josh. "You pick stuff up really quickly."

Josh smiled at her and shoved a forkful of spaghetti into his mouth. We all kept eating in silence.

It was definitely uncomfortable at the table. But I was glad Josh was there. With him around, Chloe wouldn't dare mention the videotape. And that meant she wouldn't be able to bug me about my decision.

"Okay, I'm done," Marilyn said. She turned to her sister. "You ready?"

Carolyn smiled. "Oh, yeah!" She reached under the table and pulled out a big black portable CD player. "Here we go."

With a push of a button, the music began. Everyone in the cafeteria grew quiet as the song "We Are the Champions" by Queen blasted through the room. You know, it's that song they play at ball games and stuff.

Everyone looked up, surprised. Our cafeteria is usually loud, but only with the sound of kids talking. The music got everyone's attention big-time! Already a group of kids had leaped up on their chairs. They were waving their arms back and forth in the air and singing, "We are the champions. We are the champions. . . ."

Mrs. Martinez, a science teacher, ran over and made them all sit down. The kids did as they were told. But they didn't totally calm down.

"What's this?" I asked.

"It was Marilyn's idea," Liza said. "Or maybe it was Carolyn's. I can't remember. But we burned a whole bunch of CDs on their computer, and put these stickers on the cases." She handed me a CD.

"SAVE OUR SCHOOL. LET JENNY RULE!" I read from the sticker. "Wow, that's great!"

"I designed the stickers. We figured everybody loves that song. Who wouldn't want it on CD?" Liza said.

"Totally!" I agreed. "The sticker is a great touch."

"Yeah," Chloe said, sounding sincerely impressed.

"We wanted to surprise you, Jenny," Liza said.

I smiled at her. I had the best friends in the whole world.

"I wish you guys had let me know about this last night," Josh said. "I could have bought the song online and downloaded it onto Jenny's website. We could have made it her theme song."

"Hello? Liza just said it was a *surprise*," Chloe told him angrily. "And besides, it's not like we have to tell you everything we're planning."

Josh looked at her oddly. "What's with her?" he asked Marc.

Marc shrugged and went back to studying.

A few moments later, Dana approached our table. She made a point of ignoring all of us — except Josh, that is.

"There you are, Joshie," she said sweetly. "I was looking for you."

I glanced across the table at Chloe. *Joshie?* I mouthed silently.

Chloe shrugged and rolled her eyes.

"You were looking for me? Why?" he asked her.

"To thank you for yesterday afternoon," she replied. "I can't wait to get together again today after school."

Josh looked from Dana to the rest of us. We were all just sitting there, staring.

"We were just, uh . . ." Josh began.

"Oh, they're not interested in what we were doing," Dana assured him.

"She's got that right," Chloe huffed. "We couldn't care less."

"Exactly," Dana agreed. "But, Josh, you and I still have to talk about a few problems I'm having. Do you think you can sit at our table, so we can figure it out?"

Josh looked nervously at us.

"Go ahead," Chloe said. "We're squished here, anyway."

Josh frowned slightly, then stood and picked up his tray. "Sure, no problem," he told Dana.

"Whoa," Marc muttered beneath his breath. "That's a first."

I knew what he meant. Josh was going to eat lunch at the Pops' table, with Addie, Claire, Jeffrey, Aaron, and the rest of them. I couldn't believe it.

MIDDLE SCHOOL RULE # 9:
POPS NEVER INVITE NON-POPS TO SIT WITH THEM!

I couldn't believe Josh was leaving us to go sit with them. After all, the Pops were our sworn enemies. Still, I had to wonder, if given the chance, just how many of us would do the exact same thing? Even after everything that had gone on between Addie and me, there was still a little part of me that wished I could be one of them.

But I wasn't. None of my friends were. *At least not until today, anyway.*

"I am so dreading getting on that school bus this afternoon," I said, watching Josh and Dana sit down at the Pops table. "How am I supposed to sit next to Felicia and not tell her about all this?"

"Just be glad she has a different lunch period and doesn't have to see them," Chloe said. "I'm sorry I do. Looking at them is making me lose my appetite."

"It's not your fault," Liza reminded me.

"It's not your job to tell her, either," Marc told me. "It's between her and Josh."

"Will you all stop thinking about Josh! We've got a campaign to work on," Chloe reminded us. She looked over at the dancing kids, who were eagerly snatching CDs from the twins' hands. "You owe it to our class to win this election."

"Yeah. You've got to get going on your speech," Marc reminded me. "Did you and Felicia write it yet?"

"Most of it," I told him.

A furious look came over Chloe's face. "Most of it? Most

of it?" she demanded. "First, you won't let Marc use the secret weapon on our website, and now you don't even take the time to write a whole speech? You should be done by now! The election is only a few days away!" Chloe rolled her eyes toward the sky and then buried her head in her arms on the cafeteria table. "Oh, why do I bother?"

"Ah, the drama queen strikes again," Marc groaned. "Give us a break, Chloe. Save it for the play auditions."

Chloe scowled at him and then turned her attention toward me. "Jenny, you should be glad I'm your campaign manager. Otherwise nothing would get done."

"I *am* glad all of you guys are around," I said honestly. "This election wouldn't have been any fun without you."

Chloe's eyes lit up with anger again. "I can't believe you just said that!" she exclaimed.

"What?" I asked her. "All I said was . . ."

"It's not about *fun*, Jenny," Chloe interrupted me. "It's about winning!" She began pounding her fist against the table, harder and harder and then . . .

Splat! Chloe's fist came down right on an open ketchup packet. Red, gooey ketchup spurted up into the air. It landed all over her hair and face.

Liza, Marc, and I began to laugh hysterically. Marc pulled out his video camera and began shooting footage of Chloe covered in dark red goo.

"Looks like this campaign is getting bloody, folks," he joked.

Chapter
NINE

ON SATURDAY MORNING, Team Jenny (as Chloe had started to call us) gathered at my house. I was going to practice my speech. My friends were going to be my audience.

"Now don't forget to speak slowly," Rachel warned. "People can't understand if you speak too fast."

"And be sure you stop for laughter after your joke," Chloe said. "Give people the chance to love you."

"What if they don't laugh?" I asked her nervously.

"They'll laugh," Chloe assured me. "*I* wrote the joke."

"Oh, I wish you'd let me know you needed a joke," Rachel said. "I have lots of them."

"We know," Chloe told her. "But this one's better."

Rachel scowled, but said nothing. There was no point arguing with Chloe when she was in campaign-manager mode.

"The rest of the speech is pretty great, too," Felicia told our friends. "I wrote it — with Jenny, of course."

"I thought you were going to get Josh to help you, too," Rachel mentioned to me. "Where is he?"

Marilyn and Carolyn frowned and looked at the ground. Marc fiddled with his video camera. Chloe, Liza, and I exchanged glances. Rachel didn't have the same lunch period. So she didn't know what was going on with Josh and Dana.

Not that we really knew what was happening, either.

"He . . . um . . . he has a tae kwon do class," Chloe lied.

"No, he doesn't," Felicia corrected her. "That class is on Wednesdays."

"It's a . . . er . . . a makeup class," Carolyn suggested.

"Yeah, 'cause he missed a few sessions over the summer," Marilyn added.

"He didn't say anything about a makeup class," Felicia replied. "Of course, I hardly got to talk to Josh this week. He's been kinda busy."

"Gee, I wonder with *who*?" Chloe mumbled under her breath.

"What?" Felicia asked her.

"Let's get started on this speech," I said, changing the subject.

"You get started," Felicia said. "I'll be right back." She started walking toward the hall closet.

"Where are you going?" I asked her.

"To get my cell phone," Felicia replied.

As she walked out of the room, Marc glanced anxiously at Chloe. "She's gonna call Josh," he said.

Chloe grinned. "Don't worry. It's been taken care of."

"What's taken care of?" Rachel asked.

"Uh, nothing," Marc said.

"We'll tell you later," Chloe added. "Jenny, you should start your speech now."

"Yeah," Marc agreed, holding up his camera. "I'm gonna tape you. Then we can watch the tape and figure out what's working and what's not."

"Okay," I said, nervously standing up.

"Now I'm going to introduce you, just the way I'm going to do during the real thing," Chloe said, leaping to her feet. She stood up and looked at Marc. "You'd better tape me, too," she said. "I need to be sure I'm convincing."

Marc rolled his eyes. "No one cares how you sound," he told Chloe.

"Oh, yes they do. Jenny's introduction is very important. So . . ."

Just then, Felicia wandered back into the room. "That's so strange," she said. "I was sure I put my phone in my jacket pocket, but it's not there now."

"Maybe you just forgot it," Chloe said.

"I don't think so," Felicia said. "My mom reminded me twice to bring it."

"Just call Josh from Jenny's home phone," Rachel suggested.

"I don't know his number by heart. It's in my phone," Felicia explained. "Any of you guys have it?" she asked us.

"Not me," Marilyn said.

"Me, neither," Carolyn echoed.

"I have it written down at home," Liza told her.

"Don't worry, we'll get his number later," Marc said. "Just sit down and listen to Jenny's speech."

"Okay," Chloe said, as Felicia plopped down on the floor.

"Now, I'll stand up and walk over to the microphone. Then I'll wait a minute for all the applause to die down . . ."

"Applause?" Carolyn asked. "For you?"

"*Jenny's* the candidate, remember?" Marilyn added.

Chloe sighed but didn't respond. Instead, she started her introduction, "I'd like to introduce you to your next sixth grade president — a girl who is honest and kind. Someone who represents all of us. Someone who doesn't spend her whole lunch period putting on makeup in the bathroom. She's too busy thinking about how to help our school to worry about lip gloss and eyeliner. And that's the kind of person we want for class president. Ladies and gentlemen, I give you Jenny McAfee!"

"Yeah!"

"Jenny rocks!"

"Jenny! Jenny! Jenny!"

As my friends cheered, I stood up and started my speech.

"Thank you, Chloe," I said, turning to smile at her. "Can I get a copy of that for my parents? I'd like to give them that instead of my next report card." I waited for the laughter, like Chloe had told me to.

Unfortunately, Chloe was the only one who laughed.

"*That's* your big joke?" Marc asked Chloe.

"It's funny," Chloe insisted. "You guys just don't have a sense of humor."

"That's not the problem," Marc replied.

"Jenny, go on," Liza said, before Marc and Chloe could get into it again.

"I am running for sixth grade class president because I believe that we can make this the best school in the world," I said, reading from my speech. "And as the youngest kids in this school, we have the most to gain from making some positive changes right now. After all, we'll be the ones who can benefit from them for three whole . . ."

Just then I heard faint music playing. Weird. The music seemed to be coming from the flowerpot on the windowsill.

"That's my ring tone," Felicia said, leaping up from the couch and walking over to the window. She peeked into the flowerpot. "How'd my phone get in there?" she asked.

I caught a glimpse of Chloe biting her lip and kicking at the floor. So that was what she'd meant when she said it had been taken care of.

"Well, at least I've got it back now," Felicia said. "But I can't imagine how it got there."

"Maybe it fell out of your jacket pocket into the flowerpot," Chloe suggested.

"My jacket was in the other room," Felicia said. She eyed Chloe suspiciously. "You didn't take my phone, did you?"

"What do you need a phone so badly for, anyway?" Chloe asked, deliberately not answering her question.

"So I can call Josh and tell him to come over," Felicia explained.

"No!" Chloe shouted.

"Huh?" Felicia was confused.

"She . . . er . . . she just meant that we can't wait for him. Jenny's already started her speech," Liza told her.

"So? He can come over and watch the tape with us later," Felicia reasoned. "He'll have some good suggestions."

"We don't want Josh here, okay?" Chloe said finally.

"Chloe . . ." I started.

"Look, enough's enough," Chloe said. "She may as well know."

"I may as well know what?" Felicia asked.

"That Josh is definitely a spy for Addie's side," Chloe told her.

"Oh, that again," Felicia said. "Jenny and I already talked about that. And it's not true. We took a test on the computer to prove that he still likes me. Which means he can't be a spy."

"Yeah, well, did the computer tell you he ate lunch at the Pops' table yesterday and hung out with Dana after school?" Chloe continued.

Felicia looked like she was going to cry. She looked at Rachel and me. "Did you guys know this?"

"This is news to me," Rachel said.

I frowned. "She did ask him to eat at the Pops' table, but we don't really know . . ."

Marilyn smiled at Felicia. "Look, maybe it's nothing, you know?"

"But just to be safe, maybe we shouldn't let Josh hear Jenny's speech, okay?" Carolyn said, finishing her sister's thought.

Felicia frowned. "Whatever." She turned and headed toward the door.

"Where are you going?" I asked her.

"Home. I don't want to hear the speech, either."

"Come on, Felicia, stay," Marc said. "Just 'cause you're mad at Josh doesn't . . ."

"I'm *more* mad at you guys," Felicia said.

"Us?" I asked her. "Why?"

"Because none of you told me about Josh and Dana having lunch together," Felicia said. "So maybe you don't trust me, either."

"That's not it," I said. "I just didn't want you to feel bad. Your feelings were so hurt the first time we mentioned that he might be a spy, remember?"

"Well, my feelings are definitely hurt. But this time I feel bad about Josh, *and* about you keeping secrets from me," Felicia shouted. "So I guess you're not telling me only made things worse."

Talk about an understatement.

"I'm going home!" she shouted, as she stormed out of my house.

"Such a drama queen," Chloe groaned.

Marc rolled his eyes. "Takes one to know one."

"What's that supposed to mean?" Chloe countered.

I looked at both of them and shook my head. "I'm sick of all this fighting," I said. Then I headed toward the door.

"Now where are *you* going?" Chloe asked.

"To talk to Felicia," I replied.

"You can't. We have to work on this speech," Chloe told me. "We haven't even gotten through it once yet. And you have to make the speech on Monday."

I gulped. Monday was just two days away.

Chloe was right. Besides, Felicia was too mad to listen to me right now, anyway. So I read the speech over and over and over, until my mouth was dry and my tongue was tired. Then we watched the tape, talked about what changes I could make, and I read the speech again.

By the time everyone went home, I was exhausted. And I couldn't wait for the whole election to be over.

My telephone rang first thing Sunday morning — before I was even out of bed. I leaped up to answer it before the call woke my parents.

I was hoping it was Felicia calling to say she wasn't mad anymore. I'm not very good at being in fights.

"Hey, are you awake yet?" the person on the other end of the phone said.

"I am now," I said groggily. I sighed slightly. It was Chloe.

"I was thinking about your speech," Chloe said. "It's good, but it might not be good enough."

"I'm not changing my speech now," I told her. "I had enough trouble writing this one."

"I know there's no time to change the speech. And it's great — really," Chloe assured me. "I just don't know if it's good enough to win this election. People are really into being invited to a Pops party. They'll vote for Addie just for that."

"Well, we can say we'll have a victory party, too," I said.

"It's not the same thing," Chloe said. "Jen, I really wish you would reconsider using Marc's tape. We'd be doing the public a favor by showing them the real Addie Wilson."

I frowned. Chloe was right. Addie was a creep. But she hadn't always been. It made me sad to think about how my former best friend was acting these days.

"Yeah, but if I use that tape, I'll be just as bad," I told Chloe.

"Not as far as I'm concerned," Chloe assured me. "I figure all's fair in politics. If Addie had a tape like this, don't you think she'd use it?"

I didn't know the answer to that one. After all, Addie and I might be running against each other for sixth grade president, and we might not like each other anymore, but I think Addie still had some good memories of when we'd been friends. I know I did.

I had to hope those memories would keep Addie from being as mean as Chloe thought she could be.

Chapter
TEN

THE PICTURES WERE the first thing I saw when I walked into school Monday morning. They were everywhere — huge, giant color photos of me.

But these weren't pictures my friends posted on the walls. These were put up by the Pops. No one else would be so cruel.

There was a huge one of me at age nine with underpants on my head. My pigtails were sticking out of the holes where your legs go.

I knew exactly when that picture was taken. It was at a sleepover at Addie's house. Addie was originally in the picture with underpants on her head, too. But she'd cut herself out of the shot before blowing it up poster-size.

And that wasn't even the worst picture. Farther down the hall, there was a photo of me with my hair standing straight up in the air. I looked like some sort of monster.

Of course, what you couldn't see was Addie standing over me with a balloon in her hand. That picture was taken the day we'd been doing our static-electricity project for fifth grade science. There was a picture of Addie with her hair standing on end, too. But that one wasn't on the wall.

The last picture was of me with my cheeks all blown up like a chipmunk and a tiny bubble-gum bubble coming out of my mouth. My face was bright red and my eyes were bulging out of my head.

Addie's mom had taken that one. It was the day Mr. Wilson had taught Addie and me how to blow bubbles with gum. The picture of Addie had been even worse, because her eyes were crossed. But I didn't see that photo anywhere.

The last poster on the wall didn't have any pictures on it at all. Instead it read:

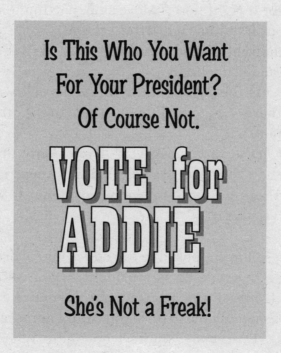

Is This Who You Want
For Your President?
Of Course Not.

VOTE for ADDIE

She's Not a Freak!

Now I was mad. Really mad. It wasn't the pictures so much — although they were really awful. It was more that Addie had used pictures of us when we were friends to make fun of me. Like the whole eight years that we were best friends was some kind of joke! I don't think I'd ever been angrier at anyone in my whole life.

Addie Wilson was a real jerk. A supercolossal jerk. A humongous mega-jerk!

"Still wanna forget about using that video?" Chloe asked me, as she walked over and stood by my side.

"I've got it right here," Marc said, patting his camera. "We can put it online right after school."

"And then call all the sixth graders and tell them about it," Chloe added excitedly.

I looked at the posters lining the walls of C wing. I had a feeling there were more just like them in the other wings of the school.

"Don't erase that video yet," I told Marc and Chloe. "Let's see how the speeches go. If Addie's speech is half as mean as these posters are, we're not going to have any choice but to use it."

"Okay, so I'm supposed to introduce my favorite candidate for sixth grade class president," Dana said, as she stood in front of the microphone during the election speeches assembly that afternoon. "But I don't really have to do that. Everybody knows who Addie Wilson is! So all I'm going to say is — here's your next sixth grade president!"

As the kids applauded, Addie stood up and waved her hand like she was some sort of queen greeting her royal subjects. Then she flashed her big, white toothy smile and began her speech.

"I guess everyone knows by now that I'm running for sixth grade president," she said. "I could stand up here and make a whole bunch of campaign promises that I'll never be able to keep, which is probably what my opponent is going to do. But that would be long, boring, and a complete waste of time. I want to keep my speech nice and short."

The kids in the audience applauded loudly at that.

Addie laughed. "Anyway, let me just tell you why I'm the perfect person to represent the sixth grade in student government. It's all about my image. We want the seventh and eighth graders to think our class is really cool. And I know you'll all agree that, of the two candidates running for this office, I'm the cool one."

I frowned slightly. I couldn't argue with Addie's logic. She sure did look cool and calm up there while she made her speech. *I* certainly wasn't calm. I was a nervous wreck. What if I burped in the middle of talking? What if I got the hiccups and couldn't stop. What if I threw up? I was feeling kinda nauseous.

"Anyhow, to sum it up, we sixth graders don't want to

be thought of as babies by the rest of the school. And since I'm really mature, I'd be the best person to represent you – the sixth grade class – in our student government. Thank you."

The kids started to clap then. Addie smiled and took a deep bow. As she turned around, she shot me a victorious look. I turned away and tried not to think about how jumpy my stomach was.

Chloe stepped up to the mike and made her introductory speech. Then, after she'd said all those nice things about me, I stood up and walked toward the front of the stage.

"Don't forget to wait for the laughter after the joke," Chloe whispered to me as she went to sit down in her seat.

I nodded, but I knew I wasn't going to have to wait for laughter. After seeing those mean, horrible posters in the hall, I'd made a few changes in my speech. And I hadn't told anyone – not even my campaign manager, Chloe – about it.

I waited for a minute, took a deep breath, and then began to read from my note cards.

"Appealing to or appreciated by a wide range of people. Relating to the general public," I read slowly off my note card. Then I looked up at the audience. "That's the definition of the word 'popular' – at least according to the dictionary. Addie Wilson may think she's the most popular girl in the sixth grade, or maybe even in the whole school, but being popular isn't about who has the best eyeliner, or who wears the most expensive clothes. It's about being able to relate to a lot of people. And according to that definition, I'm a whole lot more popular than Addie Wilson."

I could feel Addie tensing up in her chair as she sat behind me. I knew she never thought I'd have the guts to fight her over who was more popular. But I did. And I had a whole lot more to say about it, too.

" I – like most of you – care about a lot more than just makeup and clothes. And I don't think it's fun to hang out in the bathroom during lunch talking about people. But I do like having a good time – even if it means getting a little goofy or silly." I paused for a minute, just for effect. "And that includes putting underwear on my head and dancing around the room when I'm at a sleepover."

I turned around and looked at Addie. "Remember when we *both* did that, Addie? In fact, I think that's your under-wear on my head in the picture that's hanging in C wing."

The kids all laughed. Addie blushed and looked down at the ground.

I smiled and turned back to the audience. "Just like you guys, I care about Joyce Kilmer Middle School. I want to make it a great place to be. And I've got a few ideas about just how we can do that."

The rest of my speech was just the way I'd rehearsed it over the weekend. I gave my thoughts on student lounges, and a fairer method for sign-ups for clubs. I talked about getting a healthier menu in the cafeteria, and annual field days for each grade. And when I was finished, everyone in the audience was clapping. A lot of people even stood up to cheer for me.

Whoa! A standing ovation. I never thought that would happen!

I took a deep breath. I'd done it! I'd made my speech without burping or throwing up. I'd been able to make fun of myself, which took the sting out of the mean posters Addie and her friends had put up on the walls. Most of all, I'd been able to let everyone know my great ideas for how to make our school better.

I didn't know who was going to win this election, but I was certain I had done the right thing.

MIDDLE SCHOOL RULE # 10:
WHEN IN DOUBT, BE YOURSELF. THAT WAY YOU CAN'T LOSE!

"Great speech, Jenny!" Josh was the first person to congratulate me as I walked off the stage with Chloe.

"Thanks," I replied.

"Bet you're disappointed you didn't know what she was going to say ahead of time," Chloe barked at him.

"Huh? Why?" Josh asked her.

"So you could tell your *girlfriend* about Jenny's ideas for the school," Chloe said.

"My girlfriend?" Josh sounded genuinely confused.

"Yeah, you know, *Dana*," Chloe said.

"Dana?" Josh asked.

"Yes, *Joshie*," Chloe continued. "We know she's been using you to spy on Jenny's campaign. But Jenny kept this speech a secret — even from me. And now Addie doesn't stand a chance."

"I hate Dana and Addie," Josh insisted.

"Oh, yeah?" Chloe demanded. "Then why have you been eating lunch with Dana and seeing her after school?"

Josh took a deep breath, then answered, "Because I'm her math tutor."

"Her *what*?" Chloe asked. Now it was her turn to sound confused.

"Her math tutor," Josh repeated. "She was failing math, so I was teaching her after school. Everyone in the Mathletes has to tutor somebody. It's part of being in the club."

"But why Dana? Why didn't you tell us?" I asked him.

Josh shrugged. "I didn't have a choice. Dana was the one I got assigned to. And I knew it would upset you guys, so I tried to hide it."

"If you were *only* her tutor, how come Dana was acting all mushy around you — giving you candy and asking you to eat lunch with her?" Chloe demanded, not believing Josh's story.

"I don't know. Maybe she wanted you to think I was on her side," Josh suggested. "To make you mad at me or something."

I frowned. If that's what Addie and Dana had in mind, it sure had worked.

"Or maybe she was just grateful that I helped her pass her math test. But she's not my girlfriend, and I'm no spy!" Josh was practically shouting now.

I could feel the red rushing up in my cheeks. I was really ashamed. I couldn't believe I'd actually thought such awful things about Josh.

Worse yet, now Felicia believed it, too. *What a mess.* We'd all let this election get in the way of our friendships.

Well, that was going to stop right now!

"Josh, I'm so sorry," I told him sincerely. Then I turned and headed toward the back of the auditorium, where Felicia and Rachel were standing.

"Where are you going?" Chloe asked me.

"I have to talk to someone," I told her.

"But I thought you were going to stay and shake hands with people," Chloe said. "We don't have much time before tomorrow's election."

"I will," I assured her. "But right now, I have something much more important to do."

Chapter
ELEVEN

I BARELY GOT ANY SLEEP Monday night. Every time I closed my eyes, I had weird dreams. In some of them, Addie won the election, and she tortured me about it by making me run around school with giant granny panties on my head.

In some of the dreams I won, and then I actually had to be the president — which was something I didn't have a clue about how to do. I kept running around and around the school in circles, looking for the student government office and never finding it.

Either way, I was running and I didn't know where I was going. I hate dreams like that.

When my alarm clock finally rang at 7:00 Tuesday morning, I sat up in bed like a shot. Election day was here. There was nothing more I could do or say to change things. It was all up to the voters now.

It was kind of funny. I'd gotten into the race just to beat Addie and the Pops. But now that it was all over, I wanted to win because I really wanted to make Joyce Kilmer a better place to go to school. At least for most of us. The Pops already thought it was a great place. They were the ones who ruled the school.

At least they did until now . . . *I hoped.*

But I wasn't going to find out for sure who'd won until the end of the school day. That was when all the votes would be tallied, and the winner would be announced over the loudspeaker. But there were a whole lot of hours between now and then. How was I ever going to make it until the end of school?

"Are you ready to vote?" Chloe greeted Felicia and I as we walked from our bus to the school building later that morning.

I nodded. "Did you vote already?"

Chloe shook her head. "Uh-uh. I was waiting for you guys to get here. But we'd better hurry. The line in the cafeteria is getting really long."

As we turned toward the building, we saw Addie, Dana, and Claire walking just ahead of us to the school.

"Oh, get a load of her," Chloe added, pointing toward Addie. "What does she think this is? The Academy Awards?"

I had to laugh. Addie was dressed as though she were about to walk the red carpet. Her long blond hair hung down her back in a neat French braid. And instead of her usual jeans and shirt, she was wearing a really pretty dress.

I looked down at my jeans, T-shirt, and red sneakers. "I didn't know we were supposed to dress up for this," I said.

"You look exactly the way you're supposed to. You're one of the people, remember?" Felicia assured me.

"Okay, let's get this all on video," Marc said as he and Josh came up beside us. "The candidate casts a vote for herself," he announced into the camera microphone.

"How do you know who I'm voting for?" I asked him. "It's a secret ballot. Maybe I think Addie's the right . . ."

"What?!" Chloe exclaimed. "Of course you're going to vote for yourself. You have to! What if you lost by one vote? Then you'd feel awful and —"

"Relax, Chloe." I laughed. "I was just joking."

"Don't kid around about stuff like that," Chloe said, catching her breath. "It's not funny."

I walked over to the table in the cafeteria where the ballots were stacked up. Two teachers were sitting there, making sure each sixth grader only voted once. I stood there for a moment, looking at the ballot. There were only two names on it. Addie Wilson and Jenny McAffee. Quickly, I checked the box next to my name, dropped it in the box, and walked away.

That was it. All the speechwriting, cookie-baking, tape-making, and handshaking was finished. There was nothing left for me to do but wait.

That was going to be the hardest part.

Later that afternoon, our Spanish class was interrupted by a messenger from the principal's office.

"Jenny, will you go to Principal Gold's office, *por favor?*" Señorita Gonzalez said after reading the note.

"Oooo . . ." A bunch of boys in the back of the room

teased as I collected my books and headed for the door. "Jenny's in trouble!"

"*Clase*," Señorita Gonzalez warned. "*Silencio*."

Chloe shot me a questioning look as I passed by her desk. I shrugged. I really had no idea what this was all about. I knew I hadn't done anything wrong. So why was I being called to the principal's office?

It had to be about the election. As I walked down the hall, my mind began to race. Did I win by a landslide? Or had I lost so badly that Principal Gold wanted to personally let me down easy?

When I got to Principal Gold's office, Addie was already in the waiting room. I could tell by the expression on her face that she was just as nervous and confused.

"If we're both here, it must have something to do with the election," I said.

"She's probably going to let you have it," Addie said smugly.

"Me?" I asked her. "What did I do?

"You and your friends drew all over *my* posters," Addie said. "Remember?"

"I told you that wasn't us," I reminded her. "Besides, maybe she's gonna yell at *you* for putting up those awful pictures of me all over the school."

"Those weren't mean," Addie said — a little too sweetly. "I thought they were cute."

"Yeah, right," I huffed. "If they were so cute, why'd you cut yourself out of them?"

Before Addie could answer me, Principal Gold opened the door to her office. "Oh, good, you're both here. Won't you come in, girls?"

I took a deep breath and stood up. This wasn't the first time I'd been in Principal Gold's office. The last time I was here, it was because Addie and I had gotten into a food fight in the cafeteria. Principal Gold had been plenty mad at us that time. Ugh. I could feel my stomach tensing up just thinking about that day.

"Take a seat, please," the principal said, pointing to two wooden chairs on the other side of her desk. "There's something we need to talk about."

Addie and I didn't even look at each other as we sat down. We both just kept staring at Principal Gold, wondering what this was all about.

"I have the results of this year's sixth grade presidential election," the principal told us. "And I wanted to talk to both of you before I announced them."

Gulp. The principal wanted to talk to us? This couldn't be good. We were probably *both* in trouble.

"The vote was very close," Principal Gold continued. "In fact, only ten votes separated the winner from the other candidate. That means neither of you had a real majority, which is why I'd like you to consider working together on the student council. The winner of the election will be president of the sixth grade, and the other girl will be vice president. We've never had a vice president of sixth grade before, but we've never had an election this close before, either."

I looked down at my feet. What the principal was suggesting made sense — or at least it would have if it had been two different girls sitting in her office. But Addie and I working together? That would be impossible. I was pretty sure Addie would feel that way, too.

"I think that's a great idea," Addie chirped in her perky voice.

Okay, I guess I didn't know Addie that well anymore.

"I mean, as long as Jenny doesn't mind being my vice president," Addie continued. "After all, I'd still be in charge, right?"

"Actually, Addie, Jenny is the winner of the election," Principal Gold told her gently. "You would be *her* vice president."

I sat there for a minute in complete shock. Had Principal Gold really said what I thought she'd said. *Jenny is the winner of the election. . . .*

From the look on Addie's face, I was sure I'd heard the principal correctly. It was true. I'd done it! I'd stopped the Pops!

I could hear the cheers through the halls as Principal Gold made the announcement over the loudspeaker. I was standing by my locker, trying to act cool and relaxed about being the winner of the election, but inside I was just bursting. I wanted to scream and yell out that I had beaten Addie Wilson, so loud that they could hear me in China. But that would be bad sportsmanship.

Luckily, I had Chloe to do my screaming for me. I could hear her loud voice over everyone else's in C wing. And a moment later she was by my side, giving me a huge hug.

"You did it! You did it!" she screamed in my ear.

"No, *we* did it. All of us. There's no way I could have won this election without you guys," I told her.

We looked over at Addie, Dana, and Claire. They were all standing by Addie's locker with huge frowns on their faces.

"I'm going to have to work with her, you know," I told Chloe.

Chloe nodded. "That's the bad part. But the good part is you're the boss."

I shrugged. Being the boss wasn't something I was looking forward to. I wasn't very good at telling people what to do.

"So what's your first order of business?" Chloe asked me.

"I have to plan that post-election party," I told her.

"You mean the one for the people who voted for you, right?"

I shook my head. "That's not really right," I told her. "I don't want to be all exclusive and everything. It's gonna be a party for the whole sixth grade. I've already said something to Principal Gold about it. She's going to try and figure out which day we can have the party."

Chloe nodded. "So I guess you'll be pretty busy with that for the next week or so, right?"

I thought about that for a minute. "I'm not a great party planner," I admitted. "But I know someone who is. Come with me."

You should have seen the look on Chloe's face when I dragged her over to Addie's locker.

"What do you want?" Claire demanded.

"Are you here to rub it in?" Dana asked.

I shook my head. "Actually, I'm here to talk to the vice president of the sixth grade class," I explained.

"What do you want?" Addie asked me. She sounded very grouchy. Obviously, she was still mad that she'd lost the election.

"Well, you know that post-election party I talked to Principal Gold about?" I asked her.

Claire laughed. "Oh, great. Jenny McAfee's gonna throw a party."

I shook my head. "Not necessarily," I told her. "I know I'm not very experienced at throwing parties. But Addie is." I turned to Addie. "I thought maybe you'd want to be in charge of this project."

"In charge?" Addie repeated, making sure she'd heard me right.

I nodded. "Just run everything by me before you do it, so I know what's going on."

Addie studied my face. I guess she wanted to make sure this wasn't a prank. But I'd meant what I said. I was delegating. That's a very important thing for a leader to do.

"Wow. Okay. Um, sure," Addie said. "I'll get started today."

"Just remember, it's a party for *everyone*, Addie," I told her.

Addie nodded. "Gotcha."

"Okay, see ya at the student council meeting on Friday," I said. Then I walked off, pulling Chloe away with me.

"Why'd you do that?" Chloe asked as soon as we were out of Addie's earshot.

"I've got more important things to do the rest of this week," I replied.

"Like what? Order the new jukebox or pick a date for field day or . . ."

I shook my head. "I'm going to be helping you get ready for your play audition," I told her. "You need to pick a song and decide on what you're going to wear. And then we need to have you practice in front of an audience — maybe my mom can play the piano."

"Wow. You're gonna do all that for me?" Chloe asked.

"Of course. You helped me win the election, and now I'm going to help you get a great part in the play."

"I really wanted you to win," Chloe said.

"No kidding. I couldn't tell," I teased.

"I guess I went a little overboard as your campaign manager," Chloe said, looking at the ground. "It's just that . . ." She stopped for a minute and sighed.

"Just that what?" I asked her.

"Look, I know what the Pops say about me," Chloe told

me. "About my clothes and how loud I am and all that. They call me a loser all the time. I try to act like it doesn't bother me, but sometimes —"

"But sometimes it gets to you," I said, finishing her sentence. "I know exactly how you feel."

"I just wanted Addie to not be number one for once," Chloe admitted. "Kind of teach her a lesson."

I nodded. I think we'd all felt that way — just not as strongly as Chloe had.

"And I also thought you'd be a great president," Chloe assured me. "You're always thinking about ways to help out other people. Like working with me for the audition. You're a really good friend, Jenny."

"Thanks. So are you," I told her. Then I grabbed her by the arm and dragged her toward the exit. "Now come on. Let's get going. You have a lot of work to do this afternoon."

"You sound like me," Chloe laughed. She paused for a minute. "Do you think Marc will tape me singing so we can all watch it and figure out what I'm doing wrong?"

"Sure he will. Everyone's gonna want to help you," I assured her. "That's what friends are for."

In the Jungle of Middle School, What Animal Are You?

1. **If you could dye your hair any color what would it be?**

   A. Red
   B. Blond
   C. Brown

2. **When you're talking to people, do you**

   A. Touch or poke the person you're talking to?
   B. Stand still with your arms folded in front of you?
   C. Play with your hair, touch your chin, and scratch your nose?

3. When a pal tells a good joke, what's your reaction?

A. Laugh really loudly so everyone hears you.

B. Laugh heartily, but not really loudly.

C. Giggle quietly.

4. When you go to a party, what's your style?

A. Make a grand entrance, just so everyone knows you've arrived.

B. Walk in, look around for someone you know, and go over to say hi.

C. Go inside quietly and head over to a quiet corner.

5. What's your favorite pet?

A. A snake because they're so exciting and different.

B. A dog because they need you to love them, and they love you back.

C. A cat because they don't ask a lot of you.

6. What's your secret passion?

A. Motorcycles

B. Football

C. Writing

What kind of animal are you?

If you answered mostly A's, you are a tigress, an exciting, adventuresome girl who others worship and also fear. You move gracefully through your world, climbing mountains and taking chances. It's important for you to experience everything you can — it's the only way you know to enjoy life.

If you answered mostly B's, you resemble a steady, sturdy tortoise — well, only as far as your personality goes. You take things slow and steady, and are sensible and cautious. Still, you're not overly fearful. In some ways it's as though you have a shell around you, which means you aren't always the easiest to get to know. However, once people take the time to get close to you, they appreciate your good humor and levelheadedness.

If you answered mostly C's, you resemble a gentle, shy lamb. There's a side of you that finds safety in numbers and being part of a crowd. Standing out and making your presence known just isn't your style. You leave center stage for others. You're also incredibly kind. You'd never be the one to hurt someone else's feelings.

HOW I SURVIVED MIDDLE SCHOOL

JOYCE·KILMER
GAZETTE

READ MADAME X's
MOST RECENT COLUMN...

I Heard a Rumor

BY
NANCY
KRULIK

For Danny B.

Hey! Can You Keep a Secret?

Are you the go-to girl when your friends have a secret to share? Can you be trusted to keep the info under wraps or are you known for your loose lips? Take this quickie quiz and find out where you stand.

1. **You just saw your BFF's boyfriend sharing a slice of pizza (and some secretive smiles) with an attractive stranger. What do you do?**

   A. Call your BFF and tell her right away — after all, she has a right to know!

   B. Confront him and find out what's going on before telling your pal.

   C. Keep quiet. You have no idea what the deal is between these two. Why start trouble?

2. **The meanest mean girl in the whole school is bragging to everyone that she made the honor roll this marking period. But you know it's not true because you saw her last history**

test – with a big fat F on it. How do you handle this hot gossip?

A. Start spreadin' the news! It's about time everyone saw this girl for the liar she really is!

B. Keep it to yourself. You may not like the girl, but that doesn't mean you have to sink to her level.

C. Tell only your very best friends, who dislike her as much as you do.

3. **You've got the greatest news! You overheard two teachers talking about your best bud. They say she's the winner of the student council election, but they won't be announcing the results until tomorrow. What's your plan of action?**

A. Even though it's gonna kill you, your lips are sealed. It'll be even better for your friend to find out the good news in front of everyone.

B. Grab your cell and hit the speed dial. You've got to tell your friend the news and spare her another sleepless night.

C. Tell all your other friends, so you can plan a surprise victory party for your winning friend.

4. You're at a party and no one seems to notice you. But you have a secret weapon that could make you the center of attention — a juicy piece of gossip about two of the teachers in your school. You saw them together outside of school — holding hands! Do you

A. Whisper the info to a few close friends who you know will be impressed by your inside scoop.

B. Keep it to yourself: Even teachers deserve a little privacy.

C. Make your way into the crowd and fill everyone in on the news. After all, if they wanted to keep the relationship secret, they shouldn't have been out in public.

So, are you the kind of person who lets the skeletons out of the closet? Or is MYOB your motto? Add up your points to see what kind of secret keeper you are.

1. A) 1 B) 2 C) 3
2. A) 1 B) 3 C) 2
3. A) 3 B) 1 C) 2
4. A) 2 B) 3 C) 1

10–12 points: Wow! You are the most super secret keeper of all time. You could be tempted with ice cream or tortured with your dad's oldies, but you'll never tell! Just remember, while it's great to be trustworthy, some secrets shouldn't be kept. If you have a friend who may be in serious trouble, be sure to let a grown-up you trust in on the scoop.

7–9 points: Okay, so once in a while you let the cat out of the bag when you're not supposed to. Hey, you're only human, right? Still, spilling even a small secret can be dangerous. Friends have been lost over less. So if you want to hang on to your pals, keep your lips locked.

4–6 points: Well, one thing's for sure — you're not the person to tell a secret to . . . ever! You just can't keep yourself from gabbing the gossip. But there is a way to keep from spilling the beans. MYOB! You can't blab what you haven't heard, right?

Chapter
ONE

I HATE RAINY DAYS. Especially rainy Mondays. Waiting for the school bus while the bottoms of your pants are getting all wet, your sneakers are becoming soggy, and your umbrella keeps blowing inside out is not the best way to start your week. But that's what was happening to me that Monday morning.

I sighed and added another rule to my growing list of very important things that they never tell you at sixth grade orientation.

MIDDLE SCHOOL RULE # 11:

GET A LIFT TO SCHOOL ON RAINY DAYS OR
ELSE YOU'LL SPEND THE DAY WRINGING OUT
YOUR JEANS.

To make matters worse, I had to stand at the bus stop with Addie Wilson. Of course, *Addie* wasn't going to have to spend the school day in soggy jeans. She'd been smart enough to wear a skirt and waterproof boots to school. Addie was going to look perfect all day long — as usual.

At the moment, Addie was talking on her cell phone.

Probably to one of the other Pops. That's what my friends and I call Addie and her group of friends — the Pops. As in *popular*.

I think every school has its own crowd of Pops. You can spot them a mile away. They're the ones who wear the coolest clothes, have the best makeup, and only hang out with each other. Basically, they're at the top of the middle school food chain.

"No, I'm serious," I heard Addie say into her phone. She paused for a moment as the person on the other end said something. "Well, I wouldn't tell anyone but you, that's for sure," Addie said. "And we certainly can't tell Claire. You *know* she can't keep a secret."

I giggled quietly. Obviously Addie was revealing a big secret to the person on the other end of the phone.

Addie glanced in my direction, rolled her eyes, and sighed. Then she turned her back to me and began whispering to the person on the other end. "I have to talk quieter," she said. "Jenny McAfee is eavesdropping."

I was about to say that I wasn't eavesdropping, she was just talking loudly. But if I said that, Addie would know that I had been listening to her conversation. And technically, that *was* eavesdropping. So I just kept my mouth shut.

Watching Addie whisper into her cell really upset me. *I* used to be the person Addie told her secrets to — back when we'd been best friends.

But that was then. When we'd been in elementary school. Addie and I were middle-schoolers now. And ever since we'd walked through the doors of Joyce Kilmer Middle School on the first day, Addie had decided that she was too cool to be my friend.

I breathed a sigh of relief as the yellow bus finally turned the corner toward our stop. Any minute now I'd be out of the rain — and away from Addie. My friend Felicia would already be on the bus. And she always saved me a seat.

Now *I* would have someone to talk to, too.

"Over here, Jenny," Felicia called from the back of the bus as I climbed on board.

I smiled and trudged my way toward her. I wrinkled my nose as I sat down. The bus stunk — like a mix of mildew and wet dog fur.

"What a yucky day," I groaned as I sat down on the damp green plastic seat.

"Not if you're a duck," Felicia giggled. She looked down toward my feet. "Boy, your pants are really wet."

"I know," I said. I was wet from the cuffs of my pants all the way up to my calves. "I had to wait a long time for the bus."

"That stinks," Felicia said.

"It sure did," I told her. "Especially because I had to listen to Addie talking on her cell phone the whole time."

"What was she talking about?"

"Who knows?" I shrugged. "Some very important Pop secret, I guess."

"I didn't think their secrets could be important," Felicia said with a shrug.

I had to agree with her. The Pops spent all their time either talking about makeup or saying bad things about everyone else in school. I wasn't particularly interested in either of those kinds of conversations.

So how come I was dying to know what Addie had been whispering about?

That was the Pops' best-kept secret: Somehow they'd figured out how to make everyone in the school hate them *and* want to be one of them, at the exact same time.

By the time my fifth period lunch rolled around, my jeans had dried. Unfortunately they were now stiff as a board, and there was a line of mud along the bottom. They looked awful — but not nearly as bad as my hair. It was a flat, stringy mess. That's what happens to my hair in the rain. It just hangs there like limp spaghetti.

But that's not what happened to Addie's hair. As I glanced across the cafeteria, I could see that her hair still looked great. She'd pulled it back into a tight blond bun. A few of the curls had fallen from the bun and were framing her face. She looked like a model.

Eergh! It was so frustrating.

"I'm singing in the rain . . ." Just then, my friend Chloe

made her presence known by singing and dancing her way across the cafeteria toward our table. "Just singing in the rain. What a glor —"

"Somebody stop her," Marc groaned from across the table, putting his hands over his ears. "She's been singing that same song all day. You should have seen her jumping in puddles at our bus stop."

"That's what the guy did in that old movie," Chloe explained.

"You're not in a movie," Marc reminded her.

"I could be. . . ." Chloe hinted. She pointed to Marc's backpack where he kept his video camera.

"I already told you, *no*," Marc said. "My movie is a spontaneous documentary. No acting allowed."

"So I'll just jump up right now and start dancing spontaneously," Chloe suggested.

"*Spontaneous* means it happens at the spur of the moment," Marc said with a sigh. "It's not spontaneous if you plan it."

Chloe shrugged. "Your loss," she told Marc. Then she laughed and burst into song again. "The sun'll come out tomorrow . . ."

Just then, Addie and her two best friends, Dana and Claire, walked past our table. They were heading for the girls' room. That's where all the Pops hung out after they'd finished eating. None of them ever had to actually go to the bathroom or anything. They just went in there to put on makeup and gossip about people. The girls' room near the cafeteria was sort of like their headquarters.

Dana stuck her fingers in her ears as she walked by. Addie whispered something to Claire, which made her giggle. They may have been whispering, but there was no doubt they were making fun of Chloe.

Chloe wasn't bothered, she just kept right on singing as the Pops walked by. They had a busy schedule to stick to — there were lots of other people to make fun of before lunch was over.

I had to give Chloe props for how she'd reacted to the Pops. Addie, Dana, and Claire's whispers must have hurt her feelings. But she wasn't going to let them know that.

"This rain really stinks, doesn't it?" I said, changing the subject.

"Tell me about it," my friend Carolyn groaned. "No field hockey practice for me after school today."

"Can't you practice inside?" I asked her.

Carolyn shook her head. "The basketball team is practicing in the gym this afternoon."

"That's okay," Carolyn's twin sister, Marilyn, consoled her. She looked around at all of us. "We can hang out at our house after school. Maybe rent a movie or something."

"Not me," Josh said, shaking his head. "We've got a Mathletes competition on Wednesday. I've got practice."

Josh is a mega-genius. He's in sixth grade like me, but he's already taking seventh-grade math.

"Lucky you," Carolyn told Josh. "You can have practice rain or shine."

"Algebra equations are fun for all seasons," Marilyn added with a giggle.

"I can come over," I told the twins. "I barely have any homework so far today."

"Count me out," Marc said, shaking his head. "Film Club is meeting after school."

"Guess that means we can rent a chick flick, " Marilyn said with a shrug. She looked over at me. "Wanna ask Rachel and Felicia to come, too?"

I shook my head. "They've got basketball practice."

"Oh, well," Carolyn said. She glanced over toward Liza, a small, dark-haired seventh-grader who hung out with us. "Are you free?"

"Sure, I can come for a while," Liza said. "But I have to get home pretty early. I have a science quiz tomorrow."

"Cool. Chloe, how about you?" Marilyn wondered.

Chloe took a sip of her juice. "I . . . um . . . today?" she said.

The twins nodded. "When else?"

"I can't today," Chloe said. "I . . . er . . . I have play rehearsal."

"No you don't," Liza corrected her cheerfully. "They're using the auditorium for a teacher meeting after school, remember?" Liza was painting scenery for the play, so she knew the rehearsal schedule as well as any of the actors.

Chloe bit her lip slightly. "Oh, yeah," she said. "I forgot.

But . . . um . . . I still can't do anything with you guys today. I have plans."

"Well, then what are you doing?" Carolyn asked.

"I'll just have to take a rain check," Chloe told her.

Josh glanced over at the cafeteria windows. "Nice choice of words," he joked as he watched the downpour outside.

I glanced over at Liza and the twins curiously. They shrugged. Obviously, they'd noticed it, too.

Chloe sure was acting weird — even for her.

Chapter
TWO

"NO, I'M TELLING YOU, it was really strange," I told Felicia Tuesday morning while we were riding the bus to school.

"What's so weird about Chloe being too busy to hang out after school?" Felicia asked me.

"She was just being so secretive about it, like whatever she was doing after school was some big mystery," I said.

"Yeah, I guess that is kind of weird," Felicia said, nodding her head.

"What could be such a big secret?" I wondered.

"Maybe she has a boyfriend," Felicia suggested. "Someone she doesn't want the rest of us to know about."

I laughed. Felicia was really into that sort of thing. She liked to read books about dating, and romantic comedies were her favorite kind of movies.

"He could be a guy from the play," Felicia continued. "Maybe even a seventh- or eighth-grader."

"I don't know . . ." I began.

But Felicia was on a roll. She had the whole scene set up in her head. "Maybe he's an eighth-grader. Or someone who goes to another school. A mysterious stranger who came into her life . . ."

I started to laugh. Felicia was going a little overboard

now. "On a white horse, right? And his last name is Charming?" I teased her.

Felicia giggled a little. "You know what I mean." She glanced toward the back of the bus, where Addie was sitting all by herself. (There are no other Pops on our bus and Addie would never be caught dead sitting on the bus with a non-Pop.) "Wouldn't Addie just die if Chloe found a boyfriend before she did?"

I shrugged. Somehow I didn't think Addie would care. She never paid attention to anything my friends and I did. "Speaking of Addie, I've got to meet with her after school," I groaned. "We have to figure out the decorations for the post-election party."

"Is it still a luau?" Felicia asked.

I nodded. "A big one. It's not just for the sixth grade anymore, either." I sighed. Originally, the party was supposed to be for just the kids in our grade, as a celebration after our student council elections. But once the kids in the other grades heard Addie Wilson was planning it, they all wanted to join in. Imagine! Eighth-graders wanting to come to a sixth grade party! That was the power of the Pops.

MIDDLE SCHOOL RULE # 12:

ANYTHING THE POPS ARE INVOLVED WITH IS AUTOMATICALLY COOL.

"Is it hard working with Addie?" Felicia asked.

"Not too bad. But sometimes she gets bossy," I admitted.

"That's when you have to remind her that you're class president — and she's the vice president," Felicia said.

That fact still amazed me. I beat Addie Wilson in the sixth grade student council election. Sure, it was only by a few votes, but I'd won just the same.

"I'd rather we just worked as a team," I told Felicia. But we both knew Addie wasn't exactly a team player. Which was why I wasn't really looking forward to meeting with her after school.

As the bus turned into the school parking lot, Felicia and I spotted our friend Rachel waiting for us by the door. We hurried off the bus to meet her.

"Hey guys, happy Tuesday!" Rachel greeted us.

I groaned.

"We're one day closer to the weekend," she reminded me cheerfully.

"True," I agreed with a laugh. "But I wish it was Friday already."

"Speaking of the weekend," Rachel continued, "Do you guys want to go to the mall to get something to wear to the luau? My mom said she'd take us."

"Sounds fun!" Felicia exclaimed. "We should get some flower things to put in our hair."

"And I was thinking maybe a pretty flowered shirt," Rachel said.

She looked over at me. "You want to come with us, Jenny?"

"Sure," I said. "My mom said I could get a new dress or something."

"This party's going to rock," Rachel said. "I heard Addie's hiring a live band."

"What?" I asked, my eyes opening wide with surprise.

"Didn't you know?" Rachel wondered. "I thought Addie was supposed to be running everything past you before she did it."

"She was," I replied. "And we don't have enough money in the budget for a band."

"Looks like you and Addie are going to have a lot more to discuss this afternoon than decorations," Felicia said.

I frowned. This wasn't going to be fun. Not at all.

I watched as Addie and Dana headed toward the soccer field together during gym class later that day. They were walking *thisclose* to each other and whispering. Every now and then they would look over at one of us non-Pops and giggle hysterically.

Annoying much?

I did not want to go near either of them. But I knew that I had to talk to Addie. I would have done it at lunch, but she always sat with a whole table of Pops. It would have taken more guts than I have to walk over there to talk to her. This way, it was only Dana and Addie I had to face.

I hurried to catch up to them. As I came up behind Dana, she stopped and turned around suddenly. "Do you want something?" she asked, sounding annoyed.

"I . . . um . . . I need to talk to Addie," I said.

"Well . . . um . . . here she is," Dana said, imitating the nervous way I was talking.

Addie giggled slightly and then bit her lip to keep herself from laughing any harder. "What do you want?" she asked me.

"I just wanted to ask you about the luau," I said. "We're still doing decorations after school, right?"

Addie nodded.

"Also, I heard a rumor that you're hiring a band for the dance," I continued. "And the problem is, we don't have the money for live music. You were supposed to check with me before you did anything like that, remember?"

Addie bristled slightly at that. She didn't like the idea of having to check in with anyone about anything.

"Well, for starters, it's not definite yet, so there was nothing to talk to you about," Addie barked at me. "And if I do get the band, it won't cost us anything. My friend Jeffrey's older brother, Elliot, is in a *high school* band, and they'd play for free as a favor to me."

Wow. A high school kid was willing to do a favor for Addie. That was seriously impressive.

"Of course, if you don't want a high school band, and you'd rather have Mr. Jenkins play DJ again . . ." Addie let her voice trail off.

I frowned. Mr. Jenkins was a good math teacher, but he was a lousy DJ. "No, the band will be fine," I told her. "I will . . . uh . . . sign off on it after school today." There. That sounded quite presidential.

"Whatever." Addie rolled her eyes.

As I walked away, I could hear Addie and Dana giggling, which hurt my feelings. Of course, that was exactly the point.

"Hey, Chloe, there you are," I said, as I walked into Spanish class later that day. "Listen, Rachel, Felicia, and I are planning on going shopping for clothes for the Luau. You want to come with us?"

"Can't. I'm busy," Chloe said, plopping into the chair beside me.

"I didn't even tell you when we were going yet," I said. "You might be free and —"

"Not possible. I've got things to do every minute that I'm not in school," Chloe said.

"What kinds of things? We'll be going on Saturday, and there are no play rehearsals on the weekend, so . . ."

Chloe shook her head. "I'm busy," she told me firmly.

"What's so important that—" I began. But before I could finish my sentence, Señorita Gonzalez walked into the classroom.

"*Hola, clase,*" she said.

So much for finding out what was going on with Chloe.

*   *   *

I called Felicia as soon as I got home from working on the decorations with Addie. "Okay, now I'm convinced something's up with Chloe," I told her after I described our conversation in Spanish class.

"And she wouldn't tell you anything about her plans?" Felicia asked me.

"Uh-uh. Not a word. It's so not like her. Usually Chloe gives way *too* much info."

"I know," Felicia said with a laugh. "Like the time she told us that she wears underpants with the days of the week on them."

"On the *wrong* days." I giggled back. "*Definitely* TMI. That's what makes this so weird. Keeping secrets is really unlike Chloe."

"Some romances are meant to be secret," Felicia told me.

"I still don't think it's a romance," I argued. "It could be anything. Maybe she got a tutor for Spanish class. She was having a hard time with verb tenses. Or maybe she —"

"There's one way we can find out exactly what it is," Felicia suggested.

"You mean ask her?" I guessed.

"No. She'd never tell us anyway," Felicia said. "We have to see if that website you use all the time has a quiz that can help us figure it out."

I knew exactly which website she meant. It was called middleschoolsurvival.com and it had lots of really cool info on it. There were all these quizzes that told you about you and your friends. So far, the quizzes on the website had been right on target. Felicia was right. Maybe it could help us figure out what was up with Chloe.

I turned on my computer, opened up my favorites list, and clicked on middleschoolsurvival.com. Then I scanned the contents of the site. "Here's a perfect one," I said. "It's called *Is She Hiding Something . . . or Someone?*"

"Great. What's the first question?" Felicia asked excitedly.

> 1. Has your pal been especially secretive lately?
> ○ Yes
> ○ No

"That one's easy," Felicia said. "She's been really secretive. Click yes."

> 2. Have you noticed a change in her appearance lately? Is she dressing more stylishly, or with a few extra accessories?
> ○ Yes
> ○ No

I thought about the jeans and t-shirt Chloe was wearing at lunch today. The shirt said 4/3 OF PEOPLE HAVE TROUBLE WITH FRACTIONS. It was pretty funny, but she'd worn it a few times this year already. And the only accessory Chloe ever had was her backpack, which I didn't think counted.

"That's a no," I told Felicia, as I clicked the mouse.

3. Does your friend seem to be in an especially good mood — singing in the halls or smiling a lot?
   ○ Yes
   ○ No

"Yes! Yes!" Felicia squealed excitedly. "Chloe is singing all the time these days."

"That's because she's in the show," I told Felicia.

"The question doesn't ask why," Felicia reminded me. "It just asks if she's doing it. And she is."

I couldn't argue with that. I clicked the yes button.

4. Has your mysterious bud been disappearing more often than usual?
   ○ Yes
   ○ No

"That one's a yes, I guess," I told Felicia. "She's never around outside of school anymore."

"I know, I tried calling her before I called you tonight, but she didn't answer her cell," Felicia replied. "She always answers her cell."

That answered that. I clicked the yes button.

5. Has your friend been listening to a lot of love songs these days?

◯ Yes

◯ No

"All Chloe's been listening to lately is the soundtrack for *You're a Good Man, Charlie Brown*," I told Felicia. "She has to learn the songs for the show. She's in the chorus, but she also has that solo during the song 'Suppertime.'"

"That's definitely not a love song," Felicia agreed. "It's about dog food."

I giggled. "That's a no then." I said, clicking my mouse.

A moment later, the results of the quiz popped up on my screen.

> You have answered Yes to three out of five questions.
> Mostly Yes answers: Your pal is definitely hiding something. An air of romance seems to be surrounding her. Be patient. She's sure to tell you all about it as soon as she feels secure in her new relationship.
> Mostly No answers: Your friend may be keeping a secret, but it's doubtful there's a new Mr. Right in her life at the moment. You may want to let her know you're there to talk if she feels like sharing some info about what's up.

"Yeah! I was right!" Felicia exclaimed excitedly. "Chloe's totally in love."

I laughed. Felicia sure loved being right about things. She sounded like she'd just won a million dollars or something.

"I wonder who it is," she continued.

"The quiz says we have to be patient and let her tell us when she's ready," I reminded her.

"I hate being patient," Felicia said with a groan.

"Me too. But we don't have any choice. Chloe's not going to tell us anything before she's ready." I paused for a minute. "And you can't tell anyone, either. We have to keep Chloe's secret, a secret."

"Agreed," Felicia said. "This is just between us."

Chapter

THREE

"*What theater-crowd diva has a new love in her life? Seems one constantly singing sixth-grade superstar-wannabe is hiding a new man – even from her closest friends.*"

I sat at our lunch table and stared at the very first gossip column in the *Joyce Kilmer Gazette* in amazement. It was called "In the Know with Madame X." That gossip had to be about Chloe. Who else could it be?

But no one knew that Chloe was hiding a secret love – except Felicia and me.

"Yo, Jenny, did you see this?" Marilyn asked as she came over to the table. She was holding up the newspaper.

"It's gotta be Chloe," Carolyn said. "She's the only sixth-grader who sings all the time."

I looked up at the twins. They were both wearing the same green polo shirts and faded blue jeans. "What's up with the clothes?" I asked them.

"I had a math test second period today," Carolyn explained. (At least I thought it was Carolyn. It was hard to tell who was who when the twins dressed the same).

"What does a math test have to do with your clothes?" I wondered out loud.

But before Marilyn or Carolyn could explain it to me, Liza looked up and shook her head. "I hope you guys don't get caught this time," Liza said. "Remember what happened last year?"

"What happened?" I asked. "What are you guys talking about?"

"Señorita Gonzalez caught me taking her Spanish test," Carolyn explained, pointing to her sister.

"When our mom found out, she threatened to make me dye my hair red so the teachers could tell us apart," Marilyn continued. "Can you imagine what I'd look like with red hair?" She turned to her sister. "She should have wanted you to dye *your* hair. I think you'd look much better as a redhead."

I laughed at that. The twins were identical. Neither one of them would have looked particularly hot with red hair.

"Yeah. But we didn't get caught today," Carolyn pointed out. "I hope you got an A for me on that test."

"Well, I got a few wrong on purpose," Marilyn told her. "Otherwise your math teacher would have suspected something." She turned to Liza and me. "Can we get back to this Chloe situation?" she asked.

"Yeah," Marilyn agreed. "Who do you think this guy is?"

"We don't know that there is a guy, or that this diva is Chloe," Liza reminded her.

"Come on, who else can it be?" Marc asked, coming up behind the twins and putting his tray on the table.

"So you saw the article too," Liza said.

Marc nodded. "Everyone has. Madame X's article is all anyone's talking about. It's the first time there's ever been a gossip column in the school paper."

"You really think the article's about Chloe?" I asked.

Marc shrugged. "Could be."

"You live next door to her . . ." Carolyn began.

" . . . have you seen any new guys around her house?" Marilyn finished her sister's thought.

"Just her dad," Marc said. "I saw him waiting for her in their front yard when we got home from school."

Liza giggled. "I don't think that's what they meant."

"If you want to know if it's true, why don't you just ask Chloe?" Marc suggested to the twins.

"Ask Chloe what?" Chloe said, as she walked over to our table with Josh.

"Um . . . uh . . . nothing," Marilyn said, quickly slipping the school paper onto her lap.

"Yeah. We, um, forgot what we were talking about," Carolyn added.

"You *both* forgot?" Josh asked. "Isn't that taking the twin thing a little too far?"

"It wasn't anything important," Liza told Chloe. "Just stupid gossip."

"Oh," Chloe replied. "I hate that. Why don't you guys leave the gossip to the Pops? That's what they do best."

As if on cue, Addie and Dana walked right past our table. They stopped for a minute and stood behind Chloe.

"*Mwah!*" Dana said, making a big kissing noise.

Addie giggled and kissed at the air. "Oh, lover boy. You handsome mystery man."

Dana began laughing hysterically as she and Addie walked off toward their table.

"What was that about?" Chloe asked, once the Pops were out of earshot.

"You're kidding, right?" Marc asked her.

Chloe shook her head. "Nope. Haven't a clue what those two were babbling about."

"Then you haven't seen the paper today?" I asked her.

"What paper?"

"This paper," Marc said, pulling his copy of the *Joyce Kilmer Gazette* from his backpack. As he handed it to Chloe, he pulled his video camera out. Obviously he wanted to get Chloe's reaction to the story on tape.

"Oh, Marc, don't," Liza pleaded.

But it was too late. Chloe was already staring at Madame X's gossip column. As she read, her eyes opened wide.

"Now, Chloe, don't get upset," Liza said gently.

"Yeah, they don't mention your name or anything," I added. "Probably hardly anyone knows it's about you."

Chloe didn't say anything. Instead, she took a deep breath. Her hands began to shake ever so slightly, and her cheeks turned a slight pink. Then she opened her mouth wide and . . .

She laughed. Chloe *laughed.* Like the whole article was the funniest thing she'd ever seen.

"Everyone thinks this is about me?" she asked us between giggles.

"Isn't it?" I asked.

"If I have a boyfriend, it's news all right," Chloe said. "News to me!"

"Then it's not true?" I asked.

Chloe shook her head. "Of course not. Why would you guys think that?"

"Well you've been acting kind of weird lately," Liza told her.

"What are you talking about?" Chloe asked.

"Like when you wouldn't go to our house after school the other day," Marilyn told her.

"Even after you found out there was no rehearsal," Carolyn added.

Chloe shrugged. "I was busy."

"And then you didn't want to go dress shopping with Felicia, Rachel, and me," I reminded her.

"I didn't say I didn't *want* to go, I said I *couldn't* go," Chloe said. She bit her lip and looked down at her hands. "It's not the same thing."

"But you didn't say *why* you couldn't go," I explained.

"And just because of that you thought I had a boyfriend?" Chloe sounded incredulous. "You guys have huge imaginations."

"Well, you have to admit your behavior's been kind of strange the past few days," Liza said gently.

"It's totally felt like you're hiding something," I added.

Chloe sighed. "I have been hiding something," she admitted finally. "But it's not what you think."

Marc turned off his camera and looked over at her. "What's up, Chloe?" he asked, quietly.

Chloe sighed. "I didn't want to tell you guys, because I don't need anybody feeling bad for me."

"Just tell us," Josh said. "We'll be cool about it, whatever it is. Promise."

Chloe took a deep breath. "Well, the thing is, my dad lost his job two weeks ago," she blurted out. "And money's kind of tight. That's why I couldn't go shopping with you guys," she told me. "I can't afford any new clothes right now."

"Wow," I said quietly. "That stinks."

"It's no big deal. Dad's already had a few interviews, and he'll get something soon. But right now, I can't just go out and buy new stuff," Chloe explained.

"Yeah, but what does that have to do with coming to our house?" Marilyn asked her.

"Hanging out with us wouldn't have cost you anything," Carolyn added.

"Yeah, but my mom's working overtime a lot right now. So whenever I don't have rehearsal, I feel like I should go home and help out with the cooking and cleaning and stuff," Chloe told the twins.

Boy, did I feel stupid. Here Chloe was going through all this, and I'd been convinced she'd had a boyfriend. Why had I listened to Felicia?

Felicia! Boy, was I mad at her. She and I had been the only two people who had suspected Chloe had a boyfriend. I was pretty sure of that. Which could mean only one thing, Felicia had broken her promise to keep the results of that quiz secret. She'd blabbed to Madame X.

Because of that, everyone in school thought Chloe had some mystery boyfriend. And she'd had to tell us this horrible secret about her dad.

Not that Chloe seemed too upset about that. "Actually, I'm kind of glad you all know now," she said. "It really stunk having to lie to you like that."

"I wish you could have a new outfit for the dance," I told her.

"Me, too," Chloe said with a sigh. "Oh, well."

"Maybe you can earn the money," Liza suggested. "You could get a part-time job or something, on the days when you don't have rehearsals."

"I'm too young to get a job," Chloe said.

"Yeah, you have to be fifteen or sixteen to work in a store," Josh said.

"Well, there are kid jobs," Marc said. "Like delivering newspapers or something."

"You have to do that early in the morning," Chloe reminded him. "I can hardly get up for school as it is."

"There has to be something you can do," I told her. Then I got a great idea. "I know just where to find the perfect job. Call me as soon as you get home!"

*   *   *

My cell phone began to ring five minutes after I walked into my house that afternoon. I checked the caller ID. Chloe. Awesome! Now she and I could get started on her dance outfit fund.

"Hey, Chloe," I said. "Let me just turn on the computer, and we can get started right away."

"You're going to that website that helped you decide if you should run for class president?" she asked.

"Yup," I told her. "It's the website that helped Felicia and me figure out that Josh really liked her. And it's also the site that helped us figure out the Josh wasn't spying on us for the Pops during my presidential campaign."

"That site is amazing." Chloe said. "It's never wrong."

Well, that wasn't exactly true. That last quiz Felicia and I had tried had said Chloe had a secret boyfriend. But I didn't tell Chloe that. She would've been mad that we'd butted into her business. Besides, it wasn't like the website had been *totally* wrong. It did say that Chloe had a secret. It was just the wrong secret.

"Okay, here's a good one," I said finally, after logging onto the site and scanning the list of quizzes. "Are You Ready for Your First Job?"

"Perfect!" Chloe exclaimed. "Read me the first question. The sooner we get going, the sooner I'll have the cash for a new outfit."

I laughed. It was funny to hear Chloe get so excited about getting clothes. I'd never thought of her as the kind of person to care about how she looked.

I guess that was just another secret she was hiding from me.

1. Which of these best describes you?

A. Little kid person

B. Pet person

C. Book person

D. People person

Chloe thought about that for a moment before answering. "Well, I like people," she said. "But I also love dogs and little kids. Can we check all three?"

"Nope."

"All right," she said. "Then click Pet person. I like animals. They love you no matter what."

"Cool," I said, clicking B. "Next question."

2. Which is your strongest personality trait?

A. Patient and calm

B. Responsible and careful

C. Organized and detailed

D. Open-minded and free-spirited

"Oh, that's easy," Chloe said. "I'm totally open about everything."

I frowned slightly before I tapped the D. After all, Chloe

hadn't been so open about her dad being out of work. But I guess that was sort of *his* secret, and she was honoring it.

3. What is most important to you in life?

A. Human contact
B. Unconditional love
C. Mental stimulation
D. To be worshipped

"That's a tough one," Chloe said. "I like being around some people, like you guys. But being around the Pops and people like that make me sick. I guess my answer would have to be B."

"Good choice," I said, clicking the B.

4. What's your favorite subject in school?

A. History
B. Phys ed
C. Science
D. Public speaking

"Too bad they didn't give lunch as a choice." Chloe giggled. "But if I have to choose one, I guess it's history. I liked learning about ancient Egypt. The pyramids and mummies are cool."

"A it is," I said. "Okay, here's the last question."

5. What was your favorite childhood game or activity?

A. Finger painting
B. Tag
C. Reading
D. King of the mountain

"I still love to play tag," Chloe admitted. "I know it's kinda babyish, but I play with my little cousin and her friends all the time. Don't tell anyone, okay?"

"Your secret's safe with me," I assured her. I clicked the Submit Your Answers icon.

A moment later the results popped up on the screen.

You answered 2 A's, 2 B's, and 1 D.

Here's what your results mean:

Mostly A's: As a calm, cool, person who is totally in touch with her inner toddler, a career in teaching may be your best bet. Kids would benefit from your patience and genuine love of fun.

Mostly B's: For you, a life without animals would be just too rough. Consider a career as a veterinarian or a zoologist.

Mostly C's: You're a definite brainiac who tends to be happiest on your own. A career in medical research or computer science would fit your temperament.

Mostly D's: You thrive on being the center of attention in a crowd of your peers. Consider a career in publicity or sales, and you've got it made!

"Well, you got two A's and two B's," I noted. "So that means you can be either a veterinarian or a teacher."

"I always knew I was versatile," Chloe said. "With my personality I can do just about anything."

I laughed. Chloe might be great with dogs and little kids, but she wasn't good at being modest. Of course, that was what made Chloe, Chloe. We all loved her for it.

"Unfortunately, this quiz isn't going to help me get a new outfit for the dance," Chloe continued. "You can't be a teacher or a veterinarian when you're only eleven years old."

"That's true," I agreed, frowning. Then, suddenly, I brightened. "Maybe you can't be a vet just yet," I told Chloe. "But this definitely gives me an idea!"

Chapter
FOUR

CHLOE'S
Dog Walking and Grooming
Available after school
on Fridays.

$2 for a walk

$3 for a walk and bath

Call 555-4323

I USED EXTRA-STRONG TAPE to post the sign on the wooden post near our bus stop the next morning. I had a whole stack of them in my backpack. I was going to post some in school and then give the rest to Chloe and the twins to put up in their neighborhoods. Between the four of us I figured we had enough neighbors with dogs to get Chloe new clothes in no time!

"Oh, you're never going to believe this," Addie said into her cell phone. "Chloe's starting a dog walking service." She giggled. "This I gotta see."

I scowled, but didn't say anything. It wasn't worth it. I refused to give her the satisfaction of thinking that I would even *want* to eavesdrop on her conversation — again.

The bus came a moment later, and I hopped on. I saw Felicia sitting in the middle of the bus, but I took a seat up front, near Addie. I was too mad at Felicia for telling Madame X that Chloe had a boyfriend to sit next to her.

"Hey, Jenny, over here," I heard Felicia call to me.

I ignored her. I had nothing to say. Who knew what she'd blab next?

As the bus drove off, I sat by myself. I couldn't help but listen to Addie, who was sitting right behind me, go on and on to Dana about some Pops sleepover they were having on Friday night.

"I'll bring the new manicure kit my aunt sent me," I heard Addie say. She was quiet for a minute as Dana spoke. Then she started to laugh. "Well, if Claire would just stop biting her nails, she'd be able to use it, too. I swear, it's so disgusting the way she chews them and spits them out. What boy would ever want to hold her hand after that?"

Unbelievable! Claire was Addie's close friend. But here she was making fun of her with Dana . . .

MIDDLE SCHOOL RULE # 13:

NEVER TURN YOUR BACK ON THE POPS —
EVEN IF YOU *ARE* ONE!

As soon as the bus came to a halt at the next stop, Felicia came bounding up to the front of the bus. She plopped down in the seat beside me.

"Are you mad at me or something?" she asked.

"I don't know," I told her. "Should I be?"

"What's that supposed to mean?" Felicia wondered.

"I mean, did you do anything that might make me mad at you?" I asked her. "Like maybe telling Madame X our secret conversation about Chloe?"

"Who said I did that?" Felicia demanded.

"Well, somebody told her," I said. "And it was just you and me taking that quiz."

"So how do I know *you* didn't tell Madame X that Chloe has a boyfriend?" Felicia asked me.

"Because I don't even know who Madame X is," I told her. "And I would never tell Chloe's secret."

"I don't know who Madame X is, either," Felicia insisted. "And I can keep a secret as well as you. I would never have told anyone that Chloe Samson has a boyfriend!"

Just then, everyone on the bus got really quiet. Felicia had said that last part really loudly.

"She does not," I said just as loudly, so everyone on the bus could hear. I wanted to make sure that no more rumors were spread about Chloe. Then I whispered again. "She has a secret, but that's not it."

"What is it?" Felicia asked me.

I shook my head, hard. "I'm not spilling any of Chloe's secrets."

"But I swear, I didn't tell anyone about the boyfriend quiz," Felicia said. She made an X on her chest. "Cross my heart and hope to die."

She sounded really sincere. But I couldn't be sure. And besides, it wasn't up to me to talk about Chloe's dad. If she wanted to tell Felicia, that was her business.

Still, if there was a chance that Felicia hadn't been the one to tell Madame X about Chloe, then I probably shouldn't be mad at her. I'd have to believe she was telling the truth.

In the background I could hear Addie talking on her cell phone, telling Dana about how Felicia and I were fighting.

"It's an all-out geek fight." Addie giggled into her phone.

That was enough to make me stop arguing with Felicia. I reached into my backpack and pulled out one of Chloe's flyers.

"Maybe you want to bring Bruno over for a walk and

bath tomorrow?" I suggested. Bruno was Felicia's dog. He was a big, furry mutt that everyone loved.

Felicia looked down and read the flyer. "Sure," she said. "He could use a bath. He was rolling around in the grass all afternoon yesterday." She thought for a moment. "Does this dog thing have anything to do with Chloe's real secret?"

I laughed. Felicia wasn't giving up so easily.

"Well, it is somewhat related," I said. "But I can honestly tell you that Chloe's secret has nothing to do with dogs. It's purely a people thing."

"So, how many dogs do we have?" I asked Chloe as we walked to English class together the next morning. It was Friday, and our dog adventure was scheduled for that afternoon.

"I got four calls. One from Felicia, one from Marc, and the other two were my mother's friends, Mrs. Miller and Mrs. Donahue," Chloe replied. "Mrs. Miller's dog, Barney, just needs a walk. But Marc said we can give Skippy a bath. Which should be easy, because he's just a little cocker spaniel. Mrs. Donahue wants us to bathe Chester also. He's a schnauzer and not too big. Bruno's gonna be the tough one. That dog's huge."

"We can handle him," I told her. "Remember, there will be four of us, and only one of him."

"It's really nice of you, Marilyn, and Carolyn to help me with this," Chloe said.

"It'll be fun," I told her. "What time are we getting started?"

"Right after school. I'll pick Skippy up on my way home, and then you and the twins can take turns picking up the other dogs. When we have all four of them, we can take them on their walk."

"Sounds like a plan," I said.

"I figured it all out. Today we'll earn eleven dollars," Chloe said. "But I was thinking that you guys are doing so much work, we should really split the money."

"We can figure all of that out after you have enough money to get whichever dress you want for the dance," I told her.

"A few afternoons of doggie day care should earn me enough money," Chloe said.

"Awesome!" I said.

"And I owe it all to you," Chloe said gratefully. She paused for a minute and then added, "Well, you and middleschoolsurvival.com."

"Okay, here's Barney," I said, as I brought the brown-and-black German Shepherd mix into Chloe's backyard later that day.

"I've got Chester and Skippy here already," Chloe added, gesturing with the two leashes she held in her hand. "And the twins should be here any second with Bruno."

I nodded. We had decided that it would probably take

two of us to walk Bruno, since he was so huge, and sometimes he pulled on his leash pretty hard.

"I think we should take all four dogs for their walks first," I told Chloe. "Then, I can take Barney home while you and the twins start the baths."

"Good idea," Chloe said. "I've got all the doggie shampoo ready to go in the upstairs bathroom."

Just then, Marilyn, Carolyn, and Bruno came bounding into the yard. Bruno was pulling so hard on his leash that Marilyn, who was holding on to the other end, was practically flying in the air like a kite.

"Bruno, stop!" Marilyn cried. "Stop!"

But Bruno didn't stop. He just kept running around and around the yard at top speed — until Chloe pulled a bone-shaped dog cookie from her pocket.

"Bruno, sit!" she said firmly, holding up the cookie. Bruno did as he was told. He sat back on his hind legs and looked up eagerly at Chloe. She smiled and held out the cookie. Bruno gobbled it up in a second, and then sat there, staring at her adoringly.

"Wow!" I exclaimed. "The website was right. You do have a talent for working with animals."

"It's all about the food." Chloe giggled. "Okay you guys, let's go for our walks."

"Can you take Bruno?" Marilyn asked. "We're tired just from walking him here."

"Actually, it's more like he was walking us," Carolyn added.

"Fine. I'll take Bruno," Chloe said. She took his leash and then handed Skippy and Chester to the twins.

"Why don't we take them to the park?" I suggested as we left the backyard and headed down the street. "Dogs love parks."

"And fire hydrants," Chloe said, laughing as Bruno stopped at a red hydrant and lifted his leg.

"This is kind of fun," Marilyn said, as Chester walked cheerfully at her side.

"Good exercise, too," Carolyn agreed. "Mom would be happy."

I nodded in agreement. All moms have a thing about going out and getting some fresh air. I guess it's a parent thing.

"It sure is easier walking a little dog," Carolyn continued.

"You seem to have Bruno under control, though," Marilyn told Chloe. "I don't know how you're doing it."

Just then, Skippy started to bark. Marilyn jumped.

"He spotted a squirrel, that's all," Chloe told her. "No big deal."

But the squirrel *was* a big deal — to Skippy, anyway. A moment later, the little cocker spaniel yanked on his leash and took off after it. Marilyn was so surprised by how strong the little guy was that she dropped the leash, and Skippy ran off at top speed to chase the squirrel. Marilyn stood there, frozen.

"Don't just stand there, go get him!" Chloe shouted at her.

"I, I . . .I . . . he's so fast," Marilyn stammered.

"I'll get him!" I shouted, handing Barney's leash to Marilyn. I darted off after Skippy.

Boy, he was a speedy little cocker spaniel! Before I knew what had happened, Skippy had turned the corner and chased the squirrel across someone's front lawn. I ran right behind him. "Stop! Skippy!" I yelled. Then I remembered Chloe's trick. "Skippy, stop! Cookie?"

But Skippy was far more interested in the squirrel than a cookie. He kept on running, going under a hole in the fence and into another backyard. I scrambled to open the back gate, not caring that I didn't even know the people who lived there.

The squirrel raced up a tree. Skippy sat beneath it, barking wildly and leaping up and down.

Now was my chance. I hurried over to the tree, and reached for Skippy's leash. As soon as I had it in my hands, I shouted, "Gotcha!"

My shout must have scared Skippy because he started running at top speed. But there was no way he was going to get away again. I held that leash tight and ran as fast as I could until . . . *boom!* I tripped over a tree root and fell flat on my stomach. Skippy scampered for a few more feet, but I held tight, steeling myself to the ground like the anchor of a ship. When the leash couldn't stretch any farther, Skippy finally gave up.

."Skippy, I can't believe you did that!" I scolded him. Skippy looked up at me and cocked his head. Then he gave me a big doggie smile. Okay, maybe he was just thirsty or something, but it *looked* like a smile. And it melted my heart. "Okay, come on. Let's go find everybody else."

Skippy and I walked out of the yard and quickly made our way to the sidewalk. We began heading back around the corner, to where we'd left Chloe, the twins, and the other three dogs.

Just as we turned the corner, THEY appeared. Claire and Dana. In all their Pops perfection.

And there I was, covered in mud and all sweaty from chasing Skippy around some stranger's backyard.

"Nice look," Claire said, studying my grass-stained jeans and muddy T-shirt.

"I especially like the tree branch stuck in your hair," Dana added with a giggle. "You look like some sort of monster."

"Like Swamp Thing!" Claire added, laughing harder.

Just then, Skippy started to bark wildly. It wasn't a friendly bark, either. He was growling, and pulling on his leash.

"Whoa! Get that rabid dog away from me." Claire gulped, then she ran off with Dana hurrying right behind her.

People always say that dogs can sense when someone is mean or dangerous. Obviously Skippy had figured out how awful Claire and Dana were just by looking at them. He didn't care if they were Pops. He just knew he wanted no part of them. "Smart dog," I said with a grin as I patted his head. "It took me weeks to figure that out."

Just then, Chloe and Bruno came bounding over to us. "We heard all the barking," Chloe said. "Is everything okay?"

I nodded. "Skippy's a fast runner, but I caught him," I told her proudly.

"I think it's time to go home and give the dogs their baths now," Chloe suggested.

I looked down at my grass-stained clothing and muddy hands. "They're not the only ones who need a bath," I said with a laugh.

"How much of this stuff should we put in the water?" Carolyn asked as she, Chloe, and I started to fill the bathtub in Chloe's upstairs bathroom. Her parents weren't home, so we were on our own. Marilyn had gone to return Barney to Mrs. Miller. That left the three of us to give the other dogs their baths.

"Lots," I said. "Skippy is filthy from running around that yard."

"Bruno doesn't smell a whole lot better," Carolyn pointed out.

"I think we should start with Bruno," Chloe suggested. "He's the biggest, and he'll probably take the longest to dry."

"Cool." I picked up the bottle of dog shampoo, poured in plenty, and turned up the water. Before long the tub was three-quarters of the way filled with bubbling, soapy water. "You can put him in now," I told Chloe.

"Okay. Come on, Bruno," Chloe said, tapping the side of the tub. "In you go."

But Bruno didn't budge. He just stood there in the center of the bathroom floor.

"Bruno. In the water," Chloe said in a firm voice.

Bruno lay down on the floor and covered his head with his front paws.

"We're gonna have to put him in there," Chloe said. She turned to Carolyn and me. "Come on. It'll take all three of us to lift him."

Even with three people lifting him up, Bruno was plenty heavy. But we managed to get him on his feet, and then with a couple of nudges and shoves, the big guy reluctantly jumped in.

Splash! I guess I'd filled the tub a little too high, because as soon as Bruno got in, buckets of foamy water overflowed out all over the bathroom floor.

"Oops," I said sheepishly.

"*Grrr,*" Bruno growled angrily. He obviously didn't feel like having a bath. But that was what Felicia's mother had paid for, and that was what we were going to give him. I began to soap his short brown fur.

Bruno shook his head really hard. Water flew all around the room.

"Whoa, what's going on in here?" Marilyn asked as she opened the door, stepping into the bathroom and taking in the wet, soapy floor, the flying bubbles, and the wet, angry dog.

"Close the door!" Carolyn shouted at her sister. But it was too late. As soon as Bruno sensed a means of escape, he took it, leaping out of the tub and running out into the hall.

Chloe hurried after him with a towel in hand, but it was too late. Bruno was already drying his soapy fur by rolling around wildly on the hall carpet.

"Bruno, stop!" Chloe shouted. "STOP! Not on the carpet!"

Surprisingly, Bruno stopped rolling on the carpet. He stood up and stared at Chloe. "That's better," she told him.

Bruno let out a loud yelp and raced into Chloe's parents' room. He leaped onto the bed, rolled over on his back, and began to wriggle around on the comforter.

"Oh, no!" Chloe shouted. "Bruno, get off of there before my mom or dad catch you on their . . ."

"What's going on in here?" Chloe's father shouted as he stormed into the bedroom. "Why is that wet dog on my bed?"

"We were giving him a bath," Chloe explained. "And he escaped."

"It was really my fault, Mr. Samson," Marilyn said. "If I hadn't opened the bathroom door . . ."

"We'll clean everything up, Dad, I promise," Chloe said.

"You bet you will," Mr. Samson said sternly. "Starting right now."

"Well, we still have two dogs to wash first, and then . . ." Chloe began.

Mr. Samson looked at the big wet stain on his comforter and shook his head. "No more dog baths, Chloe. As of this moment, your dog care company is officially out of business."

Chapter
FIVE

"WELL, AT LEAST YOU STILL got paid eight dollars for walking the dogs," I said to Chloe as she and I walked through C wing together Monday morning. "It's a start."

"And a finish," Chloe added. "You heard what my dad said about us being out of business."

"Well, there has to be another way for you to earn the rest of the money you need for that dress," I told her. "Rachel, Felicia, and I are determined to help you. That's why we decided not to go shopping this weekend. We're waiting for you to get enough money together and come with us."

Chloe opened up her mouth to speak. But her words were drowned out by Claire's furious screaming.

As usual, a few of the Pops had gathered at Addie's locker to put on their morning makeup. They did that every day. But today, instead of giggling and gossiping, Claire looked furious. More surprisingly, all that anger was focused on her fellow Pops, not us.

"I cannot believe you people. How could you?" she demanded.

"How could we what?" Dana asked her.

"Which one of you jerks did this?" Claire shouted at

the top of her lungs as she waved a copy of a newspaper in her hands. "Now the whole school will know."

"Must be the new edition of the *Joyce Kilmer Gazette*," Chloe said. "I'll bet there's something about Claire in Madame X's column."

"Whatever it is, Claire's really mad about it," I added.

"We have to get our hands on a copy of that newspaper," Chloe said, looking around the hall until she finally spotted a stack of school newspapers at the end of the hall. She darted toward them and picked up two copies, one for me and one for her.

"What pretty Pop still sucks her thumb in her sleep?" Chloe read aloud from Madame X's column. "It's starting to make her teeth stick out. Be careful, Bucky Beaver!"

Dana looked over at Elena Ross, a seventh-grade Pop who had become friendly with Claire last year and now hung out with Addie and Dana, too. "It must have been you," Dana said.

"You were at the sleepover Friday night, too," Elena reminded her. "You saw Claire sucking her thumb. We all did!"

"I don't know which one of you decided to let the whole school know I still suck my thumb, but right now I hate all of you!" Claire shouted, storming off.

Chloe shook her head. "Her name's not anywhere in the article. No one but the Pops who were at that slumber party would have known it was Claire in that article.

She just told the whole school herself that she was the thumb sucker. How dumb is that?!"

As Chloe and I headed down the hall, the Pops continued to argue.

"I didn't even notice she was doing it," Elena told Dana. "I was sleeping, too. Maybe it was Maya. She was at the party and you know how she loves to gossip."

"Maya? You really think?" Dana asked.

Elena shrugged. "It could have been her, or you, or even Addie here. All I know is that it wasn't me."

As I watched the Pops battling it out at Addie's locker, I was struck by an amazing thought. Whoever this Madame X was, she was now the most powerful person in the school. She'd made everyone in the school suspicious and nervous. Who would be next? Apparently, no one was safe. Not even the Pops.

"Okay, how weird is this?" Josh asked as he sat down at our table during lunch and looked around the cafeteria.

"Very weird," Liza agreed in her soft voice. "They're all over the place."

I knew exactly what Liza was talking about. The Pops were scattered all around the cafeteria, instead of sitting at their usual star-studded table by the windows. Addie was with a boy named Sean from the eighth grade, a few tables away from me and my friends. Dana was sitting all by herself, pretending to read a book, while

Elena and Aaron were at the usual Pops table, and Claire and Jeffrey were over by the juice machine.

"This is great," Marc said, as he held up his camera and filmed each of the new Pop locations. "It's adding real drama to my film."

"Boy, that Madame X is something," Josh said. "With one sentence she can bring the Pops to their knees."

"It's only because the Pops are letting her get to them," Liza said quietly. "If people just ignored her column, she wouldn't have any power."

I looked admiringly at Liza. She was shy, and she didn't talk a lot, but the few things she said were pretty amazing.

"Well, I, for one, am really grateful to Madame X," Chloe told us.

Considering one of the rumors Madame X had started had been about her, I thought that was kind of a strange thing for Chloe to say. "You are?" I asked with surprise.

"Oh, yeah," Chloe said with a grin. "For once we'll have the girls' room all to ourselves during lunch!"

I had to laugh. Chloe was right. From the looks of things, there would be no meeting of the Pop gossip committee in the girls' bathroom today.

"Whoa, check that out," Marc said, moving his camera over toward where Claire was sitting. "What is she doing?"

At that moment, Claire leaped up on a cafeteria table, and blew a whistle — loud!

"Everyone, can I have your attention!" she shouted.

Of course everyone in the room grew quiet.

MIDDLE SCHOOL RULE # 14:
When Pops talk, people listen.

"I just wanted to fill all of you in on some things that didn't make Madame X's column!" Claire shouted. "There's one Pop girl in this school who sews designer labels into her discount store clothes."

"Big deal," Chloe said. "Who cares about that?"

Apparently Elena did, because she jumped up from her seat and started shouting. "I only did that once!" she insisted. "And anyway, I'm not the only one. Everyone knows Dana's Kate Spade bag is a fake. Her dad got it for her from a street vendor in the city!"

Now it was Dana's turn to get angry. "Yeah, well, at least I don't kiss my Lenny Charles poster before I go to bed every night!"

No one had to tell me which Pop that was. Addie'd had a crush on Lenny Charles ever since we'd first seen him on TV. Not that I blamed her. He was definitely the cutest guy on TV. If I had a poster with his picture on it, I'd probably kiss it, too.

But Dana hadn't been talking about me. She'd been

talking about Addie. Still, even as Addie's cheeks turned bright red, she didn't say a word. She was too smart to admit that that rumor was about her.

"Oh, horrors!" Liza whispered, giggling. "A fake purse and a crush on a movie star. How terrible."

I laughed. Liza was right. It was hard to believe the stupid things the Pops took seriously. And apparently, I wasn't the only one who thought so. Other people were snickering too, people who ordinarily wouldn't have had the guts to laugh at the Pops — at least not to their faces. But this look into how petty and ridiculous their world was definitely made people a little more brave.

I wondered how long it would last.

"I heard you guys had a really good time at lunch," Rachel said as I ran into her in the school parking lot at the end of the day. "Man, I wish I had fifth-period lunch."

"Me, too," Felicia agreed. "The only exciting thing that happened during our lunch was that Michael Newman dropped his tray."

"Not exactly Madame X - newsworthy," Rachel noted.

"Yeah, our lunch was definitely more exciting than that," I said. "The Pops were totally out of control."

"I'm telling you, things are getting weird around here," Rachel said.

Just then, as if on cue, Addie walked over to where

Rachel, Felicia, and I were standing. She had a friendly smile on her face.

Rachel was right. Things were *definitely* getting weirder by the moment!

"Um, Jenny," she said. "Are you free after school today?"

Huh?

Addie didn't seem to notice my confused, silent stare. "Because if you are," she continued, "maybe we could stay and work on the menu for the luau and take the late bus home together?"

I wasn't quite sure what to say. That was probably the nicest Addie had been to me all school year. Of course, it was probably only because all her real friends were fighting and she had nothing to do after school, but still, it was nice to hear her sounding human.

Besides, the luau was coming up and things had to get done. And as class president it was my job to make sure that happened.

"Sure, no problem," I said. "I'll meet you in the student council room in a few minutes. I just need to talk to Rachel and Felicia first."

"Oh," Addie said. She sounded a bit surprised that I wasn't going to just dump my friends right then and run off after her. "Sure. I'll meet you there."

As Addie walked off, Felicia shook her head in amazement. "Weird, huh?" she said.

I nodded. "Listen, let's talk later tonight. We still have to help Chloe come up with an idea to make money to buy that dress."

"You're right," Rachel said. "I'll call you guys and Chloe later."

I nodded. Rachel was the only one of us who could do conference calling on her phone. "About eight thirty?" I suggested.

"Cool," Rachel agreed. "Hey, do you guys know how the two telephones got married?"

"How?" Felicia asked, rolling her eyes slightly.

"In a double *ring* ceremony," Rachel answered, chuckling. "Get it?"

"Yeah, and we're giving it back," Felicia told her. "Come on, we're gonna miss our bus." She turned to me. "Good luck with Addie. I hope it's not too terrible."

"Thanks," I said. "Me, too."

"Hi, Jenny," Addie said in a voice that was so friendly I was tempted to look around the student council office for the hidden cameras.

But Addie wasn't punking me. She was genuinely glad to see me. I could tell by her eyes. They looked sort of happy, instead of angry, which was how she usually looked when I was around.

"Uh . . . hi." I answered cautiously.

"I've set everything up," Addie said, pointing to the

various piles around the room. "These paper flowers are for stringing the leis. We should give one out to everyone as they come in. I've already made a bunch. And then over there" — she pointed to a big box under the desk — "are the blow-up palm trees and beach balls. I ordered them real cheap from a catalogue, so they aren't breaking our budget or anything. And then over there are the limbo sticks and . . ."

As Addie went on and on about the directions for the luau, I had to hand it to her. She'd really made the most of the budget I'd given her. This was going to be the most amazing dance Joyce Kilmer Middle School had ever seen. Addie definitely had her talents. One of which was her ability to make the person she was talking to feel like the most important person in the world.

But why was she being so friendly to *me*? Just this morning she'd completely ignored me at the bus stop. And now she was acting like we were still best buds.

A couple of weeks ago I wouldn't have even bothered to question it. I would've been grateful for whatever crumbs of friendship she threw in my direction. But that was then. This was now. And now I had plenty of my own friends. I didn't need Addie in my life the way I used to; she'd changed too much.

Besides, Addie was totally using me. Thanks to Madame X, none of her friends were talking to each other. Which meant Addie had no one to hang out with after school. I guess as far as she was concerned, I was better than no one.

Not much of a compliment, huh?

I sat down and began stringing pink, white, and green flowers onto a cord. I pretended to focus really hard on what I was doing so I didn't have to talk to Addie anymore. I felt kind of uncomfortable sitting in the room, just the two of us and all.

"Oh, that's a pretty pattern," Addie complimented me.

"Thanks," I said, picking up some more flowers.

"This is fun, isn't it?" Addie continued. "Sort of like that time your mom bought you that new bead kit for Christmas, and we spent a whole snowstorm making jewelry, remember?"

Of course I remembered. I was just sort of shocked that she did. Addie always acted like she'd blocked out our whole friendship.

"So how's Felicia doing these days?" Addie asked me cheerfully. "I hardly ever see her anymore."

That's because you were so mean to her at camp last summer, I thought to myself. But out loud I said, "She's great. She and Rachel are on the basketball team. They might even make varsity."

"Wow, as sixth-graders? That's huge," Addie said. She paused for a minute, thinking. "How does Josh feel about Felicia maybe making varsity?"

"Josh?" I asked with a shrug. "I guess he's happy about it."

"It must be weird for him to have a girlfriend who is so good at sports, when he's not so great," Addie explained.

"Yeah, but he's amazing at other things," I defended him. "He helps Felicia with her homework sometimes."

"Mmm-hmm," Addie murmured. "You know, I noticed none of the guys you hang around with are great at sports."

The only other guy I hung around with was Marc, so I figured that was who she meant.

"Marc's okay at soccer and baseball, but he's so into his movie that —"

"He's making a movie? That's awesome," Addie interrupted. "Is he an actor?"

I shook my head. "No. He wants to be a director. He has this video camera he carries around, and he uses it to film stuff."

"What kind of stuff?"

"Middle school life," I said. "His movie's sort of like *The Real World*, except about *our* world."

"Sounds interesting."

"I guess so. He hasn't let any of us see it yet."

"Artists can be so independent," Addie noted.

I nodded. "You're not kidding. Liza's the same way. Chloe told me she won't let anyone help her paint the play scenery she's responsible for. She wants it to be absolutely perfect."

Addie chuckled. "She sounds like Claire. She won't let anyone touch her makeup."

I smiled. I couldn't believe how easy it was talking to Addie. I could feel myself falling back into our old, relaxed ways.

I know it's kind of mean, but I was glad the Pops were fighting with each other. Their arguments had given me my old friend back. At least for a little while.

"I'm telling you guys, she was totally normal — even nice," I told Felicia, Rachel, and Chloe during our conference call later that night.

"Whatever you say," Chloe said.

"Maybe it wasn't actually Addie," Rachel joked. "Did you pull on her face to see if it was real skin or just a mask?"

"Ha ha," I replied sarcastically. "This is real life, Rach, not *Mission Impossible*."

"Addie being that nice sounds utterly impossible," Felicia groaned.

"Whatever," I said finally. I was getting tired of defending Addie. Especially since I knew that by tomorrow morning she'd probably be back to her old new-self. "I thought we were going to figure out a way for Chloe to earn the rest of her money for that dress."

"Yeah," Chloe said. "That dog thing didn't work out so well."

"What else are you good at?" Rachel asked her.

"Talking," Felicia joked. "Too bad you can't make money doing that."

"I know," Chloe agreed with a laugh. "I'd be a million-aire by now."

"The website said you would be good at working with kids, too," I reminded Chloe. "Maybe there's something we could do with that."

"You could baby-sit," Rachel suggested.

"I wouldn't earn enough money in time," Chloe said.

"But if you baby-sit a few times . . ." Felicia began.

"There's not enough time," Chloe said. "I have only one free afternoon this week."

"What if you baby-sat for a couple of kids at once?" I suggested.

"That seems like a lot of responsibility. I can't imagine taking care of a few kids all at once."

"What if we all did it together?" I asked. "Sort of like a Thursday afternoon daycare. We could use my backyard for two hours. The kids could play there."

"Yeah," Rachel piped up. "Felicia and I could play sports with them."

"And I could do crafts," I said, remembering what Addie had said about the bead kit my mom had once given me. I still had tons of those beads left.

"And I could sing for them!" Chloe said.

"Or something," Felicia said quickly. "We'll think of some other activities."

"I'll make a few flyers tonight and post them around the neighborhood tomorrow before school," Chloe said. "Hopefully we'll get a bunch of kids by Thursday."

"I know we will!" I said confidently. "You'll have all the money you need. You'll see, Chloe."

Chapter
SIX

TO AN OUTSIDER, things at our school might have seemed normal the next Tuesday morning. But even though they looked that way, they weren't normal at all. Everything was just a little bit off.

For starters, Addie was at her locker, putting on makeup, like always. But she was all alone. There was no crowd of Pops fighting for mirror time.

And, as usual, Claire was wearing a new shirt, and very trendy leather boots. But today, no one was enviously complimenting her on her new ensemble. In fact, Elena walked right past her without a word.

Dana was, as always, being mean to my friends and me.

"Nice T-shirt, Chloe," she said, sticking her finger down her throat and pretending to gag. "Where'd you get that thing? The Salvation Army?"

"Yes," said Chloe, but in the bizarre alternate reality my school had entered, Dana's slam fell on deaf ears. Without any of the other Pops there to laugh or add a mean comment of their own, no one cared at all about what she had to say.

I turned to Chloe and rolled my eyes. "Did you put up

any flyers on your way to the bus stop this morning?" I asked her, ignoring Dana completely.

Chloe nodded. "Yes, and I ran into my neighbor across the street, Mrs. Wilensky. She is dropping off her five-year-old, Julia, at four o'clock on Thursday."

"That's one kid already," I said enthusiastically. "And the signs haven't even been up for an hour."

"I know," Chloe said excitedly. "At this rate we could be millionaires in a month."

I laughed. Once again, Chloe was taking things to an extreme. "Come on, Bill Gates," I teased, dragging her by the arm. "We've got to get to English class."

"You're really going to go through with it?" I heard Felicia asking Rachel as I walked down C wing toward my locker at the end of the school day. The two of them were huddled by Felicia's locker, talking with Liza.

"Going through with what?" I asked curiously.

"Rachel's going to get a haircut tomorrow," Felicia told me.

"Actually, I'm going to get them all cut," Rachel joked.

"Ouch," Felicia said. "That one hurt."

"I want a completely different look," Rachel told me. "I'm so sick of this long, straight, red mop on my head. And I want to do it before the luau next week. I'm totally ready to look different."

I was really surprised to hear that. Ever since kindergarten, Rachel had had the same hairstyle. This was huge!

"I just don't know *how* I should get it cut," she said. "What style do you guys think would look best on me?"

I shrugged. "I usually just let the person who's cutting my hair decide," I said.

"I like my hair kind of short," Liza said. "That way it doesn't get in my way so much when I draw."

"Yeah, but I don't know if short hair would work on me," Rachel said. "And if I cut it short, I want to be sure it's right. Do you know how long it will take me to grow it out again if I don't like it?"

I nodded. A haircut was kind of a commitment.

"Do you think that website you go on might have some ideas?" Rachel asked me.

I shrugged. "It's got everything else," I said.

"Okay, I'll call you as soon as I get home from basketball practice so we can talk about the ideas we find," Rachel told me.

"Speaking of practice, I'd better get to the auditorium," Liza said suddenly.

"See ya later," I said as she turned to walk away.

"So be home around six o'clock," Rachel told me. "I'm dying to hear what that website says I should do about my hair."

That night, at six o'clock on the dot, my phone rang. "Did you find anything on the website?" Rachel asked me anxiously.

"Hello to you, too." I giggled.

"Oh, sorry," Rachel said. "Hi. I'm just so excited about this."

"I can tell," I said. I headed over to the computer and switched it on.

I typed in middleschoolsurvival.com and then searched the site for hairstyles. Sure enough, there was a section called Hairdos and Don'ts. I double-clicked the link and waited for the screen to load.

"Oh wow! This is everything you need!" I told Rachel excitedly. "But it's really long. Can I forward it to you instead of reading it over the phone?"

"That would be awesome!" Rachel exclaimed. "I'll force my brother to get off the computer."

"Okay, it's on its way," I said, attaching the information to an e-mail, and hitting Send.

"Thanks Jen, you're the best," Rachel said. After we hung up, I read over the information on the website. It was pretty cool. And I knew for sure it would help Rachel decide what to do.

Hairdos and Don'ts

When it comes to your hair, you have to take things at face value. Knowing which style will look good on you means having a sense of the shape of your face. Start by looking in the mirror. Pull your hair back and get close enough that you can see your face clearly reflected in the mirror. Then, use a lipstick to carefully outline your face on the mirror. Now step away. The shape you see drawn on the mirror is the shape of your face. (Be sure to have plenty of glass cleaner nearby. Your 'rents are sure to be miffed if they see lipstick all over the bathroom mirror!)

Once you've got the facial geometry down, here's how to make sure your style is a cut above.

OVAL-SHAPED FACE: Lucky you! People with oval-shaped faces can pretty much wear their hair any way they'd like. Let your hair's natural thickness and texture determine whether it works better long or short. (As a rule, if you have thin hair, keep it short and layered to add thickness.)

ROUND-SHAPED FACE: Keep the sides of your hair close to your face and add height at the crown of your head. This will soften the fullness of your face and give the illusion of a more oval-shaped face.

DIAMOND-SHAPED FACE: Narrow-faced girls need to give their faces a rounder look. Wide bangs with a chin-length bob will do the trick.

SQUARE-SHAPED FACE: The goal for you is to soften the angles of your face. This can easily be done with long, soft bangs that extend down over your temples. Your best bet is to have either long hair or short. Medium-length hairstyles won't accentuate your positives. Long hair should extend past the shoulder, while short haircuts should have some added height at the crown of your head to give your face a more oval look.

HEART-SHAPED FACE: Chin-length hairstyles, especially on girls with curly or wavy hair, will add fullness where it's needed. A side part will soften your chin.

Most important, don't get fooled into getting your hair cut in a certain way just because that's what's in style. Do what works best for your face. After all, as everyone knows, styles are hair today, gone tomorrow! ☺

The next day at lunch, everyone was talking about the dance. "I hope we don't have to eat a pig with an apple in its mouth at the luau," Chloe said as she took a bite of her peanut butter sandwich.

"It's not a real luau," I assured her. "We're serving pizza and ice cream sundaes. But we'll have Hawaiian pineapples, and punch served in plastic coconut shells."

"That sounds sooo cool," Chloe said, relieved.

"It was Addie's idea," I admitted with a shrug.

"She's good for something, I guess," Chloe replied.

"Hey, I just got some new face paints," Liza announced. "I can paint flowers on everyone's cheeks."

"Count me out," Marc said. "I'll just throw on a Hawaiian shirt, thanks."

"Me, too," Josh agreed.

Liza giggled. "I didn't mean you guys."

As I sat there in the lunchroom, I realized how many people were obsessing over Addie Wilson's Luau. That was what people were calling it. Not the School Luau. Or even the Sixth-Grade Luau. It was Addie's party. Plain and simple.

Not that I could argue with that. Our class vice president had pretty much done the whole thing by herself. And it did sound like it was going to be amazing.

I guess the thing that amazed me most was the effect the luau was having on my friends. They were almost as excited as the Pops were.

"Are you going with Rachel when she gets her hair cut today?" Chloe asked me.

I shook my head. "Too much homework. I have a math test on Friday. And since we're baby-sitting tomorrow after school . . ."

"How many kids do you guys have for that, anyway?" Josh asked.

"Four," Chloe said. "Not as many as I would've liked, but it's still pretty good."

"It's perfect," I assured her. "There are four of us to take care of four kids. I think we can handle that."

"I hope you handle it better than you handled the dogs," Marc teased.

"Yeah, maybe you should keep the kids on leashes, too," Marilyn added.

"Not like that helped with the dogs," Carolyn added with a laugh. "But seriously, I wish we could be there to help you guys. Unfortunately, we both have to go to the orthodontist."

"And we really do need to get rid of these retainers as soon as possible," Marilyn said, clicking hers up and down in her mouth.

"It's okay," I told the twins.

"Really," Chloe agreed. "We should be able to take care of a couple of little kids, easy."

I sighed heavily. I sure hoped Chloe was right. The last thing I wanted was a repeat of our dog day.

Chapter
SEVEN

"WOW, RACHEL, YOU LOOK SO DIFFERENT!" I exclaimed first thing Thursday morning. Rachel was standing in the middle of C wing. Already a whole crowd of our friends had gathered around her. Everyone was ooing and aahing over her new 'do.

"You look so elegant. Like a model in a magazine," Liza told her.

"You seem older, too," Chloe said.

"It's a huge change. I can't believe you had the guts," Felicia added.

"Me, neither," Rachel said. "But I'm so glad I did. I love it!"

Everyone loved it. Rachel had followed the advice from the website, and framed her square-shaped face with long, soft bangs. Her hairdresser had taken about four inches off the bottom, so her hair now fell just below her shoulders. It was layered, too, so it seemed much thicker and fuller.

"What's going on here, a nerd convention?" Claire shouted out as she approached our crowd. She stopped and stared for a moment at Rachel. She opened her mouth as if to say something, but nothing came out. She just stood there, her eyes wide with surprise. A moment later, she walked away, without saying a word.

"Wow!" Felicia exclaimed. "You did it, Rach. You actually shut Claire up!"

"I think we should all go get new haircuts." I laughed.

"Not today," Chloe said. "Today's baby-sitting day."

"You guys are going to have so much fun," Liza remarked wistfully. "I wish I didn't have my tutor today."

"It's okay, you can come next time," Chloe told her. "We plan on turning this into a regular thing."

I shook my head. Once again, Chloe was being slightly over-ambitious. "Let's just get through today," I said.

Rachel, Chloe, and I hurried off the bus and ran to my house after school. We had to set up the backyard before all the little kids got there.

"It's really nice of your mom to let us use the backyard for this," Chloe said.

"She was so relieved when she heard it wasn't going to rain today. I think the idea of four little kids running around the house was too much for her to handle," I told Chloe, as I set up cups of beads and pieces of yellow lanyard on our picnic table. "This will be our craft table," I explained.

"I've got the sports center set up!" Felicia called. She pointed to a crack in the sidewalk where she'd placed a shiny penny. "We're going to play hit-the-penny," she added, holding up a pink rubber ball. "That's this game where two kids stand on either side of the penny, and try to hit it with the ball. It's one point for a hit, and two if you flip the penny over."

"That's such a fun game. I used to play with my cousins," Rachel said. She pulled a bag of hair ribbons, old shirts, and soft felt hats from her backpack and dumped them on the grass. "The dress-up area is ready," she announced.

"Wow! This is great!" Chloe exclaimed. "The kids are going to have so much fun."

"Hey," Felicia interrupted her. "If I'm doing sports, Jenny's doing crafts, and Rachel's got dress-up covered, what are *you* doing?"

"I'm going to help all of you guys," Chloe said. "The computer said I'm a natural with kids, so I want all of them to get a chance to be around me."

"Oh, brother." Felicia groaned, rolling her eyes.

"You know what I mean," Chloe told her. "I'll be the one who helps out if anything gets too crazy."

"Let's hope it doesn't," I said, remembering the dog disaster.

"It'll be okay," Chloe promised me. "Kids are much easier than dogs. You can talk to them and tell them what to do."

Just then, my mother walked out into the backyard. She was followed by two little boys.

"Jason and Michael are here," my mom announced. "Mrs. Thomas just dropped them off."

Chloe was the first to run over to the boys. "Hi there," she greeted them. "I'm Chloe."

Jason, who was five years old, stuck out his chubby hand. "I'm Jason," he said, trying to sound very grown-up.

Chloe shook his hand, and then pulled hers away quickly. "Sticky hand," she said.

"It's from my jelly sandwich," Jason told her.

"Didn't you wash your hands before you came?" Chloe asked him.

Jason shook his head. "I like to lick off the jelly," he told her, taking a big lick of his hand. Chloe made a face, but she didn't say anything.

Three-year-old Michael reached up and wiped his nose with his sleeve. "Gotta cold," he said.

"I'll get you some tissues," I said, hurrying toward the house.

"He doesn't need them," Jason told me. "He's just gonna use his shirt anyway."

I frowned. Little boys were pretty gross. I couldn't wait for the girls to arrive. I had a feeling they would be much cleaner.

A few minutes later, five-year-old Julia Wilensky showed up. She was wearing a pink tutu and white tights. She looked a lot sweeter than Michael or Jason.

"What a pretty ballerina you are," I told Julia.

"I'm a fairy princess," Julia said. She held up her sparkly, star-shaped wand.

"Oh, I'm so sorry, your highness," I apologized with a grin.

"It's okay," Julia told me. "I wear this when I want to be a ballerina sometimes, too."

"Who are we waiting for?" Rachel asked Chloe.

"Cecilia Katsalis. She should be here any minute," Chloe said. Then, turning to Julia she added, "You'll like Cecilia. She's very nice. And she's five years old, just like you."

A few moments later, a shy girl in blue jeans and a red T-shirt walked into the backyard. "You must be Cecilia," I said, walking over to greet her.

Cecilia looked up at me and started to cry. "I wanna go home," she sobbed. "I don't like it here."

Felicia raced over to her. She lived on the same block as Cecilia and had been the one to get her to come. We all hoped she could calm Cecilia down.

"We're gonna have a great time, Cecilia," she promised her. "Look at all the fun stuff there is to do."

"Can we have a water fight?" Cecilia asked. "I love water fights."

Felicia shook her head. "It's a little too chilly for that."

"Can we bake cookies, then?" Cecilia suggested.

I shook my head. "We're going to have tons of fun out here," I told her. "We can't use the kitchen."

"This is gonna stink," Cecilia groaned.

"No, it won't," Chloe told her. "We're going to have fun. Why don't you go make some nice bead necklaces with Jenny?" I raised my hand so she could see who I was.

"Don't wanna," Cecilia said.

"*I* wanna make a necklace," Michael said. "*Aachoo.*"

I tried not to look as Michael wiped his nose with his sleeve again. Then I walked over to the bead table with him and got him started stringing the plastic beads on some yellow cord.

"Do you want to play dress-up?" Rachel asked Cecilia.

"No."

"Oh, I do! I do!" Julia squealed. "Can we play beauty parlor?"

"That's one of my favorite games," Rachel said excitedly. "I have lots of hair bows you can try on. Come on. We can play together."

That just left Jason and Cecilia. "Let's go play hit-the-penny," Felicia urged, walking the two five-year-olds to the sidewalk. "Boy against girl."

"I'm gonna win," Jason announced.

"Oh, no, you're not!" Cecilia countered.

For a few minutes, everything seemed to be working out perfectly in the backyard. Then, suddenly, I heard fighting coming from the sidewalk. I turned to see what was happening.

"You cheated!" Cecilia shouted.

"Did not. I hit that penny and it flipped over," Jason yelled back.

"You were standing too close," Cecilia told him.

"Let's have a do-over," Felicia suggested.

"That's not fair!" Jason screamed.

"Is too!" Cecilia shouted back.

"Oh, yeah?" Jason growled, his eyes getting small and angry.

Suddenly, Cecilia lunged at Jason. He curled his small hands into fists. Felicia just managed to jump between them before they could hit each other.

Unfortunately for her, that was the exact moment that Cecilia tried to throw the ball really hard at Michael. Instead of hitting Michael, it got Felicia right in the eye.

"*Ouch!*" Felicia shouted, putting her hands to her face. "Now see what you two have done!"

"She did it," Jason said.

Cecilia didn't say anything.

"I'll go get some ice!" Chloe shouted, running for the house.

As I turned my attention back to Michael, I noticed he had a finger up his nose.

"How about I get you that tissue now?" I asked him.

"I'm not picking my nose," Michael explained. "I'm just trying to get the bead out."

"You stuck a bead in your nose?" I gulped.

Michael nodded. "Wanted to see if it fit. It did. Now I can't get it out!" He pulled his finger from his nose and screamed. "My nose is bleeding!" he shouted.

This was bad. *Real bad.* I grabbed Michael by his arm and pulled him toward the house. "Mom! Help!" I screamed as we ran in the door.

A little while later, everything had quieted down. Mom

had used her tweezers to get the bead from Michael's nose. Felicia had placed an ice pack over her eye. It was kind of purple, but not too bad. Chloe was quietly reading to Michael, Cecilia, and Jason. I'm not sure the two older kids really liked listening to a story instead of playing, but after all the trouble they'd caused, I think they were afraid to argue.

As I came out of the house with glasses of lemonade for everyone, I smiled to myself. The afternoon was almost over, and we hadn't lost anyone, or caused any serious damage.

By the time the kids' mothers had come by to pick them up, I was exhausted. I plopped down on the grass and took a deep breath.

"That wasn't so bad, was it?" Chloe said with a smile, sitting down next to me. "Should we do it again next week?"

I remembered Michael's bloody nose. Then I looked over at Felicia with her black-and-blue eye, and Rachel, who still sported the multiple pigtails Julia had given her while they were playing beauty parlor.

"I don't think so," I told Chloe.

"Why not?" Chloe asked. "I had fun with the kids."

"Yeah, that's because no one bled on you or hit you in the eye or knotted up your hair," I told her. "I officially retire from baby-sitting."

"Me, too," Rachel said, pulling a bow from her hair.

"That goes triple for me," Felicia added.

Chloe shrugged and looked down at the money in her

hand. "Well, I'm almost there. All I need is ten dollars more. Any of you guys have any other ideas about how I can earn some money?"

"No!" Rachel and Felicia shouted at once.

"Ouch!" I added, bumping my head on the picnic table as I reached over to pick up some of Michael's fallen beads.

I reached up and felt a small lump starting to form on my skull. That settled it. From now on, when it came to making money, Chloe was on her own. I was officially retired — at least until I was old enough to get a real job. One that didn't involve dogs or little kids!

Chapter
EIGHT

I PRACTICALLY COLLAPSED into my chair as I reached our lunch table on Friday. It was only fifth period, but I was already completely wiped out.

"What's wrong?" Liza asked me.

"What *isn't?*" I groaned. "First, I had a really rough surprise quiz in English, and then, Mr. Conte made me do a math problem up at the board — which I got wrong, of course. As if that wasn't bad enough, I got a big, fat C on my history paper, which is not going to make my parents happy."

"Oh, wow," Liza said sympathetically. "Well, just relax. You're among friends now."

"Absolutely," Carolyn agreed.

"Friends forever," Marilyn seconded. "Oh, look, there are Chloe and Marc. Boy, they're late getting to lunch."

I waved in their direction. But only Chloe could see me. Marc's view of our table was blocked by the sudden appearance of a dark-haired eighth-grader named Cassidy. I knew who she was because she had the part of Lucy in *You're a Good Man, Charlie Brown.* Chloe was a little jealous of Cassidy. Lucy was the part she had auditioned for.

Suddenly, Cassidy thrust her arms out in front of her. "Romeo, Romeo, wherefore art thou, Romeo?" she said loudly.

Marc rolled his eyes and walked right past her. He hurried over to our table and plopped down his book bag. Chloe took the seat next to him and pulled out her bag lunch.

"What was that about?" I asked Marc.

"An audition," he replied.

"For what?" I asked him.

"My movie," Marc replied sadly.

"I thought it was a spontaneous documentary," Chloe reminded him. "At least that what's you told me."

"It is," Marc said. "Or at least it *was*. I'm not making my movie anymore."

"Why?" I asked him, surprised.

Marc reached into his backpack and yanked out the newest edition of the *Joyce Kilmer Gazette*. "Madame X," he declared angrily. "That's why!"

I hadn't had a chance to read the school paper yet — not with my lousy morning. So I took the paper from his hand and read this week's "In the Know with Madame X."

There's a director in our midst, folks! Just look for the seventh-grader with the video camera lurking in the halls. He's making a movie about us — so be careful. You don't want your darkest secrets to appear on film.

"Oh, but it's okay for everyone's darkest secrets to appear in a newspaper column?" Chloe asked sarcastically. "That's what Madame X is writing about. Whoever she is, she's a real hypocrite."

"Seriously," Marilyn said.

"Big time," Carolyn agreed.

"But why does this have to be the end of your movie?" I asked Marc. "Think of it as publicity."

"Yeah, *bad* publicity," Marc groaned. "Now I can't get anyone to be natural around me," he said. "They either avoid me or audition for me. I can't make a realistic documentary that way."

"I'm not the only one who's going to be angry," Marc continued. "Just wait until Josh sees this."

"I think he already has," Chloe said. "Look."

She pointed over to the cafeteria food line. Josh was practically hiding behind his books. And he was wearing dark sunglasses.

"I think he's traveling incognito," Marilyn giggled.

"You would be, too, if you read what Madame X wrote," Marc said.

I looked down at the page. *What blond-haired, green-eyed, eighth-grade bookworm has a crush on the librarian, Miss Hopkins?* "That can't be Josh," I said.

"Not that one. Keep going," Marc said.

Which Pop girl made up an imaginary boyfriend from another school, and even went so far as to send herself text messages to make it more believable?

"Oh, that's gotta be Elena," Marilyn said. "Didn't she give herself a valentine in third grade?"

"I think that was Maya," Carolyn countered.

"It could be Dana," Chloe suggested. "She's just weird enough to try that."

"Well, no matter who it is, it's not Josh," I pointed out.

"Check out the last paragraph," Marc told me, pointing to the part he meant.

I read on.

He's a math nerd, she's a jock. This time it's the girl who is going to wind up scoring points for the school. Makes you wonder just who wears the pants in this geek un-chic relationship.

"Ouch," Liza said. "That's really not nice. It makes Josh sound like a wimpy weakling instead of a black belt."

"Why didn't Madame X mention his tae kwon do?" Marilyn wondered out loud. "He's really good at that."

"She never writes anything *good* about anyone," Carolyn reminded her sister.

"Where's Josh going?" Liza asked as she watched him head over toward the door.

"Probably to eat lunch on the stairs," Marc said. "My guess is he's too embarrassed to eat in public."

"Yeah, well, Josh will be okay. And your movie will be,

too," I told Marc. "This will blow over by next week — as soon as there's a new Madame X column."

"I don't know about that," Marc said. "The Pops are still mad at each other."

I looked around the room. Marc was right. Addie and her friends — or former friends — were still scattered around the cafeteria.

"What I don't get is how Madame X finds out her information," Marc continued. "I mean, nobody knew what my movie was about except for you guys. And none of you would tell . . ." He stopped for a minute and looked at us accusingly. "Or would you?"

"Come on, Marc. You know we would never . . ." Chloe began.

"Do I?" Marc demanded. "You were pretty mad when I wouldn't let you sing in the film, Chloe."

"Oh, give me a break," Chloe replied. "Why would I tell Madame X anything after she spread a rumor about me?"

"Okay, maybe it wasn't you. Maybe it was someone else." He glanced at Liza, the twins, and me. "Madame X hasn't mentioned any of you four," he said suspiciously. "It could be one of you."

"Me?" Liza asked him, unable to mask her shock. "I would never do anything like that."

"Me, neither!" Marilyn and Carolyn said at the same time.

"Marc, we're all friends," I assured him. "None of us would ever do anything to hurt you — or Josh and Felicia."

"Well, somebody must have told her, then," Marc said, grabbing his stuff and standing up.

"Where are you going?" Liza asked him.

"To sit by myself," Marc growled. "I don't want any more information about me leaked into the school paper."

"Oh, chill out," Chloe told him. "We're not going to reveal your deep, dark secrets. None of us even know who Madame X is."

I sighed heavily. I sure hoped we would find out soon. Maybe then we could convince her to stop.

"I just don't understand Madame X," Felicia cried to me on the bus that afternoon. "Why is she so mean? What kind of person would do this?"

"I don't know," I told her.

"And where does she get her information from?" Felicia continued. "I mean, it's like she's a fly on the wall when people are having private conversations. She hears everything! How can no one know who she is?"

"It is really weird," I agreed. "Like someone is spying on us all the time."

"It gives me the creeps," Felicia said. "I feel like I can't trust anyone. Not even my closest friends."

"That's ridiculous," I told her. "You can trust your real friends."

"Really?" Felicia asked me. "That's not how you felt a couple days ago. You thought I had told Madame X about Chloe having a secret, remember?"

I blushed. She had me there. "Yeah. But you didn't and I was wrong," I said apologetically. "I know you would never reveal a secret like that. None of us would ever be that mean to anyone."

Felicia shrugged. "I guess not," she said. But I could tell she wasn't completely convinced.

To tell you the truth, I wasn't, either.

Chapter
NINE

"THAT WAS SO MUCH FUN!" Felicia squealed as we rode the bus to school together on Monday.

"I know," I agreed. "It was so amazing that your mother let us go into the store all by ourselves while she waited in the food court."

"Well, we *are* in middle school now," Felicia said.

"And I can't believe we got to see Chloe try on a dress! I've never seen her in anything but shorts and jeans," I exclaimed. "I am so glad her parents gave her the rest of the money she needed."

"We are going to be the hottest people at the dance next weekend!" Felicia proclaimed.

Speaking of which . . . I glanced behind me to where Addie was sitting. She was all by herself, staring out the window. No cell phone conversations for her today.

The Pops must still be fighting over Madame X's column. Which meant that they hadn't been together this weekend. They all were probably just sitting at home doing nothing . . . alone. The era of world domination by the Pops had ended.

Or not. As soon as I walked over to my locker in C wing,

I saw Claire, Dana, and Elena enter the school together. They were walking in the direction of Addie's locker. And they seemed perfectly happy.

So much for my theory.

I stood there for a minute, waiting for one of them to make some snide comment about my old sneakers or Felicia's braids, but they walked right past us.

And then the strangest thing happened.

The Pops turned on Addie.

"Traitor," Claire hissed.

"Snitch," Dana growled loud enough for everyone to hear.

"Freak," Elena said, adding the cruelest cut of all.

Addie looked as though she was going to cry. But she didn't. She just looked in the mirror and smeared more pink gloss on her lips.

"Okay, so what was that all about?" Felicia asked me curiously.

"Don't ask me," I replied. "But I'll bet you anything it has something to do with Madame X."

For the first time since school began, I actually had a good time in gym class that day. With Dana and Addie not whispering to each other and laughing at everyone else, I was able to relax and really get into the volleyball game we were playing.

"Nice serve," Addie congratulated me, after one of my particularly good whacks over the net.

I looked to see if she was kidding. But she wasn't. It was a real compliment.

But I wasn't going to fall for that again. Last time Addie had been nice to me I'd almost fallen for it. I'd sat there in that student government office and talked to her all about how great Felicia was doing, and how exciting Marc's movie was. . . .

And then it hit me. *Wham!*

Addie hadn't just been nice to me because the Pops were fighting. She'd been pumping me for information.

Information she could use in her newspaper column.

Because Addie was Madame X.

It all made sense. Only a Pops insider would have known about Claire sucking her thumb, or about one of the Pops sending herself a valentine. As for that column she wrote about Chloe, well, she'd probably heard Felicia and me talking about it on the school bus. Now which one of us was eavesdropping?

Apparently the Pops had figured out Madame X's identity, too. It couldn't have been too tough. After all, while all of their deep dark secrets were in the school paper, there had never been any rumors about Addie. Which must have led them to conclude that she was Madame X. That explained why none of the Pops were talking to Addie.

MIDDLE SCHOOL RULE # 15:

KEEP YOUR FRIENDS' SECRETS. OTHERWISE YOU WON'T HAVE ANY FRIENDS!

"So, are we going to work on the finishing touches for the dance today after school?" Addie asked me hopefully as our volleyball team rotated positions.

The last thing I wanted to do was spend the afternoon working side by side with the notorious Madame X. "I think you've got it under control," I told her.

"You're not going to make me do this whole thing alone, are you?" Addie asked me. "I thought we were supposed to be working on the Luau together."

Funny, that's not how she'd been acting a few days ago. When we'd first started planning the dance, she'd tried her best to leave me out of everything. But ever since her friends dumped her . . .

I had to stop myself from thinking like that. After all, I was still class president. And no matter how I felt about Addie right now, I had responsibilities.

"Sure, fine. I'll meet you after school at the student council office," I said as the other team's server sent the ball flying over the net. I reached up and hit the volleyball really, really hard.

"Oh, good, you're here," Addie said, looking up cheerfully as I came into the student council office after my last class. She tried to smile, but I could tell she'd been crying. Her eyes were all red, and her cheeks were kind of damp.

"Something wrong?" I asked her as nicely as I could. I was really, really mad at Addie, but I just can't be mean to someone who's crying.

"N-n-no," Addie said, stumbling over the word. "I mean, not really."

I took a deep breath before I said anything else. I wasn't really sure how Addie was going to react to this. Finally I told her, "You knew they would figure it out sooner or later, Addie."

She looked at me with surprise. "I don't know what you're talking about."

"Oh, come on," I said, getting braver by the minute. "If *I* was able to figure out Madame X's secret identity, I know your friends could."

"Madame X?" Addie asked in a voice that sounded kind of fake. "You mean that gossip columnist in the school paper?"

"I mean *you*," I said flatly. "I know it was you who printed all that stuff about my friends. I know because you got all that information from me. I mean you've done some pretty mean stuff to me this year, Addie, but being nice to me just so you could find out secrets about my friends is the worst. And you twisted all my words around and made everything sound horrible."

Addie sighed heavily. There was no way she was

getting out of this, and she knew it. "Look, I *had* to write that stuff," she told me finally. "My friends were all fighting with each other about the column I'd written before that one. I figured if I wrote a lot of junk about *your* friends, then . . ."

"Then they'd start making fun of Marc or Felicia and Josh, and forget they were fighting with each other," I said, finishing her thought.

Addie nodded. "And it worked, sort of," she said. "Except now *they're* all friends, but they hate me."

"Can you blame them?" I asked her honestly. "You published all their most personal secrets in the school newspaper."

"I was just having fun," Addie insisted. "It was all a joke. No one's feelings were supposed to get hurt. That's why I didn't use any names."

"We all figured it out, though," I reminded her.

"I know," Addie admitted sadly. "And by now, Claire and Dana have told the whole school it was me who wrote the columns. *Everyone* is going to hate me!"

I stared at the piles of decorations all around the office. I thought about all the money we'd already spent on the food we'd ordered. If Addie didn't do something soon to fix this mess, it would all go to waste.

"Look, Addie, you're going to have to apologize for what you did," I told her. "Because if you don't, everyone will be too mad at you to come to the luau."

"Oh, people wouldn't do that," Addie said. "It's going to

be a great time. People will come just to dance, to hear a real band, and eat pizza."

"Most people were coming to the party because *you* planned it, Addie," I told her honestly. "Kids around here look up to you." I hated saying it, but I knew it was true. "But they won't respect you unless you come clean about all this. Just admit you made a mistake. Your friends will forgive you if you do that."

Addie started to cry again. "Do you really think so?" she whimpered.

I nodded. "I'm sure of it," I said, even though I really wasn't. There was no way to predict how the Pops would react to anything. "And once they forgive you, everyone else will, too."

I sure hoped I was right. Otherwise we were going to have one lousy luau on Friday.

That night, I sat in front of my computer, staring at a blank screen. I knew I was supposed to be doing my English homework. I was supposed to be doing thirty minutes of free writing but all I could think about was the luau. I was really worried that it was going to be a disaster. What if Addie was too chicken to admit what she had done? What if she blamed it all on someone else and only made things worse?

I had to get my mind off that party! Otherwise I'd never be able to do my homework. There had to be a way to distract myself from all this pressure.

Then, my fingers started to move as though they had a mind of their own. Only they weren't typing a paragraph. They were taking me to my favorite website. Which wasn't a bad idea, actually. If I couldn't concentrate enough to write, at least I could entertain myself with a quick quiz.

Hey, Cookie!

Everyone knows you're sweet as sugar. But does your sugary soul come with some spice? To find out what cookie you're most like, take this tasty quiz.

1. **You promised your mom you'd go shopping with her after school, but the guy you've been crushin' on just asked you to go to the mall with him instead. What do you do?**

   A. Explain that you have to do something with your mom, but you'd really like to hang with him tomorrow.

   B. Pretend you forgot about your date with your mom, and ditch her.

   C. Get your mom to give you money and promise to buy whatever she needs while you're hanging with your new fave guy.

   That one was easy. I don't break plans with people. I wouldn't want them to do that to me. (Not that my mom ever would!) I clicked on A.

2. **If you could have the perfect school schedule, which class would be first thing every morning?**

   A. Study hall — I'm not a morning person!

B. Math. I like to jump right into the hard stuff.

C. Gym class. Gotta get up and get movin'!

Definitely A. Getting up in the morning in time to make the bus is the thing I hate most in life.

3. **It's school assembly time. Everyone's piling into the auditorium. Where can you usually be found?**

A. Snoozing in your seat.

B. Giggling in the back with your gal pals.

C. Sitting in the front row, trying to pay attention. After all, you don't want to insult the speakers.

Before I ran for class president, I probably would have been one of the gigglers from letter B. But ever since I'd had to give my speech for the class president elections, I knew how hard it was to get up in front of a bunch of kids and speak. I clicked C.

4. **That huge school project is due tomorrow! What's your plan?**

A. All done. I never save stuff for the last minute.

B. *Achoo*. Think I've got the flu. I'm gonna have to miss school for a day or two ☺

C. It's time to pull an all-nighter!

My answer to that one was definitely A. But not because I like working weeks ahead of time on projects. It's just that if I don't start my work early, my dad will nag me until I do. In the long run, it's easier to just get it done.

Add Up Your Score
1. A. 1 point   B. 3 points   C. 2 points
2. A. 2 points   B. 1 point   C. 3 points
3. A. 2 points   B. 3 points   C. 1 point
4. A. 1 point   B. 3 points   C. 2 points

What's the recipe behind your personality?

4–6 points: Sugar Cookie

You're always reliable, and always delicious. That makes you special because your friends know you'll always be there for them. And just like a sugar cookie is consistent throughout, your pals can rest assured that you'll never go bitter or nutty on them when they least expect it.

7–10 points: Cream-Filled Sandwich Cookie

Everybody loves you, but for different reasons. Just like some people eat the cream first, while others prefer to shove the whole cookie in their mouths, you seem to have a little something for everyone. And like this super-stuffed cookie, you are always able to hold yourself together, even in tough situations.

11–12 points: Chocolate Chocolate Chunk Cookie with Marshmallows and Nuts

You're the wild child of the cookie aisle. Your friends never know what they're gonna get. With each bite there's a new surprise. The only constant in your life is that it's all delicious and crazy. But you might want to take a deep breath and slow down a bit. A cookie this rich could get to be too much.

With a five-point score, I was a sweet, dependable sugar cookie. That was a nice thought. But even better, I'd found a theme for my free writing essay. Quickly, I typed in my title: *Kids are Like Desserts.*
One problem solved.

The next morning, I discovered that Addie had solved my other problem as well. She'd written her apology, printed it out on paper, and distributed it to as many kids as possible.

In the Know with Madame X

Usually this column has a no-names policy. But today I'm changing that. I'm going to identify myself. I am Addie Wilson and I am really sorry I ever started writing this column. I guess I didn't realize that people would be so hurt by the things I wrote. The secrets I wrote about didn't seem so important. But, I realize now that secrets are secrets for a reason. So I apologize to all of my friends if I hurt them in any way. And I hope to see all of you at the luau on Friday.

I stood there in the middle of C wing and stared at the newspaper in my hand. I hadn't expected Addie to be this honest about what she had done.

"Pretty impressive," I said, walking over to Addie's locker.

Dana and Claire came up behind me. "She wasn't apologizing to you, freak," Dana grumbled. "Read it carefully. She apologized to her *friends*. That definitely doesn't include you."

"That's for sure," Claire agreed. She turned to Addie. "Got any more of that light brown eyeshadow?" she asked her. "I'm all out."

"Sure," Addie said, a big smile forming on her face. "Here you go."

I stood there for a minute, waiting to see if Addie would thank me for my advice. But she didn't. In fact, she basically ignored me.

Which meant everything was completely back to normal.

Chapter
TEN

"ALOHA!" I SAID, placing a floral lei around Rachel's neck as she entered the school cafeteria. I'd been doing it to everyone as they arrived at the luau.

"Whoa! Check this place out," Rachel said, looking around the cafeteria. "You guys did an awesome job."

"It was mostly Addie," I admitted. "But I *am* the one who ordered the cakes shaped like volcanoes." I pointed over to one of the snack tables, where several cone-shaped cakes with red icing dripping all over them were placed.

"Mmm, yummy," Rachel said. "Hey, do you know what one volcano said to the other?"

"What?"

"I lava you!" She laughed.

"I lava you, too," I said with a giggle. "I lava all of my friends."

"Speaking of which, have you seen Felicia?" Rachel asked.

"She's dancing with Josh," I said, pointing toward the dance floor. "Liza and Chloe are getting flowers painted on their faces, and Marc is over by the food. I'm not sure where the twins are."

"I like the purple flower on your cheek," Rachel complimented me.

"It's supposed to be an orchid," I told her.

"It's really pretty. And it matches the purple flowers in your skirt. Do you think Liza would paint a flower on my face?"

"Of course! Go ask her."

As Rachel wandered off toward the girls' room, I stepped back and took a look at how the luau was going. So far, so good. Lots of people were dancing. Addie had been right. A live, high school band was really cool — even if they only knew six songs.

As the band finished playing, Ms. Gold, our principal, hopped up on the stage. "Boys and girls," she said into the microphone. "May I have your attention, please?"

She tapped the microphone twice with her finger, but the kids in the room kept laughing, talking, and running around.

Suddenly a burst of feedback shot out of the guitarist's amplifier. Now *that* got everyone's attention!

Ms. Gold laughed as everyone suddenly turned to the stage. Even she was in a good mood tonight.

"I hope you're all having a great time!" Ms. Gold shouted into the microphone.

"Oh, yeah!" the kids all shouted back at once.

"We have two special people to thank for tonight," Ms. Gold continued. "Will Addie Wilson and Jenny McAfee come up on stage for a minute?"

I blushed beet red. I didn't want to go up on that stage in front of all those people. That wasn't my thing. I'm more of a behind-the-scenes person.

Addie, on the other hand, couldn't get up there fast enough. She raced up the stairs and took her place in the spotlight. I followed behind her, blushing all the way.

And there we were, Addie Wilson and Jenny McAfee, together again. Of course, it wasn't the same as it had once been. But as I looked out at my cheering friends, I realized that that was okay. Change could be good. I had my friends and Addie had hers. And as long as we didn't have to spend *too* much time together, we could pretty much coexist.

"Okay, everybody, let's limbo!" the lead singer of the band shouted into his microphone. Ms. Gold leaped down from the stage and took one end of the limbo pole. Mr. Schwartz, one of the art teachers, grabbed the other end. And then the music started.

"How low can you go? How low can you go?" the singer began to chant.

As I hopped into line beside Rachel and Chloe, I noticed that Addie and her friends weren't joining us.

"Guess this isn't a Pops thing," I said.

"They think it's beneath them," Rachel joked. "Get it, under the limbo pole? *Beneath . . .*"

"I get it," I said with a laugh. But I didn't really. I mean, I understood the *joke.* What I didn't understand was why the Pops always thought it was uncool to have fun.

Not me. I could sink pretty low, if it meant having a good time. And to prove it, I bent over backwards and slid my way under the limbo bar.

"Go, Jenny!" Marc cheered me on, as he filmed the limbo contest. Obviously, he wasn't letting Madame X get in the way of his making his movie anymore.

I looked around the room. My friends were all laughing, smiling, and having a great time. So was I. This was the perfect night: amazing friends, yummy food, and lots of fun. I was the happiest I'd ever been in my whole life.

I opened my mouth wide and let out a loud yell. "Middle school rocks!" I shouted. And I meant it!

Are You Too Cool for School?

Take this computer quiz and find out how you score on the diva meter!

1. **How do you react when a friend is fifteen minutes late meeting you at the movies?**

   A. You're kind of annoyed, but you'll get over it as soon as you get your popcorn.

   B. No big deal. It was fun to people watch in the lobby as you waited.

   C. You get your ticket and go in without her. You're not going to have a lousy seat just because she's late!

2. **What kind of animal are you most like?**

   A. A fun-loving puppy who always wants to go out for a walk.

   B. A sweet and simple goldfish, happily swimming around in her bowl.

   C. A finicky kitty with a passion for caviar.

3. **Your family is planning a vacation and your brother suggests camping. What's your first reaction?**

   A. You'll go along with it — as long as you get to stop at a water park along the way. You love those log flume rides!

   B. Sleeping under the stars sounds like so much fun. First dibs on the marshmallows!

   C. Unless camping means a hotel with cable TV, you're not going!

4. How long does it take you to get ready to go to a school dance?

A. About two hours — you've got to iron your new skirt, wash and dry your hair, put on a little blush, lip gloss, and eye shadow, and find a cute pair of shoes in your closet for dancing.

B. You can be ready in five minutes. A clean pair of jeans, a cute shirt, a little lip gloss, and you're good to go.

C. Two weeks, minimum. That's how long it will take you to buy a new outfit, make an appointment to get your hair cut, and invite the girls over to give each other manicures.

The Diva Meter
So how much of a pampered princess are you?

Mostly A's: Although you like the finer things in life, you're not opposed to a little low-maintenance fun. You've managed to strike a great balance in your life!

Mostly B's: There's not an ounce of diva blood flowing through your veins. But maybe you should consider thinking about yourself a little every once in a while. You deserve it!

Mostly C's: Girl, you put the D in diva. That's D for demanding. Tone it down a bit, and give in from time to time — you might get more back than you expect!

NANCY KRULIK HAS WRITTEN more than 150 books for children and young adults, including three *New York Times* bestsellers. She is the author of the popular Katie Kazoo Switcheroo series and is also well known as a biographer of Hollywood's hottest young stars. Her knowledge of the details of celebrities' lives has made her a desired guest on several entertainment shows on the E! network as well as on *Extra* and *Access Hollywood.* Nancy lives in Manhattan with her husband, composer Daniel Burwasser, their two children, Ian and Amanda, and a crazy cocker spaniel named Pepper.

Log on to my favorite Web site!

www.middleschoolsurvival.com

You'll find:

- Cool Polls and Quizzes
- Tips and Advice
- Message Boards
- And Everything Else You Need to Survive Middle School!